The New Era of Prince Malock

Book Three in the Prince Malock World

by Timothy L. Cerepaka

An Annulus Publishing Book

Annulus Publishing, Cherokee, Texas, 2014

Acknowledgments

I would like to thank my uncle, James Wilhite, once again for helping me get this novel into publishable shape. I would also like to thank my family for supporting me while I wrote this novel.

Chapter One

WHEN THE WHIRLWIND STRUCK, Prince Tojas Malock—Crown Prince of Carnag, son of Queen Markinia and King Halock, and member of the Brotherhood of Heathens—was thrown from the top deck of the *Clockwork Heart* and likely would have hit the deck below and broken his back if Hana had not appeared out of nowhere and caught him by the collar of his shirt before he fell out of her reach. The sudden stop jolted his spine, almost ripped him out of his shirt, but then Hana pulled him back up with surprising strength and dumped him onto the deck even as the winds screamed around them with the force of an explosion.

Shaking, Malock got to his feet and looked at Hana, whose Monmouth cap had been knocked off her head when the wind struck and whose long, golden hair flapped about in the wind. The smokestacks of the *Clockwork Heart* sent columns of smoke and flame into the air, but the whirlwind continued to howl and blow about the ship. In fact, when Malock looked out over the lower deck, he saw the wind scoop up one of the automaton sailors and hurl it off the ship into the now-raging sea that surrounded them on every side.

"What's going on here?" Malock shouted, trying to make his voice heard over the sound of the raging winds. "Where did this whirlwind come from?"

Hana shook her head and said, "I don't know. But if I had to guess, I'd say it was one of the gods. Possibly Niham or maybe—"

A strong gust of wind—almost tornado-like in strength—cut her off just then. The gust actually sent her skittering back, her boots scratching against the metal floor, but she grabbed the railing before it could knock her off, which she clung to for her very life.

Malock looked up at the sky. A large black storm cloud had gathered overhead, a storm cloud that looked awfully familiar to him. He ran to the railing and leaned over, ignoring the dangers the whirlwind posed, and squinted as far into the distance as he could, trying to spot what he believed to be the source of the storm.

But alas, no matter which direction he looked, Malock didn't see anything except for the ever-rising waves, the darkening sky, and the automatons below, scurrying to and fro, trying to avoid being swept overboard by the furious sea or getting caught by the wind that had already claimed the lives of one of their brothers.

Pushing his flapping hair out of his face, Malock looked over his shoulder at Hana and shouted, "Why would any of the gods attack the *Clockwork Heart*? The Mechanical Goddess is one of them, isn't she?"

Hana winced as a particularly powerful burst of wind swept through, but she still managed to throw the most annoyed look at him. "Have you forgotten about what the gods think of you or are you just stupid?"

Malock would have said that he had neither forgotten what the gods thought of him nor was he stupid, but he never got the chance because a massive wave crashed into the port of the *Clockwork Heart*, tall enough to reach the ship's highest deck. Tons of water splashed over him and Hana, causing him to gasp from the sharp coldness of the seawater. The groaning of the ship sounded far worse than any sound prior, but it hadn't yet gone under and Malock doubted that it would because he didn't think that the Mechanical Goddess would let it.

Hana teleported next to Malock; at least, he thought she did because he didn't see her move next to him. She grabbed his left arm as she said, "We've got to go below deck before things get worse!"

Without waiting for his opinion, Hana dragged Malock away from the safety of the railing down the metal stairs leading to the lower deck. Another crashing wave—this one coming from starboard —struck even harder than the last, throwing both Malock and Hana headfirst down the stairs. Malock twisted in midair to land on the deck on his back, but even so his head banged against the metal and a moment later Hana fell on top of him, the impact of her fall knocking his breath straight from his lungs.

At that moment, two mechanical hands reached down and hauled the two to their feet. Malock shook his head and looked at the owner of the hands. It was one of the automatons, the one who wore a long red scarf around its neck and carried a crescent blade at its side. If Malock's memory was correct, this one was called Calir or something like that.

"Thanks, Calir," said Hana, before the ship shuddered, causing her to grab the automaton before she fell again. "Does the Mechanical Goddess know who's attacking us?"

Calir swiftly shook its head, then pointed to the deck under their feet.

"Of course," said Hana, as if Calir had just said something obvious. "We should get below deck. That's where we were heading, actually."

Calir nodded and then ran past them toward the bow. It drew its sword as it did so, like a soldier going to war.

"Where's he going?" Malock said, raising his voice over the violent winds.

At that moment, rain started pouring, prompting Hana to raise her hands over her head and shout, "Don't know, don't care. Come on!"

She once again grabbed his arm and dragged him toward the hatch. She kicked it open—a surprising feat, considering that the hatch was made of thick, heavy metal—and immediately began climbing down the stairs leading below. Malock followed soon after, but before he could get down completely, another huge wave struck and sent tons of water cascading into the open hatch. The water slammed into his legs, causing him to fall on his bum and roll down into the bottom. At the same time, the hatch above shut itself and a *click* indicated that it was now locked.

Panting, Malock sat up and looked down at his soaked clothes with disappointment. While he had chosen these clothes—a gray boat cloak with a white cotton shirt underneath—primarily for their practical value and not their aesthetic appeal, he still didn't like how they clung to his skin like a second skin.

He brushed his sopping hair out of his eyes as Hana, who had somehow managed to keep dry, said, "Kano."

Malock looked at her. "What?"

Hana pointed at the water which was rapidly escaping through the vents in the floors. "Kano has to be behind this. Massive waves, terrible storms ... it's obvious, once you think about it."

Malock glanced up at the closed hatch. The crashing of the ocean waves reverberated through the thick metal bulkheads, mixed with the groaning of the ship itself. "Of course. I'm surprised it took her this long to—"

The sound of feet beating against the metal floor cut him off and the next instant Jenur Takren stood in the doorway. Like Hana, she was completely dry, but she did have a long chicken leg in her right hand, like she had just been eating. Her short dark hair was brushed back, making her gray eyes look larger than they were.

"What's going on?" said Jenur, looking from Hana to Malock and back again. "Did we run into a storm?"

"Not any old storm," said Hana. "We think Kano is behind it, but honestly I wouldn't be surprised if the Rain God is helping. He's held a grudge against the Mechanical Goddess ever since she saved you and Malock here."

Jenur frowned when she looked at Hana. "How come you're still here? Shouldn't you be top deck where you could get knocked off by the waves? Accidentally, of course."

Though Malock was fairly certain that no one in the room could use pagomancy, the temperature in the room seemed to drop by about a dozen degrees when Hana glared at Jenur.

"For a former Dark Tiger, you certainly aren't very subtle," Hana said.

Malock groaned internally. Ever since they had left the Northern Isles, Hana and Jenur had been at each other's throats anytime they were near each other. He knew their personal history well enough not to be surprised by it, but whenever he was caught in the middle of their arguments, like he was now, he was reminded of the few times he had seen stray cats fighting in the streets of Port Blasan. That the two had not yet torn each other apart was a miracle, though Malock was not sure how much longer this 'miracle' would last.

"Subtlety's never been my strong suit," said Jenur. "Because unlike some people, I prefer to confront my problems personally, rather than blackmailing others into doing it for me."

"Is this really the time?" said Malock as he squeezed the water out of his boat cloak. "We should really—"

"Shut up, Malock," said Hana and Jenur in perfect unison, prompting him to do just that.

Then Hana said to Jenur, "At least I didn't kill someone's family member."

"You really just love bringing that up, don't you?" said Jenur. "He's not even really dead, is he? Can katabans actually die or did his spirit just go to wherever it is you katabans go when you don't have a physical body?"

"It doesn't matter," said Hana. "The point is, your hatred of me is irrational and annoying. Drop it."

"Irrational and annoying?" said Jenur. "Why, if we weren't on the

Mechanical Goddess's ship, I would—"

She was interrupted when the ship suddenly lurched to port, causing all three of them to stagger against the left bulkhead. This was followed by the sound of something large clanging against the deck overhead, though due to the lack of openings, it was impossible to tell what had fallen.

"Look, I understand that you two aren't the best of friends, but for the love of the Powers we should really go deeper into the ship," said Malock. "You know, away from the attacking gods? You can continue your arguing later or something, okay? We have better things to worry about right now."

Jenur huffed, turned around, and walked back the way she had came. Hana glared at her back as she left, then followed. Feeling that maybe they weren't going to murder each other after all, Malock went after them both.

They soon entered the dining room of the *Clockwork Heart*, a long room with an equally long oak dining table running down the center of it. To Malock's surprise, neither the table nor the chairs had been knocked over by the ship's sudden movements. A quick glance at the furnitures' legs revealed that they had been nailed to the floor.

Unfortunately, the same could not be said of the food. A jug of water had been knocked over, its liquids spilled onto the white tablecloth that covered the table. A plate of eggs lay on the floor, its glass shards scattered and mixed with the eggs. A faint coffee scent filled his nostrils and a quick glance down toward the other end of the table revealed that Rint's coffee cup had been knocked over.

Only two people were seated at the table, on the right side, both gripping their seats for dear life. One was a male aquarian with small tentacles hanging off his face like a beard, who sat similarly to Jenur. He was Quro, Jenur's adoptive father. Malock didn't know him very well, but the aura of experience and wisdom he gave off reminded Malock of Banika Koiro, his first mate back on his old ship, so he trusted Quro well. Quro kept a cool expression on his face, although the way he held onto his seat made it clear that he was not quite as confident as he appeared.

Sitting next to Quro was an old man named Rint Dolan, a fisherman who was the older brother of Kinker Dolan, another fisherman who had been a member of Malock's crew on his first voyage to World's End. Unlike Quro, Rint was not taking this well at all. His head was bent low near the table and he was literally trembling in his boots.

"What's going on out there?" said Rint when he spotted Jenur, Hana, and Malock. His question was addressed to Jenur. "A storm?"

"An attack," said Hana as she took a seat at the end of the table. "By some of the other gods, probably. My money is on either Kano or the Rain God or, far more likely, both."

Rint's eyes bugged out. "Two gods? Good grief, they really want to kill us, don't they?"

"I don't see why they would," said Quro. "It's not like we're doing anything wrong. We're trying to save the world. I would think they would like that."

"I think they're angry about Nimiko," said Jenur, glancing at the floor. She had taken a seat about a dozen chairs down from Hana. "They're probably trying to free him from us."

"Took them long enough to try," said Hana as the ship shook briefly. "I doubt they'll succeed, though. In order to get to the hold, they'd have to kill the Mechanical Goddess, an act which is forbidden by the Treaty."

Another thundering *boom* from above made Rint actually duck his head underneath the table, while Quro frowned. "My understanding of the whole northern/southern gods situation is sketchy at best, but what is to stop these gods from ripping the Mechanical Goddess open, but without actually killing her?"

"She wouldn't let them," said Hana. "Simple as that."

Malock took a seat near Hana; just in time, because the ship lurched forward. An ikadori peach slid past Malock off the edge of the table and onto the floor. It then slid down to the far end of the room, bumping against the steel door that was currently closed.

"You sound very confident about your Goddess," said Quro.

Hana nodded. "That's because she is very intelligent and cunning. Seeing as this ship is part of her body, she designed it in such a way that anyone who tries to break a hole in her hull would kill her. So I hope you can see why I'm not worried."

"Brilliant," said Quro. "I never thought I'd say that about any gods—much less this one—but that is brilliant I will admit."

"So we're safe?" said Rint, peeking out from under the table hopefully.

Hana leaned back and put her hands behind her head. "Of course we are. Especially since the Mechanical Goddess placed us all under her protection. The other gods can still touch us, but they can't kill us."

Rint let out a relieved sigh and climbed back onto his chair. "That's good to hear. I was really worried there for a—"

A loud *clang* echoed nearby, causing everyone at the table to look at the door from which Malock, Jenur, and Hana had just come through. Though the door stood firmly shut and locked, a large dent had been punched in it. Without speaking, everyone got to their feet and stepped away from the door, save for Rint, who hid under the table.

"What ... what is it?" said Jenur, her hand reaching for the knife strapped to her leg.

Hana gulped. "Maybe a servant of the other gods."

"But how did it get down here?" said Malock, trying not to sound afraid as he backed up. "Wouldn't the Mechanical Goddess or her automatons keep it out?"

"How the heck am I supposed to know?" said Hana. By now, she was halfway down the table. "It's not like I'm omniscient or anything."

Clang. Another dent, this one larger than the last, appeared in the door. The outline of the dent vaguely resembled a gigantic fist. Malock wished he had brought his sword with him because, as it currently stood, he was completely defenseless.

"What are we standing around here for?" said Jenur. "Let's go before that thing—"

WHAMP. The door went flying off its hinges, going so fast that Malock barely registered it. He dropped to his hands and knees just in time, however, to avoid getting hit. The door flew over his head, almost scraping his scalp, and crashed with a loud crunching sound at the back of the room. Alarmed, Malock looked over his shoulder and saw that the now-broken steel door had crashed into the other door at the end, effectively blocking off their only exit.

Then Malock heard a grunt and turned his head slowly to see something standing in the doorway. At first, he was not sure what he was looking at. He saw fists as large as boulders, a hog-like snout, boiling red skin, a cape as yellow as the midsummer sun, and two glowing red eyes that focused on him.

The creature—whatever it was—stepped through the doorway, breathing heavily through its snout. It resembled an ape in stature, as it walked with its front fists before it acting as its forelegs. The sound of thunder clapping and the wind tearing through the sky followed it, which added to its terrifying appearance.

"What is that?" said Jenur, pointing at the weird creature. "A pig ape?"

Hana shook her head. "No. It's a—"

"It?"

It was a moment before Malock realized that the voice had come from the creature. Its red eyes had drifted over to Hana and looked at her like it was offended.

"Did you just call me an it?" said the creature.

"Sorry," said Hana. "I mean, *he's* a katabans. Obviously."

The creature snorted. "Good. I am glad that you corrected yourself because I was about to say—"

Malock never did get to learn what the katabans was about to say because at that moment a ceiling panel opened up above it. Then a massive metal pillar slammed down on him with lightning speed. But rather than explode into guts and blood, the katabans actually caught the pillar on his back, though he was almost slammed into the floor by the sheer force of it.

"Oh, oh," said the katabans, sweat running down his face as he fought against the pillar. "I see the Goddess is awake after all. No ... ugh ... problem. I expected it."

The katabans grunted again and, with what appeared to be no effort at all, launched the pillar off his back. The pillar flew straight up back into the ceiling out of sight and Malock heard what sounded like pipes and gears being smashed as the pillar flew up. Bits of broken gears and smashed pipes rained from the hole in the ceiling, dropping onto the katabans' head, though he appeared about as bothered by it as if it were a light drizzle.

"By the way," said the katabans as he brushed some of the mechanical bits out of his short red hair, "you can call me Vurango, servant of the Rain God."

"You don't look like a katabans," said Jenur, her eyes darting between Hana and Vurango. "You look like a pig ... ape ... thing."

Vurango grunted again. "I had little choice over the form I was given. The Rain God plucked my spirit from the ethereal and gave me this body that he made. I am not complaining, however, because it is very strong, as I just proved."

"How did you even get here?" said Malock. "The automatons and Mechanical Goddess should have stopped you cold."

Vurango spat something out of his mouth. It rolled across the floor to Malock. A quick glance showed Malock that it was a half-eaten screw.

"Blech," said Vurango, sticking his tongue out. "The automatons fell easily, but I am not the only one in this attack. Other katabans are attacking the ship even as we speak. I was the only one who managed to break through the army of machines that was protecting this hatch."

"Others?" said Rint with a gulp. "How many others?"

Vurango ignored the question. "Enough babbling. Which one of you is Prince Malock?"

Malock stood up and said, "That would be me."

Vurango grimaced when he looked at Malock. "I see you suffer from the Burn of Grinf. And here I thought you were just born ugly."

The normally dull, ever-present burning pain in Malock's face flared up at those words, causing Malock to clutch his face. "Why do you want me?"

"To kill you," said Vurango. He looked around the room and said, "And I may as well kill the rest of you while I'm at it." He said that in the same tone of voice that a street cleaner used when he decided to do a little extra, dirty work that he had no reason not to do.

Vurango charged at Malock, but Malock rolled out of the way underneath the table. He crawled quickly under the table until he emerged on the right side. The others had joined him on the right side of the table, but Vurango had skidded to a stop and was now glaring at them all like he was thinking of all the ways he could kill them.

"Do you want to die?" said Vurango. "Because a mere table and chairs will not stop me."

Vurango then jumped onto the table, but before he could do anything, Hana jumped onto the table as well and kicked him in the face. The blow must have been stronger than it looked because Vurango actually went staggering backwards onto the floor, while Hana shouted, "You guys, get out of here! I'll deal with—"

Apparently she hadn't hit him hard enough because one of Vurango's huge fists reached up from the floor, wrapped around her waist, and lifted her off her feet. Then Vurango himself stood up, looking more angry than ever as Hana beat his arm with her hands and feet in an attempt to get him to let go.

"That was a good hit, Hanarova," said Vurango as he wiped blood off his chin from where Hana had hit him. "But not good enough."

He threw Hana to the side. She smashed into the far wall, near the blocked exit, and fell to the floor with a dull *thud*. Her body actually left an imprint in the metal wall, which explained why she didn't get up.

"Now, then," said Vurango, turning to face Malock and his friends. "I believe it's about time that I—"

A couple of *swooshes* was the only warning Malock got. The next moment, Vurango was clutching his throat, blood leaking through his fingers as he gasped for air, while Quro stood there holding his hand up.

"Dragon shark scales," said Quro, when the others gave him curious looks. "Now we need to go before he recovers. Go!"

Malock didn't hesitate. He ran down the room, with Jenur, Rint, and Quro right behind him, but before he could reach the unblocked exit, Vurango appeared there. Malock had to skid to a halt to avoid running into the katabans, but he was too late. Vurango reached over with one massive fist and grabbed Malock, lifting the Prince off his feet as he glared at him. Blood still ran down Vurango's chest, but somehow that didn't seem to bother him. The dragon shark scales didn't appear to bother him, either.

"Let him go!" Jenur shouted, but before she or Quro or Rint could do anything, Vurango swiped at all three of them with his left fist, knocking them all over and on top of each other.

While they struggled to untangle each other's limbs, Vurango looked up at Malock with pure loathing. He clearly couldn't talk because of the scales in his throat, but that didn't stop his eyes from telling Malock everything that he was thinking.

Then Vurango's grip around Malock's body constricted, causing Malock to gasp for air. It was like being crushed between two huge, thick boulders. In fact, Malock felt like he was going to explode any minute now. He tried fighting back, but due to the lack of air, he succeed only in patting Vurango's fist and weakly kicking it once. His vision began to darken, while the scent of wet fur and mud—which his air-deprived brain realized was coming from Vurango—filled his nostrils, making thinking impossible.

Just as Malock thought he heard something crack, Vurango roared in pain and dropped Malock. Too weak to land properly, Malock fell on his back. His body felt like a crushed tin can, but he did manage to look up and see Vurango had whirled around, revealing the automaton Calir clinging to his back. Calir had driven his sword directly into Vurango's spine, causing blood to gush out from the wound even as Vurango cursed and roared in a language Malock didn't understand.

Finally, Vurango reached behind his back and grabbed Calir. He threw the automaton off his back, but Calir managed to twist in midair and land on the table. Vurango turned to face Calir, his pig-like face making him look as though he was going to slaughter everyone.

"I see ... I see I didn't smash ... didn't smash all of the automatons who tried to stop me," said Vurango. With his throat cut open and the sword still embedded in his spine, it was a miracle that he was still living at all, much less capable of speaking. "Not ... not a problem. I'll kill you and finish off Malock, just as I was ordered—"

The clicking and clanking of gears caused Malock to look over his shoulder. A panel on the wall behind him had slid away, revealing a dark opening that appeared entirely empty. Vurango noticed it, too, because he turned to look at it and said, "What is—"

Without warning, a gigantic, spiky spear shot out of the hole. Vurango didn't even have time to react. The spear shot straight through his chest, the force of the blow sending him flying backwards. He slammed against the wall opposite, the spear still sticking out of his bloody chest. He no longer moved or breathed, and his face was now frozen in perpetual shock.

Calir jumped down from the table. The automaton inspected Vurango's corpse; at first, Malock thought that he was making sure Vurango was dead. Then Calir shoved his hand into Vurango's corpse, causing more blood to pour out, and a few seconds later pulled his sword out of the body. With Calir's back facing him, all Malock could see was the automaton inspecting his blade, perhaps to make sure it was in good condition, and then sheath it at his side. The sword was incredibly bloody, absolutely covered in the stuff, and the metallic scent of blood filled Malock's nostrils, making him sick to his stomach.

Then Calir turned and bent over Malock. Malock tried to say, "Thank you," but after getting crushed almost to death, he could barely utter even one syllable.

Not that it was needed. Calir just hovered one of his hands over Malock's body, almost like he was casting a spell, and then glanced at his hand. Then Calir stood up and, without another word, ran out of the room back to the hatch. A moment later, Hana staggered into Malock's view. Blood leaked from her crown and her right arm appeared entirely dislocated, but she otherwise looked quite good despite being thrown into a metal wall by a superhuman spirit.

She cast one disgusted look at Vurango's corpse and then turned to look at Malock. "How do you feel?"

Malock just said, "Unnhhh." It was about all he could say.

Hana raised an eyebrow. "Didn't catch that. Is that a mortal word for 'okay' or something?"

Malock didn't know if Hana was being sarcastic or not. He just shook his head, which he figured was a lot less ambiguous.

"I see," said Hana. She looked at the blood on the floor and wall and grimaced. "That's going to take a while to clean."

"Unnhh," said Malock again. He was trying to tell her to stop stating the obvious, but his tongue didn't really want to work.

"Guess I'd better go check the situation top deck," said Hana. "I'll be back in a minute. You just stay there, now. You look way too beat up to go anywhere."

With those words, Hana was gone, running out the open doorway. Malock gritted his teeth, thinking of all of the choice insults he wanted to say to her, but with his body still recovering, he kept his mouth shut. He would tell her how he felt about her later.

Chapter Two

SKIMIF WISHED THAT HE had not chosen this day to stage another protest in front of the Temple of Grinf. With the sun blazing hot and no close body of water with which he could use to moisten his skin, Skimif felt more and more like the fried fish he usually saw on sale in the markets of Port Blasan. His fellow Heathens looked as uncomfortable as he did, especially Aqur, who was frequently pouring water on her head from her water jug. The human Heathens didn't suffer the same way, but they were sweating nonetheless.

As terrible as the heat was, however, it was not nearly as bad as the dozen huge, bulky men in red armor, equipped with spears and shields, marching on the Heathens. The sunlight glinted off the helmets of the Justice Enforcers, and though Skimif assumed that he should be afraid of them, he could not help but wonder just how hot they were in that heavy armor. It had to be at least ninety degrees out and that armor didn't look very cool.

By contrast, Skimif and his fellow Heathens were unarmed. No swords or spears or axes or even knives, not so much as a stick with which to defend themselves. This was largely because Skimif didn't want people to think that the Brotherhood was composed of violent terrorists. Their protests had always been peaceful and he planned for them to stay that way.

Skimif looked at his fellow Heathens. Aqur was standing next to him, carrying a large sign with the words *THE DAY OF THE GODS IS COMING* written in large lettering. Her green eyes had narrowed on the incoming Enforcers.

"Whatever they do, keep your cool," Skimif said. "Pass the message on to the others."

Thankfully, Aqur didn't argue this time, even though he could tell that she wanted to. She whispered the message to the next Heathen, who then passed it onto the one by his side, until soon every Heathen knew Skimif's message. He could feel the nervousness flowing among them, but the Brotherhood had so far managed to avoid getting into violent confrontations with the Enforcers and Skimif intended for it to stay that way.

The Enforcers stopped about ten yards away from the Heathens. Their faces obscured by their helmets, it was impossible to tell what the Enforcers were thinking. Skimif remembered quite vividly what happened the last few times the Enforcers had confronted the Heathens. Several of his followers had already been arrested, a sobering thought, though he tried not to let it bother him too much because the Brotherhood was far bigger than the current group that was with him. Even if he himself was arrested, he knew that the Brotherhood would continue on regardless. Their message was powerful and true, and powerful and true messages were not crushed easily.

The lead Enforcer stepped forward. She was clearly a squad captain, based on the golden helmet she wore. She didn't appear to be General Farig, the woman in charge of all of the Justice Enforcers on Carnag, but that was to be expected, as General Farig was not the kind of general to lead her troops into battle.

Having never seen this particular Enforcer before—though admittedly, Skimif could not be sure, as few of them ever removed their helmets and they all had a very similar build, so he wasn't good at distinguishing them—he didn't know what to expect. A sense of nervousness arose in his body, but he pushed it down. Right now was not the time to freak out, especially not in front of his followers. He had already done enough of that in private when he had learned about the end of the world a week ago.

"Why haven't they arrested us?" Aqur muttered.

Skimif glanced at her, but only briefly, as he didn't want to take his eyes off the Enforcers for too long. "What?"

"The Enforcers," said Aqur, in the same low voice. "They could easily take us if they have to. We're unarmed and outnumbered. They've been trying to get you, in particular, for weeks."

"Maybe they're afraid of starting a riot," Skimif said out of the corner of his mouth. His eyes were still focused on the Captain. "Lots of people are becoming sympathetic to our cause."

Aqur cast a quick look around the street before the Temple, a frown on her jellyfish-like face. "There aren't too many people around here who would cause a riot. Although, if push came to shove, I certainly would, if it meant saving you from their grasp."

Skimif didn't smile at that, mostly because the Enforcers were still staring at them. He didn't know what they were thinking or planning, and he wasn't going to let them know what he was thinking, either, although if they had any telemancers or psychimancers among them —which he doubted, as the Justice Enforcers were not known to use those kinds of mages—his facial expressions meant nothing either way.

"You," said the Captain, her voice slightly distorted through the helmet. "Skimif of Tunya."

Skimif frowned. "That's me, yes."

A few passersby had stopped to watch the scene, but they were the only ones who did so. The vast majority of Carnagians simply walked by, largely because some of the Enforcers were glaring at the citizens, as if it were now a crime to stop and watch the confrontation playing out in front of the Temple of Grinf. Though Skimif wondered if it had at least partly to do with the fact that the people of Carnag were not nearly as united in their hatred of the Heathens as they appeared.

"I am Captain Banika Koiro," the Captain said. "I and my squad were sent to send you protestors away and to deliver a message to you, Skimif of Tunya."

Skimif exchanged a quick look with Aqur before returning his attention to Captain Koiro. "Deliver a message? From who?"

"The King and Queen of Carnag," said Koiro. "They have intended to deliver this message to you for a while now, but due to the recent death of Princess Raya Kabadi of Shika, and the even more recent disappearance of Prince Malock, they have been delayed from doing so."

Skimif knew that Malock hadn't actually disappeared, but he

didn't say anything. Over the last week since Malock had gone to World's End to find the Powers, the Justice Enforcers had become even more strict. Nearly every building in the city had been searched by the Enforcers in their attempt to find the Prince, but since Malock had last been seen on Shika, there was even more anti-Shikan hate in Carnag than ever. In fact, from what Skimif knew, most Carnagians hated the Shikans far worse than the Heathens, which was both comforting and disturbing. Aqur had even informed him of rumors going around suggesting that the King and Queen of Carnag were planning to declare war on Shika, but whether there was any truth to those rumors, Skimif didn't know. He hoped there wasn't, however, because a war with Shika would certainly throw a wrench in his plans.

"And what is this message you have to deliver?" said Skimif. "I am listening."

"The message is this," said Koiro. She pulled a folded letter from her breastplate and unfolded it neatly. She then began to read: "*To Skimif, leader of the Brotherhood of Heathens: As the rulers of Carnag, we have taken a great interest in your message. That is why we are inviting you to come and debate Grinfian monk Yamaru Domaha at the Stadium one week from today just after lunch. You will be given an opportunity in which to share your views with a wider audience, including to members of the Carnagian Royal Family itself.*

We await your response,

King Halock and Queen Markinia."

That must have been the end of the message because Koiro folded the letter up, gently replaced in its envelope, and slid the envelope back into her armor. She then looked at Skimif expectantly.

Skimif blinked. "The King and Queen have invited me to a public debate? At the Stadium?"

"That's what the letter said," said Koiro, patting her crimson breastplate, where the letter was stored.

"And what will happen if I refuse?"

Koiro didn't say anything. She just rested her hand on the sword sheathed at her side, while her fellow Enforcers stood erect, as if awaiting their Captain's command.

"Don't do it," said Aqur under her breath, so low that only Skimif could hear her. Her eyes were on Koiro. "It's a trick."

"You think I don't realize that?" Skimif muttered in return, now privately wishing that he hadn't left behind his sword, Pointy, at the hideout. "Of course it's a trick. I'm not naïve enough to believe that the King and Queen don't have some kind of plan in place to arrest me."

"The King and Queen gave me their word that you would not be harassed at the event," said Koiro. It was as if she had heard what he said, which meant she either had great hearing or had simply gotten lucky. "We Justice Enforcers were given orders not to harass you, unless the Brotherhood causes a public disturbance of some sort that requires action on our part."

"Can you guarantee that others will not try to harm us?" said Skimif.

Koiro's form remained rigid. "As I said, I can only guarantee that the Justice Enforcers will not bother you."

"Then what's the point of this debate?" said Aqur, a slight growl to her voice. "I cannot honestly believe that the King and Queen of

Carnag—easily the two most ardent followers of Grinf in all of Carnag—value a debate that could bring our views to a wider audience than ever before."

One of the Justice Enforcers took a step forward. He was larger than the others, wearing armor that appeared to have been especially designed for his bulk. And rather than the standard sword and shield equipment that all Enforcers carried, he gripped a massive battle ax in his right hand. Skimif wondered how he had failed to notice the giant of a human until now, but it didn't matter because Koiro raised a hand and the Enforcer stepped back, albeit reluctantly.

"I would think it rather obvious," said Koiro, her voice tinged with a hint of condescension. "King Halock and Queen Markinia have never been ones to support Heathen views; however, they have always been ones to value intelligent public debate in order to educate the public. Unlike the warlords of Ruwa or some other backwards eastern island, the King and Queen of Carnag have always valued fair play."

As a farmer, Skimif had never had a very thorough education; a pithy saying from his grandfather here ("Never trust the neighbor with yesterday's crops"), a lesson in math there ("If you planted sixteen rows of seaweed and only harvest eight at the end of the month, then you've got half less than you can raise a family on and half more than you can feed yourself with"). Indeed, he had spent much of the last few months attempting to correct that imbalance by reading whatever books he could get his hands on, which had been a difficult feat because reading had not been something he had been taught, although his skill in that area had grown in leaps and bounds since a reading teacher had joined the Brotherhood a while back. He still considered himself a simple aquarian, one who happened to believe that most people were not out to get him.

But even he could detect the fraud in Koiro's words. Ever since the Brotherhood of Heathens had revealed itself to the general Carnagian population, Skimif and his fellow Heathens had spent much of their time avoiding getting captured by the Justice Enforcers. Even when the Heathens held peaceful protests or gatherings, the Enforcers always showed up to try to arrest whoever they could lay their hands on. If the King and Queen truly cared about giving a fair hearing to all points of view, then they wouldn't have tried to shut down the Heathens' public demonstrations in the first place.

Reaching for his water jug, Skimif said, "Do I have to make this decision right away?"

Koiro's fingers wrapped around the hilt of her sword. "I was not told there was a deadline, but if I were you, I would think twice about rejecting this offer. This would be the perfect opportunity for you to spread your views without worrying about us Enforcers bothering you."

Skimif popped open the lid of his jug and drank from it briefly. Though his throat was dry, his skin was drier. He refrained from dumping the water all over his body, however, as he knew from experience that most humans didn't appreciate it. The last thing he needed to do was give the Enforcers a reason to arrest him.

"I would like to speak with my brother and sister Heathens first," said Skimif. "If that is all right with you."

Koiro's helmet blocked her face, but her voice was clear as she said,

"Certainly. I would suggest not doing that for very long, however, because the King and Queen expect an answer soon."

Skimif gathered his Heathens together in a circle. To make sure the Enforcers wouldn't attack them while their backs were turned, Skimif had a few of the Heathens face the Enforcers. With all of the Heathens close together, the stench of the drying bodies of the aquarians and the sweating bodies of the humans combined to make an awful smell that Skimif, nonetheless, did his best to ignore.

"Don't do it," said Aqur. "I know I already said that, but—"

"But it's the truth," said one of the other Heathens, a bald-headed man whose name escaped Skimif's mind at the moment. "Even I can see that this is all a setup."

"I know, I know," said Skimif, glancing over his shoulder at the Enforcers, who, true to their word, had not moved an inch from their current position. "This whole thing is very fishy. I would not be at all surprised if this turned out to be a way to get us cornered in one spot so they could arrest us all or something."

"Then why not just reject them outright?" said Aqur. "Tell 'em that you're not interested and that the King and Queen can go eat mud for all you care."

"That might get them angry," Skimif said. "But while that idea sounds great, I am not so sure I want to reject their offer just yet."

"Yeah," another Heathen broke in, this one a female human. "Because if you did, I bet the Enforcers would just attack us. Probably drag us down the street to the prison or something."

"They didn't say they would do that," said Skimif.

"But they implied it," said Aqur. "Didn't you see that big guy?

They really hate us."

"That may be true," said Skimif. "If it is, I don't have much choice but to accept, now do I?"

"You'll regret it," said Aqur. "All of us will, I'm sure of it."

Skimif had to look over his shoulder again, this time letting his gaze linger on the weapons that the Enforcers held. He remembered well the actions the Enforcers had shown against him and his fellow Heathens over the past few weeks. He wondered if he and his fellow Heathens could run away and escape the Enforcers, but when he noticed a glint of red in the shadow of a nearby alleyway—the armor of another Enforcer, hiding in the shadows, perhaps to attack them if they behaved in a way the Enforcer didn't like—he realized that there was nowhere they could run to.

And of course, Skimif realized that in the end, it didn't matter what he said or did. The Powers were coming to destroy their creation. When they would get here, he didn't know, but he did know that they were coming. He still remembered the traumatic visions he had experienced merely a week ago. True, Malock and the others were going to stop them, but he didn't have any confidence that they could, even if they had two gods on their side. The Powers drew closer and closer to Martir ever day. He could sense them, though why, he wasn't sure.

"All right," said Skimif, turning his attention back to the others. "I've made my decision. Do I have all of your support?"

"Depends on what your decision is," said Aqur. "If you're going to agree to the offer—"

"I am," said Skimif, looking at her hard. "Do you disagree with that?"

Aqur pursed her lips. "Yes. I do."

Skimif looked at his fellow Heathens. "And? Do the rest of your support my decision?"

All of them looked uncomfortable at being asked the question. He could tell that they didn't agree with it at all, that they thought he was foolish for agreeing to it. But none of them spoke up, and he realized that he didn't really need their approval. After all, with the end of the world coming soon, this particular decision didn't really matter in the long run because there wasn't going to be a long run ever again.

So the Heathens broke their circle and turned to face the Enforcers.

"Well?" said Koiro, though her voice was less impatient and more curious. "What's your decision?"

Skimif took a quick sip from his water jug again, just to moisten his throat, and said, "My decision is this: I will attend the public debate with monk Yamaru Domaha. I only ask that you keep your word and not harass or bother any of my fellow Heathens who may attend to watch."

Even as Skimif spoke those words, he could sense his fellow Heathens behind him silently disapproving. In fact, he doubted that any of them would actually attend the event. And to be honest, he wasn't sure if he would, either, because for all he knew, the Powers might arrive before then and render this entire conversation moot.

Koiro nodded and said, "I will deliver this message to the King and Queen without delay. Remember, the debate will be exactly one week from today, in the Stadium, after lunch."

Skimif nodded in return. "I will be sure to remember that date."

With that, Koiro turned and walked away. Her fellow Enforcers followed her, though the big one from before hesitated for just a moment longer. He cast a hateful gaze at Skimif—easy to tell even with the helmet he wore, because the Enforcer's hand firmly tightened around the handle of his ax.

Then the Enforcer resumed following his Captain and cohorts, the clinking of their metal-toed boots against the street announcing their presence for anyone to hear.

As he watched them go, Skimif looked up at the sky. He hoped that he had made the right decision, but when he turned around and saw the less-than-enthusiastic expressions on his fellow Heathens' faces, he began to doubt himself.

Chapter Three

EVENTUALLY, MALOCK BEGAN TO feel well enough to get up and check on the others. He discovered that, while Jenur and Quro had taken Vurango's blow without suffering anything more serious than some nasty bruises, Rint had fractured his left knee. They didn't have any real medical supplies on hand to treat his knee, so they just sat Rint in the least painful position they could and tied a part of the tablecloth around his knee to keep the swelling down. Even then, Rint kept groaning in pain. Malock would have gone and found someone to help, but he knew that all of the automatons were currently top deck defending the ship from their attackers. And seeing as none of them knew where the medical supplies were kept on this ship, they were forced to wait out the fight in the dining room. That wouldn't have been such a bad thing if Vurango's corpse hadn't smelled like rotting bacon, his stench getting worse and worse with each passing hour, forcing them to move down to the very end of the dining room, away from the exit, which they had failed to close because the door had been knocked off its hinges by Vurango and it was too heavy to move back into place. They just hoped that none of the enemy attackers would take advantage of the open doorway to come running in.

"Do you think they're still fighting up there?" said Jenur, looking up at Malock, rubbing a bump on her forehead. "Can you hear anything?"

Malock raised his head to the ceiling, tilting it to the right, as that was the ear he happened to hear the best out of. The low hum of the Mechanical Goddess's engines reverberated through the air, but he could not tell if there was any fighting going on top deck or not. The metal plating on the ceiling was too thick and the sound of the engines too loud.

With a shrug, Malock said, "I don't know. Best we can do for now is wait until someone comes down."

Quro, who was sitting against the wall, patted the floor and said, "The ship has stopped shaking."

Malock looked down. Quro was right. The floor of the dining room was still.

"Maybe Kano gave up," Rint said, anxiously rubbing his hands together.

"She certainly seems to have stopped rocking the ship," said Quro. "The only question is, why? Did she really give up, as Rint said, or is there another reason for it?"

No one knew the answer, so for the next ten or twenty minutes, the party of four sat in silence. Every time a sharp noise rang out, the whole group would look up. Malock hoped for Hana or one of the automatons to appear, but with each passing minute, that hope slowly turned to despair. He had no idea what kind of forces the other gods had marshaled against the Mechanical Goddess. She was probably not dead, but that didn't mean she couldn't be incapacitated.

Or worse, they made a deal with her, Malock thought. *I can see it now: 'Give us Nimiko or we will kill all of your automatons.' She'd probably throw us in for good measure, seeing as she would have no reason to carry us anymore.*

Of course, that was silly paranoia. At the start of this journey, the Mechanical Goddess had made it very clear—through her servant Hana—that she was going to stick with Malock and the others to the end. Unlike the rest of the gods, the Mechanical Goddess wanted to save the world. Though she had not been happy upon learning about Nimiko's capture (mostly because she, as a southern goddess, disliked the idea of any god being at the mercy of mortals), she had understood why they had taken him with them and had shown no interest in freeing her older brother. For that Malock was grateful, as he had no doubt what Nimiko would do to them if the God of Light was free.

Then again, Malock thought about all of the things the Mechanical Goddess had done to them in the past. Feeding several of his crew mates to her siblings, allowing her servant Hana to manipulate Jenur instead of being straight with her about what the Mechanical Goddess honestly wanted her to do (a thought which made Malock grind his teeth in anger sometimes, as it was because of the Mechanical Goddess's mishap that Princess Raya, Malock's friend, had died), and probably other things Malock didn't even know about. Add her status as a southern goddess to the list and Malock was starting to believe that she had appeased her siblings by coming to some sort of agreement with them that might hurt him and the others at some point.

He looked at the others. Jenur held one hand over her black eye, Quro was rubbing his arm, and Rint was quietly grumbling about his shattered kneecap. If the Mechanical Goddess had actually betrayed them—and it was not a thought he wished to see realized—none of them were in any condition to fight back. Not even Jenur could defend them, and she was easily the best fighter out of them all.

Maybe I should just have faith in the Mechanical Goddess, Malock thought. Then he caught himself. *What am I thinking? I'm a Heathen. Heathens don't have faith in the gods. The better word would be trust, although even that is stretching it a bit.*

The more Malock thought about their current situation, the more he found himself regretting it. True, he was on a mission to save the world, which he supposed was a noble goal, but he had left without informing his parents. No doubt they were panicking, maybe even inching toward war with Shika. He had left them a note, which he had given to one of the servants of Castle Shika prior to his and Jenur's departure from the island, but whether they had read it or not, he didn't know.

Moreover, he had left with the Mechanical Goddess. Originally, he and Jenur had planned to have Nimiko teleport them to World's End, but the God of Light had refused point blank to do such a thing, mostly because he was a stubborn, nihilistic idiot who was still sour about being caught by a bunch of mortals. Had the Mechanical Goddess not offered them a ride down south, there was a good chance that Malock and Jenur wouldn't have even made it this far.

Not that Malock was pleased about the Mechanical Goddess, mind you. When he had learned of what Hana had threatened to do to Rint and Quro if Jenur did not comply with their demands, he had been enraged. He even challenged Hana to a duel, but she rejected the offer and pointed out how useless it would have been even if she had accepted it. Her exact words were, *How would getting killed by me bring back Raya or undo anything? You mortals can be really stupid sometimes, you know that?*

Needless to say, Malock would have socked her right there if he and Jenur hadn't needed the Mechanical Goddess's services. He did wonder why the Mechanical Goddess had deceived Jenur, but he supposed that even the gods who were on their side were not exactly the kindest or most considerate of individuals. He had learned that much from his first voyage to World's End.

The groaning of the ship caused all of them to jump, including Rint, but as soon as he did, he cursed far more foully than the entire crew of the *Iron Wind* put together. Whenever Malock looked at Rint, he had a hard time not thinking of Kinker. He wondered why Rint had bothered to come along at all, seeing as he was not a very brave man and could not fight or anything, but he supposed that, as Martir was Rint's world, too, the old fisherman had reason enough to join them on their cruise to the Void.

Quro the Thinker was another mystery passenger to Malock. True, he had gotten to know Quro fairly well after the two weeks they had spent going south, but the aquarian was still an enigma to him. It was probably because of Quro's identity as a Dark Tiger, a revelation that had alarmed Malock when he first learned of it. The Dark Tigers had a well-known reputation for killing politicians and rulers; in fact, one Dark Tiger had tried to kill Malock's father, King Halock, years ago when Malock was only ten. The attempt had been foiled thanks to the timely arrival of the Justice Enforcers, but from what Malock had been told, the Dark Tiger had come very close to killing his father, supposedly bringing the tip of his blade up to the King's neck while he slept.

But Quro had shown himself to be an honest fellow who didn't show any interest in assassinating Malock or anyone else. Seeing as Malock was Jenur's friend, he supposed it made sense, but he still felt skittish around Quro anyway. He would have felt the same way around Jenur, if he had not learned that she had quit the Dark Tigers a while ago and had no interest in ever returning to that lifestyle.

As for why Quro had come along, he said he had done it to keep an eye on Jenur. He said that as her father he wasn't going to let her go off on her own again, possibly to die, not when he could protect her. Jenur had actually argued with him—quite loudly, Malock remembered—about that, but in the end, Quro had won. Although how helpful he would actually be, when no one knew what lay beyond the Void, Malock didn't know.

Finally, Hana stepped through the door-less doorway. She looked tired, her long hair hanging from her head like vines from a tree.

"So?" said Malock, pushing himself away from the wall and walking up to the table. "What's going on?"

"The other gods have left," said Hana. She wiped sweat off her forehead. "They're no longer attacking. The Mechanical Goddess told me that she managed to beat them off."

"Is she sure about that?" said Jenur, nervously glancing at the ceiling. "'Cause I'm not sure I want to go out there if I could be killed by a god."

"She's sure," said Hana. "Said that it's unlikely they'll return because she hit them pretty hard. That, and she invoked the Fifth Clause of the Treaty."

Rint looked up, peering over the top of the table so he could see Hana better, his anguished face frowning in confusion. "The Fifth Clause? What does that mean?"

"It basically means that none of the other gods can attempt to attack the Mechanical Goddess," Hana said. "Basically, by invoking the Fifth Clause, the other gods are not allowed to harm the Mechanical Goddess for a week. After that, they can do what they like to her, except kill her, obviously."

"Well, why didn't she invoke the Fifth Clause before?" said Malock. "Would have saved us a lot of time and grief."

"Because she didn't need to, obviously," said Hana, rolling her eyes. "The Mechanical Goddess is all about efficiency. She doesn't waste something as important as the Fifth Clause when there is no need to."

"I guess you make a good point," said Malock. "What kind of damage did the *Clockwork Heart* endure?"

"Nothing we can't repair," said Hana. "Though we lost a lot of automatons in the battle. Lots of dead katabans too, though we've already cleaned up most of them and dumped their bodies into the sea."

Malock grimaced and looked at Vurango's corpse, which still had the thick spear embedded in its chest. "I assume the Mechanical Goddess took care of most of them, like she did to Vurango here?"

"More or less," said Hana. "There are all sorts of neat little traps in this ship. Even I don't know even half of them and I've worked on it for years. Doesn't help that she's always adding new ones or improving the old ones."

"Why didn't you tell us?" said Rint as he looked worriedly around the room. "What if we accidentally set off a trap without realizing it?"

"Not possible," said Hana, shaking her head. "The Mechanical Goddess isn't one to create those kinds of traps. Only she can activate her traps. So, unless you've angered her somehow, you don't have to worry about ending up like this idiot here."

She gestured at Vurango's bloody corpse as she said that.

"Speaking of Vurango, we should really get this removed," said Hana. She looked over her shoulder and shouted, "Automatons, get this corpse out of here. It's stinking up the place."

A moment later, two automatons entered the room, pulled the spear out of Vurango's corpse, and then lifted up the corpse with ease. While they carried it away, a third automaton appeared with a bucket and mop and began moping up the blood and guts that remained where Vurango's corpse had lain. In just a few minutes, this automaton accomplished his task, for when he lifted up his mop and bucket and left, the area was practically spotless, almost shining in its cleanliness. The spear itself retracted back into the wall where it had launched from and the panel slid back in place, thus making that spot look like how it had before Vurango appeared.

Then Hana snapped her fingers and another couple of automatons entered the room. She pointed at the steel door that had been punched off its hinges, which they immediately ran over to. The duo lifted up the door in a similar manner to how the other two lifted up Vurango's corpse and soon they had taken the door away, perhaps to fix it, though Malock couldn't be sure.

"There," said Hana, folding her arms satisfactorily. "What did I tell you? The Mechanical Goddess and her servants are efficient, if nothing else."

"That's nice," said Rint. Then he groaned. "But you know what would be nicer? Someone actually healing my kneecap. Can your automatons or Mechanical Goddess do that?"

Hana cracked her knuckles and said, "They can't. But I can."

She moved around the table, brushing past Quro and Jenur (Jenur a little harder than Quro) on her way to Rint. When she reached the old man, she placed her hand on his shattered left kneecap. Before anyone could react, a brief yet bright light shone, and when it faded, Rint looked exactly the same as he had before. The only difference was that he did not appear to be in pain anymore.

"Wow," said Rint, bending his knee experimentally. "How did you do that?"

Hana stood up and turned around. "I know some panamancy, even though I'm not a follower of Atikos. You kind of have to when you're in my position, since the Mechanical Goddess knows little about how to heal organics, and her automatons are just as ignorant."

Rint now looked at Hana with the kind of awe that most people normally reserved for the gods themselves. "Well, I would like to thank you anyway. You're much kinder than I first thought."

Hana didn't appear to hear him because she was already walking back to the exit. "If any of you would like to come top deck and see the damage, you're welcome to, but I'm not sure you'd like to."

Although Vurango's corpse may have been taken away and the spot where it had lain cleared of all traces of blood, the horrible stench of death still filled Malock's nostrils. And based on the expressions on the others' faces, they, too, could still smell it.

So Malock said, "I'd like to come. Need some fresh air after all we've been through."

"Same here," said Jenur.

Rint got to his feet, using one of the chairs set around the dining table for support, and said, "I'm going back to my cabin, I think. After all of this excitement, I need to rest."

Quro rubbed his side and said, "I'm tired, too. So I'll just head on back to my cabin as well."

Malock had a hard time believing that the Mechanical Goddess was okay when he, Hana, and Jenur emerged from the hatch onto the surface of the *Clockwork Heart*. Deep dents in the deck that resembled the outlines of knuckles made the surface uneven, although as he watched the dents unbent themselves, which Hana informed him was the Mechanical Goddess's body at work healing itself. She explained it was similar to how the body of an organic being would naturally heal a wound on it, which made Malock realize—not for the first time—that he had been sleeping in the belly of a goddess for the last two weeks, a thought which disturbed him greatly.

Furthermore, the bodies and body parts of dozens of automatons were scattered everywhere—far more than Malock had thought manned the ship, though when he thought about it, the Mechanical Goddess had never told him how many she had. One automaton was little more than a smoking wreck, appearing much like it had been struck by lightning. About six or seven undamaged automatons were going around collecting the parts in huge metal crates that they rolled around on tiny wheels. Malock wondered if any of the automatons felt any sadness when they saw the corpses of their brothers; then again, they were mechanical, so he doubted it.

The highest deck of the *Clockwork Heart* still stood, but it had clearly taken a few hits. An entire layer of metal had been ripped off its left side, revealing a complicated, though skeletal, framework of wires, gears, pipes, and other things Malock couldn't identify. One of the large smokestacks had a large hole in the center, which a couple of automatons hanging off ropes were busily covering with what looked like a thin sheet of metal.

"Boy, she looks like she took a lot of hits," said Jenur, scratching her chin as she looked around at the ship's deck. "Did you say it was Kano and the Rain God who attacked?"

"I didn't actually see either of them, mind," said Hana with a shrug. "But the Mechanical Goddess sure is a lot more creative with her insults than I thought she was. Makes your old ragtag group of sailors look like refined gentlemen."

Malock scratched the back of his head. "Were there any other gods?"

"Niham, Goddess of the West Wind," said Hana. "Kano's wife.

41

Looked like she and the Rain God combined their powers to make a very powerful storm."

"What are they going to do with all of those parts?" said Malock, gesturing at the automatons pushing the huge crates around.

"They'll rebuild the ones that can be rebuilt," said Hana. "The rest will be put in storage in the hold to be used as spare parts later. Anything else will be junked. The Mechanical Goddess doesn't like wasting anything even remotely useable."

"You mean it doesn't bother her at all that some of her 'children' are dead?" said Malock. "Not even slightly?"

"You'd have to ask her yourself," said Hana. "If I had to say, I'd say that it probably doesn't bug her much. It's not hard for her to make more automatons. They're very easy to make and easy to rebuild if they get blown apart, like those ones did."

"She's not much of a caring mother, then, is she?" said Malock.

The other smokestack—the one that hadn't been damaged in the attack—exploded with smoke and flames, causing Malock and Jenur to start. The smoke and flames spewed for several seconds, burning through the air and sending ash everywhere. The ash lightly rained down from the sky onto their clothes and onto the deck of the ship itself.

Dusting the ash off his shoulders, Malock said, "What was that all about?"

"The Mechanical Goddess didn't like your accusation," said Hana. "She thinks of herself as being far more caring than you say she is."

Deciding it best not to argue with a goddess, Malock said, "How much longer until we reach World's End?"

"Oh, I'd say probably about three or four days, assuming nothing else goes wrong," said Hana. "That little attack from the other gods slowed us down a bit, but not too much thankfully. Still full steam ahead."

"We're just going to go straight past World's End, though, right?" said Jenur. "Because I don't think the gods want us setting foot there."

"That's the plan," said Hana. "We go past World's End to the Void, and from there on, you and Nimiko will make the rest of the journey without us."

Malock frowned. "Wait, you mean the Mechanical Goddess isn't coming with us?"

Hana nodded, as if this was an obvious fact. "Of course. She may want to save the world, but she hates going into the unknown without at least some idea of what will happen. Not even the gods know what lies beyond the Void, after all."

"None of them do?" said Jenur, leaning forward slightly. "Are you sure?"

Hana put her hands behind her back and stared out into the sea. A strong wind blew off the starboard just then—not strong enough to blow them away, but enough to blow in the salty scent of the sea around them. "Well, I guess that is something of an exaggeration. There is one god who went beyond the Void and returned. We don't talk about *him*, though."

"Why not?" said Malock. "If he's gone beyond the Void and returned, then surely we should go to him and ask him what he saw, right?"

"That's just the thing," said Hana. She turned her attention back to Malock and Jenur, a frown across her thin lips. "He's difficult to find, to put it mildly. As in, not even the other gods know where he is half the time. Hell, most of them aren't even sure he's actually a god or if he's ... something else."

As an automaton pushed a heavy cart past them, the metal parts within clinking together, Malock said, "That's ridiculous. How can you not be sure if a god is actually a god? There are no other beings on Martir who are on that same power level at the gods. Even our most powerful mages don't come close to being mistaken for gods."

Hana took off her Monmouth cap and rubbed her forehead. "You'd think, but there are things even in this world that the gods don't understand. Such as the beast that sleeps on the bottom of the ocean, which the gods call the Sleeping Beast."

"The what?" said Jenur.

"The Sleeping Beast," said Hana. "None of the gods know what its purpose is or why it sleeps there. Even Kano doesn't know. Best they can figure is that the Sleeping Beast was created by the Powers and put there, though whether even that much is true is anyone's guess at this point."

Malock shuddered and looked down at the deck beneath his feet. "How big are we talking?"

"Big as Stalf," said Hana. "And don't worry, none of the gods have ever tried to awaken it. Henim, the God of Dreams, did try to see what it dreams about, but he found out that it doesn't dream about anything at all. Most of the time, the gods try to pretend that this creature don't exist."

"Let's go back to the main subject, then," said Jenur, a hint of nervousness in her voice. "That one god you said, the god who might not actually be a god. What's his name?"

"Like most southern gods, his actual name is unpronounceable on a mortal tongue," said Hana. "Even the other gods aren't sure what his real name is. So they just call him the Mysterious One."

"The Mysterious One, eh?" said Jenur. "Sounds like a very melodramatic name, if you ask me."

"It's the only name they could agree on," said Hana with a shrug. "His mysteriousness is one of the few aspects about him that everyone agrees on."

"So where is he?" said Malock.

Hana sighed heavily. "Didn't you listen to what I said earlier? None of the gods know where he is. He's so mysterious that he doesn't even have a temple on World's End devoted to him, like the other gods do. Nor does he have a statue in the atrium of the Temple of the Gods. A few gods even deny his existence entirely, though no one ever listens to them."

"What domain does he preside over?" said Malock. "If he's a god, surely he controls something in Martir, doesn't he?"

"This is about the only other thing anyone knows for sure about him," said Hana. "He is known as the God of Mystery and Magic. In fact, the only solid fact about his existence is that, during the Godly War, he slew the original God of Magic and took over his domain, as was common during that period."

Jenur gulped. "Does that mean he eats humans?"

"How should I know?" said Hana. "He doesn't even employ any of us katabans as his servants. If he does have any tasks that need to be done, he probably does them himself."

Malock scratched his chin. "If no one even knows that he exists or what his name is, how do any of the gods know that he's gone beyond the Void or not?"

"A katabans fisherman said he spotted a being entering the Void once, while he was out fishing," said Hana. "It's a disputed sighting, however, because he's the only witness of this person and his description wasn't very detailed. Said it was a very thin, boney person who he saw from a distance. Still, who else would even try to cross over to the Void?"

"Why would the Mysterious One even do that?" said Jenur. "Was he looking for something?"

"Hell if I know," said Hana. "That was a long time ago and, like I said, I've never actually met the Mysterious One, so I've never been able to ask him if it's true or not."

"It certainly would be nice if we could talk to him," said Malock. His eyes swept over the horizon, though he could not yet see the black, starless wall that would signal the beginning of the Void. "If he has actually passed through the Void, then he might be able to warn us of any dangers that we should avoid."

Hana chuckled. "Good luck with that. No one knows where he is, and even if we did, he's probably not going to tell a bunch of mortals about what's beyond the Void, even if you ask him nicely."

"She's got a point for once, Mal," said Jenur in a reluctant voice. "We'll just have to go straight ahead and hope we don't die. I mean, we'll have a god with us, won't we? Nimiko will probably be able to defend us."

Malock shook his head. "No. If there's even the slightest chance that we could go into the Void with knowledge of what lies within, I say we should take it. We need to find the Mysterious One and get him to tell us what he saw."

"That would be nice," said Jenur. "But Hana said that no one knows where he is. I know Hana usually struggles with telling the truth and all—"

Hana glared at Jenur, but the former Dark Tiger didn't seem to notice.

"—but for once I figure she's being honest and that we should listen to her."

"There must be some clue as to his whereabouts," said Malock. "If he's still on Martir, then we can probably reach him somehow."

Hana opened her mouth, probably to tell Malock that searching for the Mysterious One would be a waste of time, when the *Clockwork Heart* groaned beneath their feet. The ship shuddered and then another column of smoke shot out of the undamaged smokestack. Hana closed her mouth and tilted her head to the side, as if listening.

"It's your lucky day, Mal," said Hana, looking up at him. "The Mechanical Goddess actually agrees with you. Not only that, but she says she has an idea of where the Mysterious One might be and that we could stop by there on our way to World's End."

"Really?" said Malock. "But I thought—"

Another shake and shudder of the ship. Then Hana said, "She

says it's just a rumor, but there's an island a few miles to the east that is supposedly where the Mysterious One lives."

"What's it called?" said Malock.

"Doesn't have an actual name," said Hana. "But the Mechanical Goddess calls it Bleak Rock. She says it's totally uninhabited and generally avoided by the rest of the southern gods because of its unusual nature."

"Unusual nature?" said Malock. "What's so unusual about it?"

"She was vague about it," Hana admitted. "As she usually is whenever she talks about a subject she knows better than anyone. Hate it when she does that."

"Bleak Rock sounds like a great place to visit," said Jenur as she leaned against the railing around the hatch. "Is it between Island of Doom and the Isle of Depression? Or am I confusing it with the Place of No Return?"

"You're being a smart aleck, that's what you are," said Hana, glaring at her. "And not a very clever one, either, I might add."

Jenur rolled her eyes. "Whatever."

"I take it you don't want to go there, Jen?" said Malock.

"Who *wants* to go to a place called Bleak Rock?" said Jenur. "But if the Mysterious One is there and if he does happen to know what lies beyond the Void, well, I guess it would be worth taking a detour to see if he would be willing to share his knowledge with us."

"Then it's settled," said Malock, rubbing his hands together eagerly. "We'll go to Bleak Rock to find the Mysterious One. After that, we'll head to the Void."

"Hold on," said Jenur, glancing at the hatch. "Shouldn't we ask

Dad and Rint if they agree to it? I mean, I don't think they'd object, but—"

Malock waved off her concern. "I'm sure they'll understand. Besides, we don't have a lot of time to waste coming to an agreement on an issue that allows little room for debate. They won't mind once we find the Mysterious One and we find out more about the Void from him."

Jenur shook her head and said, "You sound just like how you did on our first voyage to World's End."

"And is that a bad thing?" said Malock. "Someone needs to be in charge around here, after all. Without strong leadership, a group can't function properly."

"Unless that 'strong leadership' has a history of making dumb, hasty decisions, that is," Jenur said. "Like using a deck of playing cards to determine the identity of a spy."

Those words felt like a slap to the face to Malock, but he said, "I thought I already apologized to you for that?"

Jenur held up her hands in a pacifying way. "I'm not holding it against you or anything. Just saying that these kinds of decisions might be better made after we consult everyone else, you know?"

Malock's hands balled into fists briefly before uncurling again. "Well, if Quro and Rint wanted to be part of this discussion, they shouldn't have gone to bed. I'm just doing what I think is best not only for us, but for the whole world. Do you object to that?"

"No," said Jenur. "But—"

"Then there we go," said Malock. "The Mechanical Goddess will take us to Bleak Rock. We'll stay there for less than a day, most likely, and if we can't find the Mysterious One during that time, we'll just keep going to the Void."

The more he spoke, the more captain-like Malock felt. And he liked the feeling. It was better than the self-doubt and worry that had dominated his mood over the last month or so. That was certain.

Jenur folded her arms across her chest and said, "You know what? Do what you want. I'm not really in the mood to argue with you anyway. I'll just go and see if Dad and Rint are awake. I'll tell them what we're going to do."

With that, Jenur climbed back down the hatch. Malock watched her go until she disappeared entirely. Then he turned to Hana and said, "Do you think she's angry with me?"

"The ways of mortals are mysterious to me," said Hana, her voice dripping with sarcasm. "The better question to ask is, does it matter?"

Malock shrugged. He supposed it didn't, but that didn't stop him from thinking about it just the same.

Chapter Four

SKIMIF SAT ON THE cot in his room, rubbing his temples. He raised his hammerhead shark-like head to look up at the writing on the walls of his room. He had spent the last hour trying to read it all, but every time he did, his eyes would hurt and his brain would start to ache. His own inadequacy as a reader made it even more difficult, thus causing him to give up and try to rest.

Emphasis on *try*. His single cot was springy and hard, which he normally did not complain about but which now seemed to be causing him back problems. Additionally, the gloomy, dank nature of his room—which was actually the basement of an abandoned building, located near the center of Port Blasan—was starting to get to him, even though it hadn't bothered him before.

He stood up and started walking around his room again, his eyes scanning the writing that he had written during that strange trance-like state he took whenever the Powers sent him a vision. He glanced at his hands, which were no longer stained with the blue paint that he had used to write with, and was amazed that he could have written so much with only his fingers.

The end of the world is near, Skimif thought. *The rest of this writing doesn't make much sense, but that much is clear to me.*

The only two people Skimif had shared this knowledge with were Prince Malock and Princess Raya. And now—with Malock gone on a possible suicide mission and Raya, unfortunately, dead—only he knew about it.

Then again, the gods also knew about it, no doubt. And as usual, the gods were doing nothing about it. He had never taken the gods to be nihilists, but he supposed that even they didn't know what to do when faced with the possible end of all existence. Maybe they weren't quite as brave as they made themselves out to be.

Skimif stopped at the stairs leading up to the exit and looked at the door at the very top. His fellow Heathens didn't know about this. He had wondered if he should tell them, but he didn't want to panic any of them. He still had to put on a strong face, show to his brothers and sisters that his belief in his message was as strong as ever.

And of course it was. Skimif was still no fan of the gods. He fully intended to keep preaching his message until every mortal on Martir ceased worshiping the gods. That meant he would have to confront his own fears of public speaking and his own doubts that invaded his mind any time he thought about how close the end of the world was.

The only question was how long he could keep this up.

It might not matter in the end, Skimif thought. *If Malock and the others fail, then we're all going to die anyway.*

And then there was that other thing, which he had not chosen to reveal to Malock, Raya, Aqur, or any of the other Heathens. It was still something that he had a hard time wrapping his head around, if only because he was unable to explain it. It had only started manifesting around roughly the same time that he had received that vision from the Powers. He had done his best to hide it, but he knew that at some point he wouldn't be able to do that anymore.

He looked around his room. He was alone. If Skimif wanted to, he could test it again and no one would ever know. Assuming, of course, that he wouldn't lose control of it, though he thought that was a silly fear because he had never lost control of it before. And with the door to his room locked and with the only pair of keys in the room on his belt, Skimif decided it would be safe to test it. Maybe he would understand it better if he did.

Skimif stepped into the middle of his room, where his sword named Pointy still stood embedded in the ground. He removed Pointy and tossed the sword onto his cot, then stepped in the spot where Pointy had been and closed his eyes.

A hint of electricity in the air went up his arms and spine, making him shiver. The floor beneath his feet rumbled slightly, like a dormant volcano, but he controlled that because if he shook the building's foundation then the other Heathens would inevitably notice. And then the occupants of the other buildings nearby would feel it, too, no doubt, and they would call in the Enforcers and then things would get ugly very quickly.

Then he felt it in his hands, warm and writhing. He almost opened his eyes, but then kept them closed. Fear of what he would see coursed through his very soul, making him regret ever even trying it. Still, he opened his eyes anyway to see what he had created.

In his hand was a long, slimy snake. Its thin body was pure black, from the tip of its head to the tip of its tail, with bright red eyes that looked up at him. In disgust, Skimif dropped the snake onto the floor, but as soon as it hit the stone, it evaporated into mist and smoke.

For a long while, Skimif stared at the spot where the snake had evaporated. He still didn't quite know what had happened. He didn't know why he could create snakes (and possibly other things, though he hadn't yet tried to make anything else). He suspected the Powers had granted him that ability, but why, he didn't know. He was beginning to suspect that the Powers could be just as arbitrary as the gods, if not more so.

Then there was a knock at the door, sudden and rapid, causing him to jump. When he landed, he accidentally caused the floor to shake under his feet, but just slightly. After cursing himself for doing that, Skimif looked up the stairs and shouted, "Who is it?"

"It's me," said Aqur's voice, slightly muffled by the door. "Aqur. There's some urgent news that you need to hear. Right away."

Even through the door, Aqur's voice was uncertain and even fearful. Frowning, Skimif climbed the stairs, unlocked the door, and opened it to find Aqur standing there. Her green eyes were wide with fear, so wide that they almost disappeared into the green bandanna wrapped around her head that signified her membership of the Brotherhood of Heathens.

"What's the problem?" said Skimif. "Have the Enforcers discovered the location of our hideout?"

"No," said Aqur, shaking her head. "You'll have to hear it from Ower. He's the one who saw it."

"Saw it?" said Skimif. "Saw what?"

Aqur shrugged helplessly. "Again, you'll have to talk to Ower. He's in the living room describing it to the others even as we speak."

An ominous feeling swept over Skimif, almost making him want to turn right back around and head back down into his room. Nonetheless, he followed Aqur down the hall into the living room, where a dozen or so of the other Heathens sat on the floor or stood near the sofa, where a young Carnagian boy—wearing nothing but some pants with rolled up legs and a sleeveless brown shirt—sat.

"Ower?" said Skimif as he and Aqur entered the living room, causing the rest of the Heathens to turn and look at them. "What's going on?"

The young boy looked at Skimif, his eyes just as fearful as Aqur's, if not more so. Ower was perhaps twelve or thirteen, easily the youngest Heathen on Carnag. As far as Skimif knew, the boy didn't have any parents, which was why Ower had sought out the Heathens, as he seemed to think that the gods had murdered his parents or were tied to their deaths.

However his parents had died, Ower had shown himself to be highly intelligent and hardworking, which he had proven by locating the Heathens' hideout all by himself and threatening to tell the Enforcers if they didn't let him join (there had been no debate that night about adding him to their ranks).

So when Skimif saw just how shaky Ower looked, that ominous feeling from before increased exponentially.

"Sir," said Ower with a gulp. He was actually sweating, which didn't help Skimif's nerves at all. "I was just out on the streets, you know, keeping an eye on those Enforcers and listening in on their private conversations when I saw it."

Despite the ominous feelings rising in him, Skimif found himself annoyed by Ower's vagueness. "Aqur already told me about 'it,' but she wasn't very specific. What is 'it'?"

Ower gulped. "A giant, flying monster. Not a bird or anything I've ever seen. Looks almost like a lizard, except with wings and stuff. Like a dragon."

Skimif flashbacked to the vision the Powers had given him a couple of weeks ago. In his mind's eye, he saw dozens of giant creatures—very similar to what Ower described—surging out of the Void, slashing their claws through the air as they tore apart buildings in World's End and others cities in Martir.

Remaining as composed as he could, Skimif said, "That sounds hard to believe. Where did you see it?"

"Just past the Fountain of Justice," said Ower with a shudder. "Don't know where it came from. I was just sitting there, eavesdropping on some Enforcers, when it flew out from behind a building and ripped off the roof of another building. Tossed the roof into the building next to it and took off before any of the Enforcers could take a shot at it."

"Did you recognize it at all?" said Skimif. "Did anyone else identify it?"

"No one did," said Ower, shaking his head. "Lots of people saw it. There was a biomancer who claimed that no such creature had ever been seen before, so I don't think even the mages know what it is."

Skimif stroked his chin. *I know exactly what it is,* he thought. *It's an envoy of the end.*

Knowing how the others would take those words if he spoke them, however, Skimif said, "Does anyone know where it went? There aren't a whole lot of places a creature that big could hide without being found."

"That's just the thing," said Ower. "When it vanished behind a building, I followed it 'cause I wanted to see where it was going. When I looked behind the building, I didn't see hide nor tail of it. Like it completely disappeared. Like a ghost."

Aqur folded her arms across her chest. "Impossible. Something that big couldn't have just up and vanished. You must not have followed it correctly."

"I did follow it correctly," said Ower, his tone slightly annoyed now. "I did. And it was the scariest thing of my life, let me tell you. The Enforcers, they also chased it, but they couldn't find it either."

"So a giant flying lizard appears out of nowhere, rips the roof off of a building, throws the roof at another building, and then disappears?" said one of the other Heathens with a snort. "That sounds like a story a kid would make up just to scare his friends."

"It is one hundred percent real," Ower said. "I could even show you the spot where it attacked. And you could talk to the witnesses, too, if they're still there. They'd back me up."

"Why isn't the entire city in an uproar about this, then?" said Aqur. "I can't see the Carnagians taking this very well, not with everything else that has happened recently.

"The Enforcers are keeping it hush-hush," said Ower. "They blocked off the area and are getting some etimancers to fix the building before anyone sees it. Overheard a couple of them talking about it before I ran to tell you guys."

"That won't stop the witnesses from talking," said Skimif. "News travels as fast as lightning in this city. If your story is true, it won't be long before everyone is talking about it."

"What if it attacks again?" said Aqur. "If it does, there's no way the Enforcers or Royal Family could hide it. They'd have to do something about it."

"That would be a good thing," said another Heathen. "Maybe they'll be so distracted by this monster that they'll stop bothering us."

"That may be why they're covering it up," said Skimif. "With Prince Malock's sudden disappearance, the rise of the Brotherhood, and the Justice Enforcers' harsh crackdown on lawbreakers in recent months, I'd imagine that the Enforcers' numbers are stretched to the breaking point just trying to keep it all together."

"But that still doesn't answer what that monster is," said Aqur. "There aren't any giant flying lizards on Carnag. Sure, the tunneler snakes in the north are pretty large, but they tend to keep to themselves and certainly can't fly."

"I don't know," said Ower with a shiver. "Never seen anything like it in my life. Don't really want to again."

While the other Heathens speculated about the creature's identity, Skimif looked up at the gray, decaying ceiling that was missing a few tiles.

The end is almost here, Skimif thought. *Malock, please hurry up. There's not much time left.*

Chapter Five

AS JENUR DID EVERY day, she descended deep into the hold of the *Clockwork Heart*, making her way through the hallways of the ship's interior. Though the walls and ceiling started out with metal panels, the further in she went, the more exposed the pipes became, until eventually she walked through a dimly lit hall with pipes that ran bare along the walls. Smoke and steam rumbled through the pipes; in fact, Jenur had to be careful to avoid touching them because she had learned from experience that she would burn herself if she did.

Her job was pretty simple. Somebody needed to head down to the hold, where Nimiko, the God of Light, was kept, and check on him daily. None of them were actually concerned about his well-being or anything like that. They just needed to make sure that he was in no position to escape.

As Jenur climbed down a metal ladder on her way to the hold, she thought, *Then again, if Nimiko ever did get free, wouldn't the Mechanical Goddess let us know?*

Of course, Malock didn't trust the Mechanical Goddess, at least not completely. He had given Jenur this job because, he had said at the time, he wanted someone he could trust keeping an eye on Nimiko. And Jenur understood that. The Mechanical Goddess may not have been as bad as the other southern gods, but she still wasn't entirely trustworthy in Jenur's eyes.

Especially after her servant threatened to kill my dad, Jenur thought as her foot touched the floor and she let go of the ladder's rungs. *And manipulated me into almost killing one of my friends.*

Jenur shook her head in disgust as she turned and walked down the narrow walkway that would take her to the hold. Rint and Quro had told her that they had not been treated unkindly while held captive by the Mechanical Goddess, but that did nothing to make Jenur feel any friendlier toward her. Or toward Hana, for that matter. Jenur just couldn't stand the idea of losing more people close to her, especially not after Kinker.

Without thinking, Jenur slammed her fist against one of the pipes. The smoke flowing through it must have been warmer than usual because heat shot up Jenur's arm, forcing her to remove her hand and blow on it to cool it off. She hadn't meant to do that, but when she thought about Kinker, her body immediately reacted. She didn't think the Mechanical Goddess would even notice, largely because Jenur hadn't left so much as a dent in the piping.

There's no reason to act that way, Jenur thought as she continued down the hallway, holding her aching, burning fist in her other hand. *You've done all you've can for Kinker. You saved his brother's life, after all. Kinker's gone. The best you can do is move on. If only it were that easy.*

Eventually, Jenur emerged out onto the catwalk stretched above the hold, her nose taking in the stale, metallic scent that was present in every room in the ship. The hold of the *Clockwork Heart* was massive, far larger than the hold of the *Iron Wind* had ever been. Gigantic metal crates containing supplies dotted the hold, clustering in groups of twos and threes. All of the crates were bolted to the floor. A couple of automatons were walking among the crates, lifting up the lids to check their supply levels, but the automatons didn't seem to hear her footsteps echoing off the metal catwalk as she made her way to the other end of it, where a simple metal staircase would take her to the bottom.

When she reached the ground floor, Jenur couldn't help but feel very small, as the hold's open space was almost like standing outside in an open field. She then made her way to the west end of the room, where a dozen or so crates blocked off a cage that glowed softly. Of course, Jenur knew that it wasn't the cage itself that glowed, but rather its single inhabitant.

She climbed on top of the small crate and stood on it, looking down at the cage. She said it to its occupant, "You're awake."

Sitting cross-legged on the floor of the cage—his wrists shackled to the floor by thick Void metal chains—was a bald-headed, thin man who glared up at her. His entire body glowed, giving off a light similar to that of the sun's, which made it almost impossible to look at him directly. His white shirt and brown trousers made him look less like a god and more like a peasant. Under ordinary circumstances, Jenur wouldn't have wanted to be anywhere near him, but with the Void metal chains and the Void metal cage, she was not intimidated by his stare.

"I heard fighting," said Nimiko. His eyes flicked to the cage ceiling above his head. "Felt the ship shake."

"Couple of other gods attacked," Jenur said with a shrug. "Tried to get Malock. But the Mechanical Goddess scared them off with the Fifth Clause."

Nimiko grunted. "Always hated the Fifth Clause. A cheap trick, if you ask me."

"I didn't write it," said Jenur with a shrug as she sat down on the crate. "Anyway, it's a cheap trick that saved our lives, so I'm not complaining about it."

Nimiko stood up in his cage, though he had to slouch slightly due to the chains not being long enough to allow him to stand. He may have been a god, but to Jenur, he looked quite pathetic. Part of her even wondered if he would eventually pass away, though when she remembered that the gods literally could not die unless they were killed by another god, she dismissed that thought right away.

"What do you want?" said Nimiko. "Have we reached World's End yet?"

"No," said Jenur, shaking her head. "We're actually headed to some island called Bleak Rock. We're going to find the Mysterious One."

Nimiko raised a thin eyebrow. "Why?"

"Because he's supposedly the only god to ever go to the Void and return alive," said Jenur. "At least, that's what Hana told us."

Nimiko smirked. "And of course you believe Hanarova because she's been such a trustworthy individual, hasn't she? Hasn't tricked you or deceived you ever, I'm sure."

"Nice try," said Jenur. "But I see what you're doing. I'm not going to sabotage the ship because you said so."

"I'm not trying to make you do anything," said Nimiko, scratching his left calf. "After all, I, too, want Martir to survive. I have a vested interest in making sure your voyage succeeds, despite my earlier hesitation. Which is why I demand to be freed."

Nimiko stepped forward, but he couldn't step forward very far because the Void metal chains were too short. He still glared up at Jenur, however, his eyes shining brilliantly and forcing her to look away to keep her eyes from being damaged by his brightness.

"Sorry," said Jenur, holding up a hand to help protect her vision. "But Malock says you gotta stay put until we reach the Void. Captain's orders."

"Captain's orders," Nimiko sneered. "As if I give a crap about your 'captain's' orders. I am the first god, the oldest of them all, and I demand to be treated with respect."

"I know, I know," said Jenur. "But the answer is still no. Now if you'll excuse me, I have to leave, since I now know that you're still as stuck-up and bitter as ever."

Jenur stood up and was just about to jump down from the crate when Nimiko said, "Hold it."

For some reason, Jenur obeyed his command, even though she didn't want to. She looked over her shoulder at Nimiko, who still stood, slouching slightly, in the cage. A curious expression had crossed his face, though there was something vaguely sinister about it as well.

"What?" said Jenur, not even bothering to hide the annoyance in her voice. "Do you want more leftovers from dinner or something?"

Nimiko stuck out his tongue. "Of course not. I merely have a question I wish to ask you. Yes, you, specifically, Jenur Takren."

Jenur didn't like it when people she didn't know very well used her full name. She thought about just blowing off his question, but something about his tone made her curious.

"All right," said Jenur as she turned around to face him. "What's the question?"

Nimiko sat back down on the floor and rolled his shoulders. "I was wondering if you would like to ascend to godhood someday."

Jenur froze. Against her will, her mind flashed back to when Malock had told her that Kinker had been destined for godhood. Why had Nimiko asked her this question? Did he somehow know about Kinker or was it just an idle question on his part?

"Why do you ask?" said Jenur, keeping her tone level.

Nimiko stretched his legs, which were as thin as sticks, and said, "Oh, I just thought that a broken mortal like you might prefer godhood. Not that being a god is any easier than being a mortal, mind you, but with all of the problems you face in your life, apotheosis might be just what you need."

"You don't know me," said Jenur, her tone sharper than she had intended. "You don't know me at all. You don't know what kind of problems I face. And don't call me 'broken,' either. I'm as a whole as anyone else."

Nimiko closed his eyes, but his eyeballs still glowed enough to be seen through the lids. "Rint has been talking to me, telling me all about you and Quro and the others. He doesn't know everything about all of you, but he knows enough to be an interesting conversation partner. So I know some of your history."

"Rint is—?" said Jenur, but she shook her head. "The idiot. Why is he talking to you?"

"He's the only mortal on this ship who doesn't have some kind of apathy or enmity toward the gods," Nimiko pointed out. "He's not one of my followers—prefers my sister Kano, Powers know why—but he still has respect for the gods in general. Respect, I might add, that you ought to learn from him."

"I'm going to have a long conversation with Rint about sharing other peoples' personal information without permission after this," said Jenur. "A *long* one."

Nimiko shrugged. "You still haven't answered my question. Godhood or not?"

"I am perfectly happy being a mortal," said Jenur. "That answer enough for you?"

"Good enough, I suppose," said Nimiko. "But I think you may have answered too hastily. Have you even given the subject some thought?"

Jenur peered at him suspiciously. "What are you trying to pull? Are you trying to tempt me with unlimited power or something?"

"You seem to think I'm like the southern gods," said Nimiko. "Did you forget that we northern gods, despite what you Heathens think, are pro-human? That the only reason you mortals still exist is because I and my other northern siblings defended your people during the Godly War?"

"Yeah, I guess that's true," said Jenur. "But that doesn't mean I have to worship you. Not when you northern gods have shown yourselves to be pretty petty, what with killing Princess Raya and all that."

"That was Hollech's servant, not me," said Nimiko, folding his arms across his chest. "The point is, as a northern god who has always held humanity's best interests at heart, I see no reason at all for you to treat me the way you do. It is almost like you consider me mud beneath your heel."

"I've never been much of a respecter of the gods," Jenur said. "Always been a heathen, though never a member of the Brotherhood. And by the way, you still haven't said why you're offering me godhood."

Nimiko put his hands on his knees. "It's what I said earlier. Right now, the Dark Tigers will kill you if they find out you're alive. They might even know it already, seeing as your father is with you and hasn't reported back to his master yet."

"I can take care of myself," said Jenur. "I was thinking of heading to the Great Berg or some obscure island in the west, where the Dark Tigers usually don't go."

"And live the rest of your life in fear that they may find you?" said Nimiko. "That doesn't seem like much of a life to live to me. Well, I suppose if you were a mouse it might, but even rodents don't live their every waking moment afraid of being killed by their former comrades."

Jenur reached for her knife, but stopped when she remembered that she couldn't actually kill Nimiko with it. Raising her hand up, Jenur said, "I'm just going to live undercover, change my name and start a new life. Dad won't tell Wirm about me. He promised."

"Promises are easily broken, Jenur," said Nimiko. "Especially when torture is applied to them. I've heard much about the ruthless Dark Tigers. I don't doubt they will find a way to make Quro talk once it becomes clear he is hiding important information from them. And then what will you do?"

Jenur scowled. "You're getting ahead of yourself. I mean, I don't even know if the world is going to survive. I'll figure that out when we get there."

"Short term planning has always been a skill you mortals possess," said Nimiko. "But it blinds you to the long term, which is what truly matters in the end."

Jenur turned around again. "Look, you just sit here and be a good quiet little god while we find your brother who may or may not exist. I really have to go."

"Fine," said Nimiko. "But just remember: As a mortal, you must always live in fear that your fellow mortals will kill you. As a god, you need never fear anyone else again, not even your fellow gods."

Jenur didn't even look back at him when he said that. She just jumped down from the crate and made her way back to the stairs, walking past the automaton inspectors who were digging through a crate full of guns and blades, as the light from Nimiko grew dimmer and dimmer.

Me, a goddess, Jenur thought. *What a ridiculous thought. I doubt being a goddess is nearly as great as Nimiko made it out to be. He's just trying to trip me up for some reason.*

Nonetheless, when Jenur reached the catwalk, she stopped about halfway to the other side and looked out over the hold to Nimiko's end. His light still shone, but far more dimly now. And Jenur had to admit that, whatever Nimiko's motives were, he had hit upon a very important desire of hers: namely, safety.

And if godhood could offer me safety ...

Jenur shook her head again and continued walking across the catwalk. Right now, she had more urgent matters to worry about. Like the end of the world, for example.

Chapter Six

TWO DAYS LATER, THE island known as Bleak Rock came into view of the crew on board the *Clockwork Heart*. It was the Mechanical Goddess who announced its existence. When she spotted it, she sent a column of flame and smoke into the air out of both smokestacks, which Hana translated as meaning that Bleak Rock was now within sight.

So Malock, Jenur, Rint, and Quro made their way to the ship's bow to try to get a glimpse of the island. For some reason, a heavy mist hung low in this part of the southern seas, initially making it hard to see, although they could hear the waves of the ocean crashing against it. But eventually, the mist parted, revealing an island that Malock had not expected to see.

A tall, thick rock stood out of the ocean. It resembled a mighty spear breaking through a wooden shield, with the tip shining in the sunlight. The 'island' had no real beach or docks. Only a giant rock protruded out of the ocean, with what appeared to be an entrance nestled high near its top, though that could just be a cleft for all Malock knew.

"That's Bleak Rock?" said Quro. "It doesn't look much like an island to me."

Hana had joined them and was leaning against the railing of the *Clockwork Heart*'s bow, her chin in her hand. "Legend says it used to be bigger, but when the Mysterious One took up residence here, he sunk the beaches and made the waters vicious to outsiders."

Malock looked down into the sea as it parted before the *Clockwork Heart*. "The waters don't look any more vicious to me than the waters in other parts of the southern seas."

"Like I said, it's just a legend," said Hana. "But there is definitely something off about this place. Can you feel it?"

Malock shrugged. "No. What would this 'off'ness feel like?"

"Hard to describe," said Hana. "It's a bit like the normal laws of physics and magic just don't apply around here. I mean, you can still cast spells and such, but it really makes me feel uncomfortable. Maybe you mortals can't feel it, but I can."

"Is the Mysterious One violent?" Rint asked, his eyes locked on the approaching rock. "The southern gods eat mortals, don't they? What's to stop him from eating us?"

"Like I said, I don't really know anything about him," said Hana. "He did fight on the side of the southern gods ... I think. I mean, he's been known to hang out here and no one has ever reported seeing him cross the Dividing Line, so ..."

"So maybe we shouldn't be here at all," said Rint. "We should just keep going onto World's End."

"Actually, we're perfectly safe," Jenur said. She gestured with her head toward the ship's smokestacks and said, "The Mechanical

Goddess has us under her protection. Means the other gods can't so much as touch us."

Malock frowned. "The Mechanical Goddess told Vashnas that, too, and we know how that turned out, don't we?"

"She's telling the truth this time," said Hana. "The Mechanical Goddess has no plans to betray any of you whatsoever. You're just being paranoid."

Deciding it would be better to avoid arguing the point, Malock said, "So how are we going to get onto Bleak Rock? If it doesn't have a beach, it's not like we can just waltz on up it, now can we?"

"Easy," said Hana. "We've got a ramp that we'll just lay out across the gap between the ship and the rock. So we actually will be able to waltz on up it."

"Who's going?" said Malock, looking at the others. "I know I am, but is anyone else going to come?"

"I'll stay here," Rint said as he stepped away from the railing. "Just in case, you know, something happens."

Malock nodded and looked at Jenur. "You coming?"

She opened her mouth, obviously to say yes, but then Quro said, "No. I'll go in her place."

Jenur whipped her head to look at her adoptive father, who was now leaning against the railing. "What are you talking about? You can't make me stay here."

"It's too dangerous," Quro insisted. "We have no idea what to expect. And while you may be an adult, I am still your father. I spent four months thinking you were dead. I am not going to spend another four minutes worrying that you might be killed in there."

Jenur threw up her hands. "We've had this discussion already, Dad. I am perfectly capable of defending myself."

"Actually, I think Quro makes a good point," said Malock, glancing at Bleak Rock, which gradually grew larger the closer they drew to it. "There's no telling what might be in there or what the Mysterious One—if he's there—might do. You're the only one who can handle Nimiko, besides myself. Can't risk losing both of us."

Jenur looked at Malock in utter disbelief. "Oh, come on. I've been through worse than this and come out of it okay."

"It's still too risky," said Quro. "I would listen to Malock if I were you. He was your captain at one point, wasn't he?"

"But I'm under the Mechanical Goddess's protection, same as everyone else," said Jenur. "Even if the Mysterious One hates mortals, he won't be able to hurt me."

"What if he has servants?" said Quro. "Servants who might be under his protection and who might see nothing wrong with attacking invaders?"

"Then I'll slit their throats and teach them not to mess with me," said Jenur, patting the knife strapped to her leg.

"I think your father has a point," said Rint. "Remember Vurango? He almost killed us."

Jenur glared at all three of them with all of the annoyance she could muster. In fact, she glared at them so hard that Malock thought she was going to pull out of her knife and force them to take her.

But then Jenur sighed, brushed the strands of her dark hair off her forehead, and said, "All right. I'll stay here with Rint. I'd rather not, but hey, I clearly can't take care of myself. It's not like I led a mutiny that overthrew one of the most dangerous pirates in the world or anything, oh no. I'm just a weak little girl who can't take care of herself."

She then stomped off before any of them could stop her. Malock watched her go, feeling ill about her departure, while Quro just shook his head, as if in disappointment.

"She really wanted to go, didn't she?" said Malock.

"She's always been stubborn and independent," said Quro. "Though I assumed you would have known that already, seeing as you and her have known each other for a while now."

Rint shuddered. "I don't see why anyone would want to go up there, to be honest. I don't even understand why you two do. Can't you just send a couple of automatons up there to scout ahead?"

"The Mechanical Goddess wouldn't allow that," said Hana. "She's not very keen on possibly losing more of her children, especially so soon after the other gods' recent attack."

Malock turned to face Bleak Rock again, the cool mist rolling off his burning face. "The Mysterious One might not even show up if he sees a bunch of automatons. Maybe he would think the Mechanical Goddess is trying to invade his domain. Besides, I don't trust the automatons to ask the right questions or get the right facts. When you want a job done well, you've got to do it yourself."

When the *Clockwork Heart* got close enough, Hana ordered about a dozen automatons to set up a long, wide ramp leading from the top deck of the ship (where the wheelhouse was) to the entrance of Bleak Rock. The automatons achieved this with their usual efficiency, laying out the huge ramp in about ten minutes.

As soon as they did that, Malock and Quro climbed up to the top deck and made their way across the ramp. Malock had a pistol hanging off his belt, while Quro carried his dragon shark scales (and probably other weapons, too, though Malock couldn't see them because of the Dark Tiger's robes). Neither of them expected to fight, but if they had to, they were prepared.

Crossing the makeshift bridge was easy, though Quro looked nervous the entire thirty seconds it took for them to cross it. Malock didn't understand why, as the bridge was firm and there was no wind blowing about, so when they stepped off the bridge onto Bleak Rock itself, he asked Quro, "Afraid of heights?"

Quro grabbed onto an overhanging rock and looked at Malock. He seemed to be trying to avoid looking down. "Let's just say I've had some bad experiences with bridges and leave it at that."

Malock raised an eyebrow, but said nothing more about the matter. He turned to look at the entrance before them, though it wasn't much of an entrance. It was much closer to a slit in the rock, apparently carved out by someone at some point. It was wide enough for the two of them to slip through one at a time, of that he had no doubt, but it was so dark on the inside that he couldn't see anything. He didn't even know if there was a staircase leading down or it was just a straight, abrupt drop.

"Got the lantern?" said Malock, glancing at Quro.

Quro unhooked the lantern from his belt, held it up, and said, "Got it."

"Good," said Malock. "Because it looks like we're going to need it."

Quro pulled a match out of his pocket, but then stopped and looked at Malock. "What are we going to say when we run into the Mysterious One?"

"Ask him what's beyond the Void, obviously," said Malock. "Why does it matter?"

"Just curious," said Quro as he struck the match against the rock wall, causing it to light. "And what will we do if he turns out to be as violent as the other southern gods?"

Malock rubbed his face because the burn had flared up again. "Run. Not much we can do against him, if he's as bad as the other gods."

Quro looked at Malock like he was not at all reassured by his answer. "I guess that's all we can do when faced with the wrath of the gods, isn't it?"

Malock ignored his response. "Let's just go in already. If the Mysterious One is here, we don't want to let him get away." He held out a hand and said, "Give me the lantern. I'll go first."

Quro handed the lantern to Malock, who then proceeded to enter the narrow entrance. He had to duck his head to avoid scraping it against the top of the entrance, but as soon as he entered, he sensed that it would be safe to stand up. As soon as he did, he held up the lantern and looked around the place.

Either the lantern was not as bright as it should have been or the interior of Bleak Rock was huge because Malock could not see any further than five or six feet before him. Part of him wanted to turn back and get a better light source, but something about this place told him that it wouldn't have mattered if he had managed to bring the entire sun in with him. The darkness was oppressive, reminding him of the Tunnel of History, though unlike the Tunnel of History, Malock didn't feel any intelligence nearby except for his own.

So Malock took a step forward, but as soon as he did, his other foot slipped and he fell on his backside and went sliding down a steep incline. The incline was smooth, but he rushed down it at a frightening speed, his hair billowing out behind him as he screamed. He couldn't see anything, even though he still held the lantern, and didn't know when the incline was going to end until, without warning, he slammed into solid rock with enough force to make his whole world spin.

He fell on his back, stunned, as Quro's voice floated down from above. "Malock? What happened? Are you okay?"

Though he couldn't be sure, Malock thought his nose was broken. At least the pain in his nose burned, burned along with his face, causing him to groan as he lay there. It wasn't completely dark, however, because the lantern had somehow managed to stay lit, but it had fallen out of his hand when he slid down the incline and now lay somewhere just outside of his reach. He tilted his head to the right and spotted the lantern lying on its side only a few feet away.

Quro's voice rang out from above, echoing in the cavern and making Malock's head hurt even more. "Malock? Are you okay? What happened?"

"I fell," Malock said as he inched toward the lantern. "Watch your step. It's a steep incline, like a slide. You should go back."

"No way," came Quro's voice. "I said I was going to come with you. I'll just need to be careful about how I go about getting down there, that's all."

Malock looked around the area. "But I don't see any way we can get back up. If we're both stuck down here—"

"The Mechanical Goddess will figure out a way to save us, if we get stuck," said Quro. "And if she tries to abandon us, Jenur will make sure she doesn't."

"All right," said Malock. "Just let me move out of the way. I'm right at the bottom here and if you slide down now, you'll end up running into me."

"Right," came Quro's voice again. "You just shout when you're out of the way."

Grunting, Malock sat up and half dragged himself off to the right, where the lantern was. When he was certain that he had pulled himself out of the way, Malock looked up the slide and saw Quro's silhouette standing against the entrance. It wasn't nearly as high up as Malock had thought.

"You can slide down now," Malock shouted.

A moment later, Quro slid out of the darkness and into the light of the lantern. Unlike Malock, he had slid in a more controlled manner, standing upright and coming to a controlled stop before he could crash into the wall. Malock felt slightly envious of Quro's grace.

"You look terrible," said Quro when he saw Malock. "I mean, worse than usual. You've got gunk and grime all over your cloak."

Malock looked down at the boat cloak he wore. Mud and dirt clung to the front and back, causing Malock to attempt to wipe them off. Unfortunately, the layers were too thick to wipe and so he gave up, deciding he would make sure to get his clothes washed once they returned to the *Clockwork Heart*.

"Where do we go from here?" said Quro.

Malock raised the lantern. To their right was a thick, rough wall, with no doorway or hallways or anything. When he pointed the lantern to the left, however, there was what appeared to be a hallway they could enter, albeit a rough one with an uneven floor.

"To the left," said Malock. "But we're going to have to be careful. Don't want to slide again unexpectedly, after all."

"I'll lead," Quro said, reaching for the lantern. "After what you found—"

Malock pulled the lantern away from Quro's reach. "No, I can do it. You should probably get your weapons out, however, in case we need them."

Quro's tentacled face frowned, then he shrugged and said, "Fine by me."

So Malock walked past Quro and soon the two were walking through a narrow stone hall, with a ceiling just high enough that Malock's scalp didn't scrap against it.

The walls were cool and damp, making Malock feel like he was underwater, even though as far as he could tell, he and Quro weren't below sea level yet. The opening seemed to go straight ahead, neither down nor up, though the two continued to walk carefully because they did not want to fall again. This made their progress much slower than it should have been, causing Malock to wish he could see their surroundings better so they could walk faster.

As they walked, there was no sound at all, save for Malock and

Quro's footsteps that echoed off the wet stone floor. Malock couldn't even hear the waves outside, which meant that the walls were either extremely thick or the sound was being blocked somehow. He suspected it had something to do with the strange nature of the island, but he tried not to dwell too much on it because the complete lack of sound made him more nervous than he would ever admit.

They walked slowly for what felt like hours, until eventually Malock's foot met midair. He almost fell forward, but Quro grabbed him by the collar of his shirt and jerked him backwards before he could fall head first.

"Whoa," said Malock, his heart beating fast. He looked over his shoulder at Quro and said, "Thanks for the save."

"No problem," said Quro. "But is that yet another slide you were about to fall down?"

Malock held out his lantern as far as he could without falling over. The bright orange light reflected off of a set of wet stone steps that went down well beyond the lantern's glow. The steps appeared as if they had not been used in a while and were very narrow. Also, the walls widened around here; in fact, when Malock spread out his arms, he could not reach wall on either side of him. Not only that, but the staircase seemed to cross over some kind of pit, though it was impossible to tell its depth due to the shadows.

"Looks like a staircase," said Malock. "But we're gonna have to be careful. The steps are narrow and the walls are far apart, so watch your step."

So the two started down the steps, moving even more slowly than they had before. One step at a time, the bottom of Malock's boots splashing the shallow water that was gathered on each step, Quro's shoes following. Each step echoed before dying into the darkness on either side of them. Malock wished he knew how far down the pit on either side was, but he didn't intend to stop and find out.

Every minute, Malock expected something to happen. The islands in the southern seas, after all, were not exactly tropical, slow-moving paradises where travelers could rest, party, and drink. So far, the worst that had happened was him tripping and sliding down the first incline. They had not seen or heard anything else; in fact, the entire island seemed completely uninhabited, as if it had been forsaken by every living thing on Martir.

He thought about bringing this up with Quro, but something about the utter quietness of Bleak Rock made him keep his mouth shut. What could Quro say, anyway? Talking was useless. They just had to keep walking until they found the Mysterious One, wherever he was.

After several minutes of walking, they reached the bottom of the steps. Here they found yet another entrance, similar to the one they had used to enter Bleak Rock, except wider. It looked like a natural formation, at least until they got close enough for the light of the lantern to reveal what looked like pickax marks in the edges. It was the first sign of civilization that either of them had seen yet, aside from the staircase, and Malock now felt excited, like any minute now they would find the mystery god.

Passing through the entrance, Malock and Quro emerged in a large, square room, though it was not nearly as large as the room that the staircase was in had been. In fact, it was small enough that the lantern's light illuminated every corner of the place, but to Malock's eternal disappointment, the lantern revealed nothing more than four smooth, featureless walls, with a ceiling and floor that were similar in their lack of features.

"Is this the end?" said Malock. His voice sounded odd in the silence of the room.

"I don't see any doors or exits," said Quro. "Perhaps there's a secret switch around here that could open a trapdoor of some sort?"

"Worth a look," said Malock. "But you know, I have a feeling that the Mysterious One would be a lot easier to find if he was here."

"If even the gods haven't been able to find him, it shouldn't surprise us that we'd have some difficulty," said Quro. "But I wonder how we will know when we have found him."

Malock looked at Quro. "What do you mean?"

Quro stroked his chin as he said, "I am no expert on the southern gods, but if they are anything at all like the Mechanical Goddess, then most of them don't look very human. Correct?"

Malock nodded, then rubbed his face, which had chosen that moment to start burning again. "Spot on, actually. Most of the southern gods I've seen look nothing like humans."

"If that is the case," said Quro, "then could it be that we may have already seen the Mysterious One without even realizing it?"

Malock chuckled. "Trust me, Quro, when I say that we would know if we had seen the Mysterious One. While the southern gods generally don't look very human, it's kind of hard to mistake a cloud of murderous leaves for anything but a hungry deity."

"True," said Quro. "But the Mysterious One, if Hana's information is correct, doesn't draw attention to himself and generally shuns contact with other people, even with his fellow gods."

"Well, then what do you think he might look like?" said Malock. "Is he the island itself? The damp air? The floor on which we walk?"

Quro shrugged. "I have no idea what he may or may not be. It's just a theory."

"I have no patience for theories," said Malock, shaking his head as he took one step into the room. "Or myths or anything but rock solid fac—"

A cold breeze blew past Malock and Quro, so harsh and so gelid that it felt like the snow on Stalf. It made Malock gasp, especially when the cold clashed with his burning face, while Quro actually fell to his hands and knees as if he had tripped over something. Even stranger, the breeze felt like the breath of a person, as if a giant human was blowing in the room. Yet when Malock turned around (slower than usual due to his freezing joints) to see the entrance, he saw that the entrance they had taken was completely blocked off.

"Oh no," said Malock. His voice had dropped to a whisper and he hadn't even realized it. "That is not good."

Shivering, Quro stood up and pounded his fists on the wall where the exit had once stood. He then ran his fingers along the door's outline, or where it had once been, but then he cursed in Aqua and turned to face Malock. His skin was bluer than usual now, as if his blood was running cold.

"No use," said Quro. "We're trapped. Someone clearly doesn't want us to leave."

Malock gulped. "Do you think—"

His question was interrupted by the sound of footsteps behind him. He whirled around, the lantern swinging in his hand, and saw that a new exit had opened directly across from the entrance they had used. In fact, this new exit looked exactly the same as the one that had just been closed up, though he focused less on the similarities and more on the footsteps that echoed from just beyond the doorway.

Malock immediately reached for his pistol, despite not knowing if it would be helpful against whatever was coming, while Quro drew out his dragon shark scales. The two stepped back, making as little sound as possible, but the pace of the footsteps didn't slow down or speed up. Whoever was coming clearly was in no hurry to get there.

Then a hooded, robed figure entered the circle of light tossed by the lantern. The gray robes that the figure wore were so long that they completely covered its body, even its hands and feet. The long hood covering its head made it impossible to tell what the being's face looked like, even when it looked directly at Malock and Quro. A terrible, yet oddly familiar, stench of alcohol and seawater wafted off the being's form, causing Malock to feel sick to his stomach.

"Who are you?" said Malock, gripping the handle of his pistol, his finger resting lightly on the trigger.

The hooded figure looked from Malock to Quro and back. Then it turned around and began walking back into the darkness from which it had emerged, at the same pace as it had previously. This time, however, it made a clear gesture with its right hand, encouraging Malock and Quro to follow it.

Seeing as they had no choice, Malock and Quro went after the hooded being, though they exchanged a look before doing so. Malock privately wondered if this being was the Mysterious One, but even if it was, he made sure that his pistol's barrel was not blocked. A pistol might not do much against a god, but it was better than nothing.

The hooded being took them down a spiral hallway of sorts. As usual, the walls were high and narrow, which the hooded being did not seem to mind at all. It just walked at the same slow pace as usual, forcing Malock and Quro to slow down to avoid overtaking the being. It had not spoken one word since its appearance, nor had Malock or Quro. As usual with this place, Malock felt that to speak would be to break some great law, which would invite terrible retribution from a wrathful god.

If the Mysterious One is here, then that might not be an entirely inaccurate feeling, Malock thought, *even if he's no Grinf.*

After a few minutes, the trio reached the bottom of the spiral hallway, which ended in an open doorway. The being passed the threshold first, followed by Malock and then Quro. As soon as they entered, a sudden chill entered Malock's bones, making him shiver, while behind him Quro grunted.

"What was that?" Quro muttered.

Though Quro's voice was low, it sounded extremely loud in the deep silence, causing Malock to lower his voice even further when he responded. "No idea. Maybe the—?"

He cut himself short when he noticed that the hooded being had disappeared. Fear rising in his stomach, Malock thrust his lantern this way and that, trying to illuminate the room they had walked into, but no matter where he pointed it, the lantern showed no sign of the hooded being's presence.

"Where did he go?" Quro asked. "He couldn't have just up and disappeared, could he?"

"No telling," said Malock. "This might be a good time to run."

"Now, that I agree with," said Quro. "Let's—"

A sudden blue light—tiny and round—shone from the other side of the room. It was followed, in rapid succession, by dozens of more lights, similar in color, that ran across the top of the room's walls. The sudden lights revealed that Malock and Quro stood in a large chamber, similar in size to the throne room back in Carnag Hall, but without all of the fancy details that made the throne room what it was.

Four stone pillars stood in each corner of the room, like massive support beams. In the center of the room was a highly detailed circle of green paint, like a part of a ritual. Lying in the center of the green-painted circle was a human-like skeleton, its arms and legs stretched out and its bones as white as sand.

And standing just beyond the circle was the hooded being. The hooded being stood there, its head bowed slightly, almost as if it was listening to the skeleton.

Malock stepped forward and said to the hooded being, "Are you the Mysterious One?"

The hooded being shook its head. It then pointed at the skeleton on the floor.

"Is *that* the Mysterious One?" said Malock.

The hooded being nodded.

"You must be joking," said Malock.

The hooded being again shook its head.

Malock looked down at the skeleton. Its white bones looked bluish in the glow of the lights on the walls, but that didn't make it look any more alive. In fact, it looked like it had been dead for years, decades even. He bet that if he so much as laid one finger on it, it would crumble into dust.

"I don't believe it," said Malock. "I know the gods can come in a variety of shapes and forms, but I would think that it would be more obvious, if this god was indeed the Mysterious One."

A low clicking sound—like that of a crab's teeth chittering together—entered Malock's ears. It took him a moment to realize that the sound was coming from the hooded being. It was the first sound that the hooded being had made so far, and it was a familiar sound, reminding Malock of the time when the Gray Pirates first attacked his ship.

"Doesn't matter if you believe it or not, gold blood," said the hooded being, whose feminine, yet harsh, voice was instantly recognizable to Malock. "Truth is, this is the Mysterious One, or at least his preferred form when he's not elsewhere in our wide world."

Malock gasped. "No way. Garnal Gray?"

The hooded being reached up, the sleeves of her robe falling down her arms and revealing her claw-like hands, and pulled the hood down. Garnal Gray's crab-like face looked a little odd in the blue light, but there was no mistaking it for anyone else.

"Long time, no see, gold blood," said Garnal. "How was World's End? I heard you lost a couple members of your crew there."

"Wait a minute," said Quro. "Garnal Gray? The Captain of the

Gray Pirates?"

"*Former* captain, tentacle beard," Garnal corrected. "Lost most of my crew to the gods, and then lost the rest of them to Malock's murderous band of wannabe pirates. And now here I am, alive and well, though hardly whole."

"But how did you even get here?" said Malock. "I thought for sure you would have been killed somewhere in the southern seas after we let you walk the plank."

"As usual, gold blood, you were quite wrong," said Garnal with a nasty laugh. "I did try to head north, seeing as I didn't want anything to do with these damn seas, but whilst swimming in the ocean I got caught in a current and almost died."

"Who saved you?" said Malock.

"The Mysterious One, of course," said Garnal, gesturing at the skeleton again. "Dragged me out of the sea and brought me into here. I was terrified at first, mostly because I didn't know anything about him, but when the Mysterious One explained to me who he was and what he wanted to do, I felt a little better."

"The Mysterious One actually spoke to you?" said Malock. "I was told he never spoke to anyone, not even to his fellow gods."

"I didn't say he was easy to understand," said Garnal. "You are pretty slow, gold blood, so I don't expect you to understand this right away. After all, I'm sure you are used to having your tutors explain difficult to grasp concepts to you, rather than letting you work them out yourself, right?"

"Get on with it," said Malock. He was now starting to remember just why he hated Garnal. "Do you serve the Mysterious One now?"

"Of course," said Garnal. "He promised to keep my life safe so long as I committed my life to his service."

"The fearsome leader of the most successful pirates in history has committed her life to a god?" said Malock. "Here I thought you hated the gods for what they did to you and your crew."

Garnal's eyes glowed briefly, though whether they actually did glow or they just reflected the blue lights, it was difficult to tell. "I may not be the gods' biggest fan, but I am a pragmatist first and foremost. I had nothing to gain from rejecting the Mysterious One's offer. I would have died, and I'm no fan of death unless I'm inflicting it on my enemies."

"Wow," said Malock in his most sarcastic voice. "I guess there really is a humble person trapped somewhere within that thick shell of yours. Perhaps, when I return north, I will tell rumors about how the great Garnal Gray is now the humble servant of a god."

Much to his disappointment, Garnal didn't look at all annoyed by his sarcasm. "Do what you want, gold blood. My former life ended when I walked the plank of your floating shipwreck. At least I am still alive."

Malock opened his mouth to respond, but Quro stepped forward, pointed at the skeleton, and said, "How do we know that that is in fact the Mysterious One?"

"It's not his actual body," said Garnal. "Similar to the Mechanical Goddess and her many forms—yes, I know she's the one who brought you here—the Mysterious One occasionally takes on the form of a human skeleton to achieve certain tasks. Don't know what his actual body even looks like, though I imagine it must be a thousand times more handsome than your current face, gold blood."

The burn in Malock's face flared again, causing him to scratch it as he said, "So where is the Mysterious One now? Clearly, he's not possessing this skeleton."

Garnal shrugged. "I have no idea. I may be his only servant—though to be honest, he could have more elsewhere, I don't know—but that doesn't mean he tells me everything he does or everywhere he goes."

"Sounds like every other god out there," said Malock. "The more I hear of this Mysterious One, the more I convinced I become that he's just like all of the other gods."

"Be careful what you say, gold blood," said Garnal. "The Mysterious One has a habit of turning up when you least expect it."

Malock folded his arms. "What's the worst he could do to us? Quro and I have the Mechanical Goddess's protection. As per the Treaty, we cannot be harmed or killed by another god."

Garnal chuckled. "I must not have spoken correctly. I wasn't warning you to be careful because I cared about you. I was warning you to be careful because the Mysterious One does not respect the Treaty."

"Impossible," said Malock. "Every single god on Martir—both northern and southern—adheres to the Treaty and its clauses. That is what I have always been told. And I have never seen any god ever go against it, even though I've seen many who complain about it."

"That's just the thing," said Garnal. "The others call the Mysterious One a god, but to be honest, I suspect he's much more than a mere god. He's alien; why, he's not even from Martir."

At that, Quro leaned forward slightly. "Not even from Martir? What do you mean?"

Garnal gestured at the room in which they stood. "I mean exactly what I said. I do not believe the Mysterious One is actually a god or that he's from Martir. I've seen him do ... things no god could ever do."

"Such as?" said Malock.

Garnal gave a dark chuckle. "You don't even want to know. You'd think me a freak if you did."

"I already think you're a freak," Malock said. "And you talking like you're hiding some big mystery from us isn't helping alter my perception of you, you know."

"Fine," Garnal said. She pulled aside the front of her robes as she said, "Look and tell me what you see."

Under the blue glow of the lights, harsh, jagged gashes stood out in sharp relief against Garnal's chest. Her shell was shattered in front, with what appeared to be dried blood covering the front of her body. It looked like a master swordsman had dragged a sword through her body, cutting out chunks of flesh.

"How can you even still be alive?" Quro said, his eyes transfixed on Garnal's body. "You look like a corpse."

"That's because, for a short while, I *was* a corpse," said Garnal.

Malock almost gasped, but he didn't want to give Garnal the satisfaction of knowing she had surprised him, seeing as he suspected she was being dramatic.

Still, he let his arms fall to his side as he said, "What do you mean, you *were* a corpse? When someone dies, they're dead. Gone forever.

Even Hunuk, the God of Life, cannot bring the dead back."

Garnal brought her robe back over her chest, as if ashamed of her body. "I wasn't truthful with you earlier when I said I almost died. As it turns out, I *did* die. A ginormous sea monster—never seen anything like it—attacked me when I escaped the current. Ripped through my body like it was paper. There was blood everywhere, coloring the water crimson. Thought for sure that I was dead."

"Did the Mysterious One bring you back to life?" said Quro.

"He did," said Garnal, nodding. "Found my body floating near this spit of land and revived me, although not beautifully, as I just showed you. Still, I'm alive again and that's what matters."

The temperature in the room seemed to drop like a rock because Malock shivered. "How do we know you're not lying? What if you were just unconscious and badly wounded?"

"I showed you my body," Garnal snapped. "By the gods, gold blood, I know you royals aren't exactly the brightest crowns in the treasury, but even you must have seen that there is no good reason that I should even be talking to both of you right now."

"She's quite correct," said Quro. "Back on Ruwa, I once saw a man suffer similar wounds from a swordtooth. He didn't last even five minutes after it attacked him."

"See?" said Garnal. "And let me tell you, I've been both unconscious and badly wounded in my time, sometimes simultaneously, and what I felt when I died was nothing at all like either of that. I truly believed that my soul must have passed on to the other side and would have stayed there if the Mysterious One had not brought it back."

"Why would the Mysterious One bring it back?" said Malock. "Why would he save your life? Isn't he aware that you're nothing more than a murderous, no-good pirate whose life is worth less than sea salt?"

"Who knows?" said Garnal. "All I know is that I am grateful for his actions. It is why I am his faithful servant. And this time, I say it with complete sincerity."

"But how did he bring you back?" said Quro. "That's never happened before in the history of Martir. No one, mortal or god, has ever come back from the dead."

"I don't know," said Garnal. "That is why I think he's not from Martir. That is why I think he is greater than a god."

"Or maybe he got that information from the Powers," said Malock. "You're his servant. Has he ever told you about the time he went to the Void and returned?"

"He's never told me anything, except that he saved my life and will keep me safe as long as I serve him," said Garnal. "To be honest, I don't even know what this 'Void' is."

Malock cursed under his breath, but then said aloud, "Well, it doesn't matter if you do or do not know. So long as the Mysterious One himself appears and tells us about it, we'll be fine."

"Good luck with that," said Garnal. "It's been weeks since I last saw him. He tends to disappear for weeks at a time, always without telling me where he goes. I'm basically his housekeeper, for all intents and purposes, even though there is not much house to keep here."

She gestured at the bare walls and ceiling. "Nor do I I know when he is going to return. Might be today, might be tomorrow, might be a year from now for all I know."

"We don't have a year," said Malock. "The end of the world is right around the corner and if we don't get that information from the Mysterious One right now, then we will be severely hampered on our quest to save the world."

"The end of the world?" said Garnal. "That's the most ridiculous piece of bull that I have ever heard in my life. The world is not ending."

"Oh, yes it is," said Malock. "A friend of mine received a vision from the Powers announcing that Martir is going to be destroyed. They will not spare the lives of anyone, god or mortal."

"We're on a quest to try to convince them to spare the world," Quro explained. "Hence why we stopped here. We don't know what lies beyond the Void, which is where the Powers are, so we thought that the Mysterious One could tell us."

Garnal rubbed her left arm, almost nervously, as if she knew something that they didn't. "Well, even if what you say is true, you're still wasting your time. The Mysterious One would never tell a couple of mortals anything, especially a couple of mortals that he doesn't know. I'm his servant and I still don't know much about him. You'd have better spent your time heading to this Void yosu speak of, rather than going here."

She said that while looking at the skeleton lying on the floor, like she hoped it would get her out of this situation. This timidity made Malock suspicious.

"All right," said Malock. "What are you hiding?"

"Hiding?" said Garnal. "I'm not hiding anything. I'm just stating the facts."

Though her tone was as brash as ever, still she looked at the skeleton. She didn't raise her eyes to look at either Malock or Quro. Malock had never known Garnal to be a timid person, so this set off an alarm in his head.

"You're hiding something," said Malock. "You're not that great a liar, you know. I can see right through you. Whatever you're hiding from us, you can't hide it forever."

Garnal finally looked up at Malock and Quro. For once, her brash facade seemed to have vanished, replaced by a look of horror that Malock had never expected to see on her face.

"Don't you get it?" said Garnal. "The Mysterious One is *gone*. He's left. He sensed that the Powers were coming to end the world as we know it. He abandoned me here."

"What the heck?" said Malock. "But earlier, you said that you didn't know where the Mysterious One is."

"I lied," said Garnal, her voice returning to its usual harsh tone. "Is that such a difficult thing for you to understand? I'm a pirate. We learn to lie early on. It's how we survive."

"But why would you lie?" said Malock. "What would you gain from leading us on like that?"

Garnal raised her snapping claws as she said, "Well, with the end of the world just around the corner, I figured that now would be the perfect opportunity to get the revenge on you that I've always wanted. I just wanted to make sure you were perfectly miserable and despairing before I did it."

Malock reached for his pistol. "So you're the one who blocked off the exit."

"That I did, gold blood, that I did," said Garnal. "I wanted to make sure you couldn't escape. I didn't recognize you at first due to your uglier than usual face, but when I heard your voice I knew this was my only chance."

"Hold on," said Quro, holding up a hand. "There's no reason we should fight. If the Mysterious One has truly left, then this makes it all the more urgent that we go to the Void and convince the Powers to spare all of us. You should let us free. We don't know how much time the world has left."

Garnal chuckled. "And what will you do, pray tell, once you cross the Void? You can't convince the Powers to spare our world. If even the gods are too afraid to stand against them, I doubt we pathetic mortals could do anything."

"You're wrong," said Malock. He pulled his gun off his belt and aimed it at her. "But if you're going to fight us, then I guess we have no choice but to fight back."

"I expect no less from my worst enemy," said Garnal. "Unlike the last time we met, gold blood, I will not treat you mercifully. Your death will be quick and your blood will stain the floor of this cave for the rest of eternity, though that's not saying much, seeing as eternity is about to come to its end."

Chapter Seven

UNDER THE PALE HALF-MOON hanging in the sky, Skimif climbed up the old, rusting fire escape of an apartment building in east Port Blasan, though he tried to do it as silently as he could. But due to his lack of experience sneaking about, he still made more noise than he liked. He didn't want to awake the inhabitants of the apartment building, who as far as he knew were all asleep. If any of them woke up and looked out their apartments, they would undoubtedly not react well to seeing a stranger climbing up to the roof of their building. Especially an aquarian like himself; despite their pretensions, the human Carnagians were not nearly as tolerant of aquarians as they usually made themselves out to be.

Not that Skimif wanted to be here. He had made a point, as leader of the Brotherhood of Heathens, to avoid going out at night unless absolutely necessary, and in fact discouraged all of his fellow Heathens from going out at night unless necessary. It was all part of his long-term strategy to legitimize the Brotherhood to the Carnagian public. If they gained a reputation as people who walked the streets at night, it would just give their critics more ammunition to use against them.

But tonight, Skimif had no choice but to go out. He had to go out alone, too, which would admittedly make it easier to move around unseen but still made him feel skittish. So far, no one had seen him, but he supposed he wouldn't know for sure until the next morning, which he figured was the earliest that any rumors about the reasons for his sneaking around would reach the general public.

When Skimif reached the top of the roof, he saw no one else on the roof. It was completely flat, without any entrances or exits into or out of the building. He didn't see anywhere anyone could hide, though he climbed on top anyway. The wind was blowing, so he had to bend over slightly to avoid getting blown over by it.

The particular apartment building he stood upon—made of rock and brick, probably a couple of decades old—was not very tall. It was perhaps three or four stories tall, if that, and had the unfortunate state of being built right in the middle of a dozen other buildings that rose above it. None of the lights in those other buildings were on because Port Blasan was a city that slept at night, unlike some of the cities near the south, aside from the Justice Enforcers, who patrolled the city's streets after dark on the lookout for criminals.

Or they did in most parts of the city. A quick glance over the side told Skimif that there were no Justice Enforcers in this neighborhood tonight. One of the newer Heathens—a retired Justice Enforcer—had told him that this part of the city was usually ignored by the Enforcers due to its lack of criminal activity. Skimif supposed that the person who had sent him the letter must have chosen the spot for this meeting precisely because of the lack of Enforcers.

Just to be safe, Skimif moved away from the edge of the roof and sat down on the gravel-covered roof. He pulled out the letter that he had found nailed on the door of the Brotherhood's hideout a couple of days ago and, after doing yet another quick glance around to make sure no one was nearby, he read the letter's contents again. Due to the darkness of the night, he couldn't actually read it very well, relying more on his memory of it from having read the letter over and over again in the days since he had received it:

Skimif,

Meet me at the fifth apartment building on Third street in east Port Blasan at midnight two days from today. Assuming you do not want the Enforcers to know the location of your hideout, you would do well to heed my words.

Frowning, Skimif turned the letter over again. He and his fellow Heathens had poured over the letter for hours, trying to find any clues that might tell who had written it or why. None of them recognized the handwriting—which was curly and thin, like the writer had not been pressing down very hard on the paper—and there were no other clues on it that they could find.

Despite that, there had been no question in Skimif's mind that he should give into its demands. The most obvious fact about the letter was that it had not been written by any of the Heathens, yet somehow the letter-writer had known where to place the letter where Skimif would find it. Only a dozen or so of Skimif's most trusted Heathens even knew where the hideout was located and he doubted that any of them had leaked the secret to people outside of the group. Nor could a mage have discovered its location via topomancy; Skimif had learned, shortly after receiving his first vision from the Powers, that he was immune to being detected via magic for reasons he was not entirely sure of, an ability he had passed on to the rest of his trusted men so they could not be found, either.

As a result, Skimif couldn't dismiss it as a prank. Whoever had written the letter was most likely serious about informing the Enforcers about the hideout's location. Aqur and the others had protested against him going alone, but if satisfying this letter-writer's demands would keep the movement safe, so be it.

The sound of feet crunching against the gravel made Skimif stand up and look around. He didn't see anything at first; but then a moment later a human form appeared out of thin air, stepping out of the shadow that a nearby larger building cast upon the one Skimif stood on. The man was shorter than the average Carnagian, with pale skin that looked white as snow in the moonlight. He was almost bald and had a grin as wide as the sun. He wore a long brown poncho/cloak over his body, flapping in the wind as his bare feet crossed over the roof toward Skimif. He didn't wear any shoes, but the gravel under his bare feet didn't seem to bother him much.

"Good night, Skimif of Tunya," said the man, his grin never changing as he approached the aquarian. "I see you got my letter. I thought you might not choose to show up, but it looks like you proved me wrong. Good for you."

Skimif thrust out the letter before him. "How did you know where we live? Who are you? And why did you want to meet me alone on top of an apartment building in the middle of the night?"

"Good questions," said the man. "You're not as easily hidden as you think you are, you know. The gods know the location of all people. The mortal topomancers can't find you, perhaps, but the gods cannot be fooled by your little trick."

"It's not a trick," said Skimif. "I don't trick anyone. The Powers gave me that ability. If you have a problem with it, bring it up with them."

The man sighed. "If the end of the world is indeed soon, then I may very well get that chance. Of course, I am assuming that the Powers will not immediately turn me into a pile of ash instead, which is why we are here today."

Skimif's eyes darted to the left and right, but he didn't see anyone else. "How do you know about the end of the world? That's information we've kept strictly within the ranks of the Brotherhood."

"Master Hollech told me all about it," said the man. "The gods sense that the end is near. They're not going to do anything about it, of course, because they can't, because no one can. Prince Malock and his little band of fools may try their best, but in the end the Void will claim their lives and where will we all be then?"

"You must be a personal servant of the gods, then," said Skimif. "Tell me, what is your name?"

"Master Hollech named me Ramufa when he found me as a young boy," said the man. "Before that, I have no idea what I was called."

"Ramufa," Skimif repeated. "Aqur once told me about a freelance assassin named Ramufa the Nimble-Fingered, who also doubled as a bodyguard."

"I do—or used to do—all sorts of things," said Ramufa.

"Diversification is a great business plan, you know. So I see you already know me, but no matter. I still hold the power in this meeting. Did you come alone?"

Skimif nodded. "Of course. And before you even think it, no, I am not lying. I've never believed in lying, even to my enemies, and so I won't lie to you tonight."

Ramufa scratched his chin. "Oh, I already knew that. I did a quick scan of the area before revealing myself to you, just to make sure a couple of your friends weren't hiding like nightly eggs in a rat's cave. I only asked to see if you were as honest as the rumors make you out to be."

"I was always taught honesty was a virtue," said Skimif. "But enough of that. What have you called this meeting for? Did the gods ask you to ask me to stop recruiting mortals into the Brotherhood?"

"That is certainly an annoying habit on your part," said Ramufa, nodding. "But the gods are well-aware that you already know about their disapproval of your little group. Besides, after the assassination of Princess Raya, Master Hollech says that your movement is a lot less stable than it once was."

Skimif bit his lower lip, his teeth almost breaking his skin. It was true that the recent assassination of Princess Raya Kabadi had shaken a lot of Heathens, but Skimif didn't know how Ramufa could possibly know that. Then again, the gods always kept a close eye on their enemies, or so he had been told, which made him wonder exactly how much Ramufa knew about them.

"It looks like I hit a sore spot," said Ramufa. "I'm surprised we've made it this far, however, without you trying to throw me off the roof of this building. Didn't Malock or Jenur tell you that I was the one who killed Raya?"

Skimif almost dropped the letter, but he instead stuffed it into his coat. Then, trying not to show how angry he was, Skimif looked up at Ramufa, whose grin looked a lot more smug now, and said, "They did tell me that a servant of Hollech killed her, but they didn't tell me his name."

"I suppose Raya's death must have traumatized Malock and made him forget my name," said Ramufa. "Or maybe Jenur, that silly little girl, didn't tell him. Either way, I am very happy at how civilly you have acted toward me. It makes me feel—"

Skimif sprinted toward Ramufa, barring his teeth, but before he even moved four feet, he tripped and fell face-first onto the stone roof. Gravel and dirt entered Skimif's mouth as his face scraped against the stone, making him hack and cough as he looked down at his ankles. Two hands had somehow sprouted out of the roof and grasped Skimif's ankles tightly, which appeared to have been the source of his tripping.

"Now, now," said Ramufa, tsking. "This is not the time to fight. I know how angry you are, but I suppose no one ever taught you that attacking the people you dislike is not always constructive."

Failing to shake the hands off his ankles, Skimif looked up and started. Ramufa's arms were smooth stumps, his hands totally gone, like they had been cut cleanly by a butcher's knife. Then Skimif looked at the hands holding his ankles and realized that they were Ramufa's.

"The Thief's Way," said Ramufa. "It can let you do all sorts of interesting things with your body parts when you figure it out. Really, the only thing that limits me is my imagination, a trait which Master Hollech thankfully developed in me when I was but a small child."

Scowling, Skimif scooped up a handful of gravel and hurled it at Ramufa. The gravel clattered against his pants and feet, not even making the man flinch.

"Let me go," Skimif said through gritted teeth. "Now."

Ramufa's grin went from smug to amused. "Or you'll what? Throw more gravel at me? I suppose I didn't make it very clear earlier about what I would do if you tried to attack me?"

"You didn't say anything about that," Skimif said. "I wasn't even thinking of harming you until you identified yourself as the divine sycophant who killed Raya. You bastard."

"I should have laid the ground rules earlier," said Ramufa. "My bad. See, though the Enforcers don't usually patrol this part of the city, just a few blocks due north is a squad of Enforcers—mostly newbies, their first night on the job, very eager to prove themselves and serve Grinf, good kids—who would be just ecstatic to be the ones to bring in Skimif of Tunya, the Heathen who has blasphemed the names of the gods and done his best to shake up society. It would not take much for me to summon them here and let them take you in."

Skimif closed his fist around another fistful of gravel, but didn't throw it. "I was told that the Enforcers wouldn't bother me or my Heathens until the debate."

"And you believed them?" said Ramufa. "That's hilarious. Of course, I don't know much about this debate, as it's been largely orchestrated by Grinf's followers, and Grinf and Hollech don't get along very well due to their differences in mortality, so they may be honest."

Ramufa's hands tightened around Skimif's legs even more. His fingernails must have been sharp because real pain shot up Skimif's legs, making him almost cry out, but he didn't. He remembered the Enforcers who were just a few blocks away.

"Even if they're honest, I can't imagine any self-respecting Justice Enforcer allowing the most wanted aquarian in the Northern Isles to walk free," said Ramufa. "Especially when it is revealed that this Heathen assaulted a defenseless old man like me."

"You're not old or defenseless," said Skimif. "You look rather young, actually."

"That may be true," said Ramufa. "But so what? The point is, don't mess with me or you'll spend the rest of the night inside the nearest prison. Trust me, Carnagian prisons aren't anything to laugh at."

"Fine," said Skimif. "I won't attack you, then. Just let go of my ankles already. I think you've cut off the circulation to them."

"Do you swear on Hollech's most trustworthy name?" said Ramufa.

Skimif looked at Ramufa with disbelief. "Hollech is the God of Deception. What do you think my answer is?"

"Good enough," said Ramufa. He pulled back his arms and his hands reappeared on his stumps at the same moment that the pressure around Skimif's ankles lessened.

Skimif immediately glanced at his ankles, which were now free, and then got to his feet. He had to do it slowly, however, because his ankles still hurt and the blood hadn't yet returned to them entirely.

"Now we understand each other, I hope," said Ramufa. "You and I can have a proper, civilized discussion, like the two gentlemen we are."

"Gentlemen," said Skimif with a snort. "Right."

But he didn't attacked Ramufa. As much as he wanted to sink his teeth into the killer's neck and rip out his throat, he had no doubt that Ramufa's threat was true. Besides, he was in no mood to become wanted for an actual offense, not when he was already wanted for several imaginary ones. It was difficult not to imagine what Ramufa would look like dead, however, or the taste of his blood in Skimif's mouth. He did, however, make sure to keep an eye on Ramufa's hands, just so the freelancer wouldn't try anything with them again.

"All right," said Skimif. "What did you want to talk with me about? Are you going to tell me to give up or suffer the consequences?"

"No," said Ramufa, shaking his head. "The gods know there's nothing they can say that will make you give up. Even if they threatened to kill everyone you know and love, you'd still preach your message. I personally think you wouldn't, but unlike you, I don't question the knowledge of the gods."

Skimif didn't know whether he agreed with Ramufa or not, so he ignored the issue. "You still haven't told me what we're going to talk about. If you're not going to threaten or blackmail me, then I don't see why we're here having this conversation."

Ramufa scratched his chin. "Oh, it's nothing too serious, I can assure you. The gods—really, mostly Master Hollech, but he told me that some of the other gods back him up on this, so it's all good—want to make you an offer they think you can't refuse."

Skimif folded his arms across his chest. "What offer could the gods make for me? They have nothing I want."

"It's a simple offer," said Ramufa. "One that any sane mortal would murder a whole nation for, if given the chance."

"That sounds insane to me," said Skimif. "But tell me what it is anyway. I suppose it can't hurt to listen."

Ramufa leaned forward slightly, almost as if he was sharing a secret with Skimif. Then he glanced to the left and right and said, "Do you want to ascend to godhood?"

Skimif blinked. "What?"

"I thought I spoke clearly," said Ramufa. "Let me ask again: Do you want to ascend to godhood? Transcend your pitiful mortal form and live forever?"

"That's a ridiculous question," said Skimif, stomping his foot in anger. "And if that's their offer, then no. I'm not going to liberate my brother and sister mortals only to put them under my own rule. Besides, with the end of the world around the corner, I would not exist long enough to enjoy the benefits of godhood anyway."

"That wasn't the offer," said Ramufa. "But good to know. Master Hollech asked me to ask you that just to see your reaction." His grin widened. "Worth it."

Skimif scowled. "Then what is the *real* offer? And if it's another joke—"

"It's no joke," said Ramufa. "The real offer is this: Throw the debate."

Skimif eyed Ramufa suspiciously. "Throw the debate? What for?"

"It's pretty simple," said Ramufa. "You see, the gods want you to do your absolute worst in your debate with Yamaru Domaha. Use terrible logic, avoid giving specific examples, make sure to mumble and stutter as much as you can ... you know, all the marks of a child trying to justify their inappropriate behavior to their parents."

Skimif huffed. "No way. I'm not going to throw the debate for anyone. My fellow Heathens are counting on me to do my absolute best. I will not betray their hope."

"But you haven't even heard what the gods will do if you refuse," said Ramufa. "You sure do like to jump to conclusions without first hearing all the facts. It's a terrible flaw that can really mess up your business. Trust me, I learned that the hard way when I first started out."

"What will the gods threaten to do to me?" said Skimif. "Kill me? Destroy my friends? Or perhaps just give me a really bad rash?"

"Nothing quite so dramatic and flashy," said Ramufa, shaking his head. "The gods know that there's really not much they can do to you, seeing as the Powers draw ever nearer to Martir. Any damage they do to you—no matter how devastating—will only bring them temporary joy, seeing as they will be swept up in the great cloud of destruction that will soon descend upon us all."

"How pathetic," said Skimif. "They demand that I do something, but can't actually make me do anything? I am surprised that the gods have been worshiped for as long as they have, if this is an example of their modus operandi."

"I didn't say they can't do *anything* to you," Ramufa said. "Just that most of the usual punishments won't suffice because of your iron determination to keep going and the end of the world being right around the corner. Besides, you have that annoying protection given to you by the Powers, which makes killing you basically impossible."

Skimif didn't say anything to that. He had long suspected he had some form of protection courtesy of the Powers, so he was glad to have it confirmed. Though when he thought about it, he didn't understand why the Powers would go through the trouble of protecting him if he was going to die alongside everyone else anyway.

"But there are subtler and scarier forms of punishment that the gods could inflict upon you," Ramufa continued. "Did you ever hear the story about Remino, the God of Illusions, and the pig farmer?"

"No," said Skimif. "What is it about?"

"A simple story," said Ramufa. "One day, a long time ago, a pig farmer stole a valuable gold ring from Remino. Never one to smite mortals with thunder, as some of his siblings were wont to do when angry, Remino instead began sending a series of illusions to the pig farmer that were almost real. A vision of his wife falling down a cliff and dying, the sight of a monstrous beast lurking just out of sight, always disappearing whenever the man turned to look directly at it, and a variety of other illusions that all made the poor pig farmer fear for his life until the day he finally took it himself. Remino then got his gold ring back, so it was a happy ending after all."

Skimif legs started shaking, but he stopped them right quick. "That's a horrible story. But what's the point of it?"

"The point is, if you say no, Remino is perfectly willing to do that again," said Ramufa. "Only, he won't be the only god fooling your senses. Hamin, Goddess of the Mind, knows just which strings she needs to pull to make your sanity break into itty bitty bite-sized pieces over a slow period of time, without you ever being the wiser."

A gust of wind blew through just then, but despite the wind being warm, Skimif couldn't help but shiver. "So you're saying that Remino and Hamin will slowly chip away at my sanity, make me doubt my own senses?"

"More or less," said Ramufa, as if discussing the weather. "That will do more to discredit your movement, I imagine, than any bad performance in a public debate. The pleasure will of course still be temporary, seeing as the world will end either way, but it will still satisfy the gods' need to punish you. It's ingenious, isn't it?"

"No, it's not," said Skimif. He gestured at the sky above and said, "Your gods spend all their time devising idiotic strategies like this just to punish an insignificant mortal like me when the end of the world is just around the corner? They ought to be putting all of that so-called 'wisdom' together to figure out a way to save the world, not waste it on me."

"Don't complain to me about it," said Ramufa, holding up his hands. "I'm just the messenger. Besides, the gods know they can't beat the Powers. They think that Prince Malock and his band of fools are destined for failure. They're just trying to do everything they want to do before all of creation is swept up and tossed out like so much dust."

Skimif balled his fists, but before he could say anything, a powerful stench—like that of a rotting corpse mixed with bad eggs—

wafted on the wind into his nostrils. The scent burned his nose, making him grab his face as the flapping of two great wings filled his ears. Looking up, Skimif saw a gigantic flying creature's silhouette swooping down from the moon, its features hidden in its shadow.

Ramufa also looked up, saying as he did so, "What is that?"

The creature plucked Ramufa off the roof with its thick talons and hurled him away. Skimif watched, his body tense, as the monster threw Ramufa toward a nearby building. The servant of the gods almost slammed into it, but at the last minute he vanished into the darkness like it was water and didn't pop out, meaning that he was probably gone for good.

Not that that made Skimif feel any safer. The giant flying beast turned in the air and swooped down toward Skimif. It landed on the edge of the roof opposite him, screeching and flapping its wings, prompting Skimif to turn and run. He almost reached the fire escape, but before he could climb down it, the beast was before him again, landing with a *crunch* on the metal stairs. Skimif staggered backwards and looked for another exit, but he saw no other escape routes from the roof.

The creature now stood visible in the moonlight. It had brown, leathery skin, with a lizard-like face whose green eyes gleamed with hunger. Two long bits of flesh ran from the corners of its mouth to the back of its neck, bits of flesh that resembled the reins of a horse. Its wings were tipped with sharp spikes, while its body seemed to be as thick as a tree. Its feet were tiny and stubby, but its knife-like talons looked more than capable of ripping through his body no problem. That rank odor that had laid siege to his nostrils came directly from the creature, which made it hard for Skimif to focus on it.

As Skimif looked around, lights flickered on in the windows of other nearby buildings. In fact, a few people had already gotten up, sticking their heads out of their windows to see exactly what was going on. There were still no Justice Enforcers, but Skimif realized it would not be long before they showed up.

The giant lizard creature—which must have been the one that Ower had spotted earlier—screeched and hissed at Skimif. With its wings spread out, it looked far bigger than it actually was, but that didn't mean Skimif could beat it. On the contrary, he was quite sure that a single swipe of that creature's massive wings would be enough to break his neck and his whole body, too.

Yet I have no choice but to stay and fight, Skimif thought grimly. *I can't run, not without breaking my legs on the street. I'll just have to do my best.*

So Skimif held up his fists, spread his legs, and said, "All right, monster. You may be a herald of the end, but that doesn't mean I can't go down fighting."

Oddly, his words seemed to have an effect on the beast. It lowered its wings and ceased screeching and hissing. In fact, it looked almost docile now, like a puppy waiting for its owner to tell it what to do. Skimif didn't let his guard down, though, because he suspected this was a plot on the creature's part to lower Skimif's defenses.

All around, more people had awaken and more lights had been turned on. Skimif even heard people moving down in the streets and heard some dogs barking somewhere nearby. He wished that the people had not awoken because they were now in just as much danger of being attacked by the creature as he was.

Just as Skimif wondered when the creature was going to act, it lowered its head and looked at him, again very much like a puppy.

Does this thing seriously believe that I am going to fall for that trick? Skimif thought. *It must have a low opinion of my intelligence. Just because I didn't go to the Academy doesn't mean I'm stupid.*

Still, the creature didn't seem like it was going to attack. If it would not make the first move, then Skimif would have to. And if this display of docility was all just a ploy, then Skimif decided he might as well run straight into it.

But before he could strike, the creature opened its mouth. Then it moved its lips, in a very slow, awkward way, like it wasn't used to the motion. A single word came from its mouth, a clear Divina word that caused Skimif to shudder:

"Master."

Skimif looked at it in disbelief. The creature returned the look expectantly, as if that one word explained all of its behavior.

"Master?" said Skimif. "What does—"

A fire bolt flew out of nowhere and struck the creature in the side. The creature roared in pain and immediately took off from the roof, causing Skimif to whip his head in the direction the fire bolt had come from. On the roof of a nearby building stood four Justice Enforcers, one of whom was holding out his wand, the tip of which was smoking.

"Don't let it get away!" the Enforcer yelled, his harsh voice rising above the din of noise that had erupted in the streets below. "Kill the damn thing before it disappears again!"

Another screech caused Skimif to look up. The creature had circled back, flying directly toward the four Enforcers standing on the nearby building. The look of anger—more like pure, primal rage—on its features was thrown into relief by the light that one of the Enforcers was shining at it. The Enforcers ducked, just barely avoiding the flying beast's claws, and turned to fire more flames at it as it flew away from them.

Seeing his chance, Skimif dashed to the fire escape and made his way down it. As he rattled down the stairs, he heard people shouting and running around in the streets below, and by the time he got to the streets, dozens of Carnagians now stood in the streets. Many of them were either half-dressed or in their pajamas, pointing up at the massive winged beast that circled and roared and dodged the blasts of fire that the Enforcers hurled at it.

No one seemed to notice Skimif, which he was thankful for. As stealthily as he could, Skimif ran away from the scene of the fight, his heart racing and his skin drying. He didn't look back when the roar of the creature shook the air, nor did he even slow down. All he wanted to do was get back to the hideout and let the others know what had happened, though to be honest, he wasn't sure what just happened himself.

Chapter Eight

GARNAL SLASHED AND SNAPPED, first knocking Malock's pistol out of his hand before he could fire even one round, then almost taking off Quro's right arm with one of her claws. This left Malock almost entirely defenseless, forcing him to rely on Quro to defend him. And unfortunately, Quro was not quite as fast as Jenur was.

True, most of his blows had landed, but they hadn't done a thing to slow Garnal down. If anything, they seemed to simply irritate her, making her more and more aggressive the longer the battle went. Quro had even managed to lodge a dragon shark scale into her neck, which had done little except make her speech slightly less comprehensible than usual.

So Malock had retreated from Garnal, but that was difficult to do because Quro couldn't keep her distracted very long. Every time Malock got out of her vision, Garnal would abandon Quro and go after him instead. And every time, Quro would get her attention back on himself, although it became increasingly more difficult to do, as Quro was obviously becoming more and more tired while Garnal wasn't slowing down at all. Despite her injured body, Garnal still moved fast as lightning.

Malock hid behind one of the support beams as Garnal swiped at Quro with her claws, while Quro jumped back to avoid it. Peering around the support beam, Malock spotted his pistol lying on the floor on the other side of the room. But the only way to get it was to go directly across, which would be difficult to do because Garnal and Quro were fighting in the center of the room, near the skeleton that had once belonged to the Mysterious One.

I could make it, Malock thought. *If Quro can keep Garnal distracted long enough, I should be able to grab the gun and then ...*

His mind went blank. He had no idea how useful the gun would be against Garnal. She seemed impervious to any sort of damage, even to life-threatening blows, like several of the kind that Quro had already landed on her. He figured the Mysterious One must have done far more than merely bring Garnal back to life—perhaps made her less susceptible to pain—but it didn't matter because Malock was pretty sure that he and Quro weren't going to get out of this alive unless a miracle occurred.

And I can't rely on miracles, Malock thought. *Not right now, at least.*

Garnal swung both of her massive claws at Quro's head. Quro ducked and stabbed her directly in the stomach with one of his scales. The sharp scale dug into her flesh, but she didn't even seem to feel it because she slammed both of her claws down on his head hard. Quro fell to the ground like a stone, but he managed to roll out of the way before her foot crushed his skull. Her foot struck the stone floor, actually creating a small crater that made Malock gasp.

And she's strong enough to break rock now with her feet, Malock thought, watching as Quro rolled to his feet, his hand on the back of his head, where Garnal had struck him. *Brilliant.*

But even if Garnal was now somehow immortal—and considering how different she was now, he didn't see any reason to believe that she wasn't—he still had to get his gun and try to help Quro anyway. Better than sitting behind a pillar and hiding, in his opinion.

Garnal was now looking around the room, apparently ignoring Quro again, saying, "Where did you go, gold blood? Come out and fight me like a man. Or are you afraid of getting your shiny boots scuffed?"

By now, Quro appeared to have recovered from the blow to the head he had received from Garnal. He stuck his hands in his pockets and pulled out a handful of some kind of red dust that Malock couldn't identify.

Without uttering so much as a word, Quro ran at Garnal. Garnal turned to face him, saying as she did so, "Still awake, are ya? You'd do better to—"

Her sentence turned into a scream of pain when Quro hurled the red dust into her eyes. It must have been some kind of burning dust because she began rubbing her eyes with her claws, thus allow Quro to deliver a stunning kick to the gut that knocked her down to the floor.

This gave Malock just the opportunity that he needed. He dashed out from behind the pillar, his eyes focused entirely on the pistol. It was all that existed to him in that moment, so he was shocked when he felt thin, bony fingers wrap around his left ankle. He jerked to a stop and looked down and saw the skeleton was gripping his ankle. The skeleton was looking up at him, its eyes glowing, as if daring him to move.

"What the—" said Malock.

The skeleton yanked on his boot and Malock fell face forward. He broke the fall by holding out his arms first, but he still got the breath knocked out of him. He then rolled over onto his back as the skeleton stood up to its full height, which admittedly was not very much.

"The Mysterious One?" said Malock. "How—"

The skeleton held up its right hand. The scrapping of metal against the stone floor caused Malock to look over his shoulder. The pistol was slowly sliding across the stone floor to the skeleton, but that apparently was too slow for the Mysterious One. It yanked its right hand back and the gun flew through the air like a bee, falling into the skeleton's left hand.

It then began examining the gun like it was the most fascinating thing the God of Mystery and Magic had ever seen. It tapped the barrel of the gun, the bone clinking against the metal, and then raised the gun above its head and fired it into the ceiling three times.

In the confined room, with no windows to allow the noise to escape, the sound of the gunshots was deafening. Malock had to clasp his hands over his ears to protect his hearing. Quro had doubled over from the sound, while Garnal—her eyes still covered in that red dust —still lay on the ground, her claws over her eyes. She looked up when she heard the gunshots, however, her face turning pale when she saw the Mysterious One.

"M-Master?" said Garnal, her mouth quivering. "W-What are you doing here?"

The Mysterious One lowered the gun and turned to face Garnal. With his skeletal back to Malock, it was impossible to tell what the Mysterious One's face looked like. But Malock could see Garnal's face, which got paler and paler the longer the Mysterious One stared at her.

"M-Master," said Garnal as she got to her hands and knees, apparently ignoring the dust in her eyes. "I-I didn't mean to—"

The Mysterious One raised his left hand. A low whistling sound emitted from somewhere, which Malock suddenly realized was coming from the Mysterious One's mouth. It must have been his own way of speaking because Garnal seemed to understand it.

"N-No, sir," said Garnal. "It was all a mistake. These two ... they attacked *me*. When I told them you had left, they got angry and attacked. Honest."

The Mysterious One's head rotated until it was looking at Malock again. The eye sockets continued to glow blue, though that didn't make it any easier to read the mysterious god's expression. It stared at Malock for several seconds before rotating back to look at Garnal.

With the cracking of its finger joints, the Mysterious One gestured for Garnal to stand. This she did, trembling as she did so, but she looked relieved, too, as if everything was going much better than she expected.

"Master," said Garnal, putting her claws together in a submissive pose. "I am so glad you understand. You have always been so understanding of my mistakes. You have always been very merci—"

Another deafening shot and a bullet hole appeared in Garnal's forehead. Garnal gaped, but then her eyes went blank and she fell over backward onto the floor. The Mysterious One held the gun up, smoke rising from its barrel, which had been aimed directly where Garnal's forehead had been.

"By the Powers," Quro said. He was still on his hands and knees, looking at Garnal's corpse in disbelief. "Why—"

"She lied to me," came a voice from the Mysterious One's mouth. "And I do not take liars lightly. She knew that, and yet she still thought she could fool me."

The Mysterious One's voice was radically different from what Malock had thought it would sound like. His voice was a like a whisper, with a slight buzz to it like the voice of Messenger-and-Punisher. Why he sounded like that, Malock didn't know, and he wasn't sure that he wanted to, honestly.

"She is dead," said the Mysterious One as he walked over to Garnal, his joints creaking as he did so. "Whereas I gave her life, I can also take it away. And she knew that, and yet she still thought she could fool me."

"What did you expect?" said Malock, rubbing his nose as he sat up. "She's a pirate. Can't trust pirates."

The Mysterious One didn't respond to that. When he reached Garnal's corpse, he waved a hand above it. As soon as his bony fingers passed over it, Garnal's corpse transformed into mist that floated up toward the ceiling.

Then the Mysterious One turned to look at Malock and Quro. His expression as inscrutable as ever, he said, "Perhaps I should not have expected much from her. Perhaps I should not have revived her at all. We can only know the quality of our decisions with hindsight."

Malock stood up, brushing the dirt off his boat cloak as he said, "Yes, yes we can. Now, Mysterious One, I'm just going to cut to the chase and assume you know why Quro and I are here."

"Of course," said the Mysterious One. "You heard the rumors of my journey beyond the Void."

"Hold on," said Quro. He was still rubbing his ears, but he was no longer doubled over from the sound. "If you are a southern god, then how can you speak Divina? And perfectly, I might add."

The Mysterious One looked at Quro like he had just asked the dumbest question in the world. At least, that was how Malock interpreted the Mysterious One's face. Considering that the Mysterious One had no flesh or anything, it made interpreting his facial expressions very difficult.

Then the Mysterious One faced Malock again and said, "Let me tell you this: If you go beyond the Void, you must not—I repeat, must *not*—allow your mind to wander. Do you understand me?"

"No, I don't," said Malock. "What does that mean?"

"It should become obvious once you get there," said the Mysterious One. "The Mechanical Goddess will understand, and Nimiko, too. The Void tries to destroy anything that lives within it. It is anti-life, the very opposite of our world, which is a creation of the Powers."

"You still haven't explained anything," Malock said. "Oh, and I want my gun back, too. I didn't give it to you."

"In fact," said the Mysterious One, turning around and walking to the center of the room, "I'd say you shouldn't go beyond the Void at all. What lies beyond is madness, things that no creation of the Powers was ever meant to lay eyes upon. It would be better for you mortals to stay here and await the end than risk your very essence by going where you were never meant to go."

"Stop speaking in riddles," said Malock. "Give us some specifics."

"I already gave you the most valuable piece of information I can," said the Mysterious One, his bony feet clacking against the stone floor as he walked. "Anything more specific, and you would not believe me. The laws of this world are not necessarily the laws of the next."

"The next?" said Malock. "So there are more worlds out there? Worlds, perhaps, created by the Powers?"

The Mysterious One stopped in the center of the green circle and sat down, crossing his legs as he did so. "Under ordinary circumstances, I would have given you more help, but not today. I only took time out of my schedule because I sensed that Garnal had lied. Looks like I'll need to find a new servant."

The room suddenly rumbled, almost knocking over Malock and Quro. Then a portion of the wall on the other end of the room crumbled into dust, revealing a doorway that had previously been hidden.

"That door will take you out of Bleak Rock," said the Mysterious One.

"Wait," said Malock. "Take us out? But you haven't answered all of my questions."

"I am afraid that most of my answers would be of no help to you," the Mysterious One said. He then placed both of his hands in his lap, his fingers wrapped around the gun, and said, "Oh, and I am keeping the gun. I have never handled one before, but I see why you mortals like it. It will be the last pleasure I have before the world ends."

At that, the Mysterious One's eyes ceased glowing and the skeleton's head flopped forward on its chest as still as a stone. Not about to let a god have one of his possessions, Malock tried to walk into the circle, but found himself blocked by an invisible wall of energy. He pounded on the wall, but it wouldn't budge and it did not crack. All he could do was stare at the skeleton, which still held the gun in its lap.

"We must go," said Quro.

Malock jumped and looked to his left. Quro was standing there, looking grim, although Malock could not remember hearing the Dark Tiger move. His sudden appearance reminded Malock of Banika Koiro, the former first mate of his old ship. For a moment, he wondered how she was doing.

"There's nothing else we can do here," said Quro. "And we have no idea how much time has passed since we left. Every minute spent here is another minute that the end of the world draws closer."

"Uh, excellent point," said Malock, nodding. "We should tell Jenur and the others about what we found. And then we must go to World's End."

Quro fell into step with Malock as they made their way to the newly formed exit. "What do you think the Mysterious One meant when he said that we should not let our minds wander when we go beyond the Void?"

"I have no idea," said Malock, shrugging. "I think he was just being vague and mysterious to mess with us. You know how the gods are."

Quro looked over his shoulder at the skeleton. "Assuming, of course, that he's even a god to begin with."

"It doesn't matter one way or the other *what* he is," said Malock. "His answers were basically useless. This whole side trip was just a big waste of time. And time is all we have left."

Even so, as they walked through the exit, Malock thought he felt the Mysterious One's eyes upon his back. When he looked back to the skeleton, however, it still sat with its back to them, as motionless as the sea on a calm day.

Chapter Nine

WHILE MALOCK AND QURO were inside Bleak Rock, Jenur had walked around the top deck of the *Clockwork Heart*, watching as the automatons patrolled the perimeter of the ship, their automatonic eyes focused on the sky and sea. Hana had told her that the automatons were keeping an eye out for any gods or servants of the gods that might choose this moment to attack. That didn't make a lot of sense to Jenur, seeing as the Fifth Clause of the Treaty was still in effect, but then she remembered how the gods were always searching for loopholes in the Treaty and figured that it was better to be safe than sorry in this case.

Bleak Rock stood as foreboding as ever in the mist that surrounded it. Since Malock and Quro had entered it, no one had heard any news from them. A cold wind had blown through the area about ten minutes after their departure, but beyond that, it was impossible to know what had happened to Malock and Quro or if they were even still alive.

To avoid getting worried sick over their safety, Jenur had taken to exploring the ship. Meanwhile, Rint had gone back to his cabin, complaining that he needed to rest his old bones and that he didn't want anyone to wake him until Malock and Quro got back. Jenur had wanted to talk to Rint about his speaking with Nimiko, but he disappeared before she got the chance, so she decided to spend her time doing something else.

Yet despite her best efforts, Jenur kept finding herself drawn back to the bow of the ship, which faced Bleak Rock. The island's blank, rocky face kept her from knowing what was going on within, which frustrated her to no end. She was tempted to go onto Bleak Rock herself just to check on Quro and Malock, but she restrained herself, only leaning against the ship's railing and nothing more.

She became so engrossed with Bleak Rock that she almost jumped off the ship entirely when Hana said, "Waiting for Malock and Quro?"

Jenur turned around to see Hana. "Shouldn't you be bossing the automatons around or something?"

"We aren't going anywhere or doing anything, so I don't have anything to do," said Hana. "All the automatons are supposed to do is keep an eye out for any trouble. They don't need me to do that."

"They must not be doing a very good job of it, then," said Jenur, "because otherwise they would have grabbed you and thrown you off the ship for all of the trouble you caused me."

"You certainly didn't beat around the bush," Hana said. "I was just coming by to see what you were doing."

Jenur walked up to Hana, stopping when their faces were only a few inches apart. This allowed her to take in Hana's scent, which smelled like a rose, but that didn't endear Jenur to her at all.

"Listen," said Jenur. "The only reason I even tolerate you is because there is a lot more at stake than our own conflict. That doesn't mean I think of you as a friend; actually, I barely even think of you as an ally."

Hana leaned back, looking rather off-put. "Your breath is disgusting, you know that? Haven't you been brushing your teeth at all?"

"Is that really all you have to say?" said Jenur. "Really?"

Hana stepped back and held up her hands. "Hey, you were the one who snapped at me. All I wanted to do was see what you were doing."

Jenur didn't sense any deception in Hana's words, but that didn't make her feel any better. "Right, right, sure. Do we have any plans for what to do if Malock and Dad don't return?"

"The Mechanical Goddess has thought through this very issue in depth," said Hana, looking relieved, as if she thought Jenur wasn't angry with her anymore. "We're just going to head straight to World's End."

"You mean we're going to abandon Malock and Dad?" said Jenur in horror.

"Only if they don't return," Hana said. "Because hey, if they're gone, then they're gone, and there's nothing we can do about it."

Jenur looked back over at Bleak Rock. The entrance that Quro and Malock had entered was partially obscured by the mist, which didn't help her nerves much.

"Why couldn't we send in a group of automatons to rescue them?" said Jenur. "Would that be so difficult?"

"It would be a waste of time," Hana said. "The Mechanical Goddess doesn't like to waste time. After all, Malock and Quro technically aren't needed, after all. You and Rint could take Nimiko into the Void by yourselves."

"I guess that's true," said Jenur, scratching the back of her head. "But still. If there's even the slightest chance they're still alive—"

"Oh, they definitely are," said Hana, nodding. "But the simple fact is that the Mechanical Goddess says we've wasted enough time as is and she's not interested in getting yet another one of her siblings angry at her because of what some mortals have done. Remember, the Fifth Clause only lasts ten days and we've already wasted two."

"Then I'll just go and convince the Mechanical Goddess myself," said Jenur. "Or maybe I'll just go to Bleak Rock on my own. I'm not afraid of some—"

The sound of crumbling rock caused Jenur to look back at Bleak Rock again. About a dozen yards or so below the first entrance, a large portion of the island's rock wall was falling away, splashing into the ocean loudly. Both Jenur and Hana ran to the railing and leaned over to see what had caused it. A thick mist had descended over the new hole, though Jenur managed to spot the familiar outlines of two figures through the mist.

Then the mist parted, revealing Malock and Quro standing in a hole. Both of them looked tired and somewhat surprised, as if they had not expected the wall to come crumbling down before them.

"Malock!" Jenur shouted. "Dad! Hey, you two!"

It took the automatons only minutes to adjust the ramp so it would connect with the new hole, rather than with the old one.

Despite how tired the two looked, Malock and Quro had no trouble climbing the ramp and onto the ship itself.

"Are you two all right?" said Jenur, anxiously rubbing her hands together as they stepped onto the main deck. "Did you find the Mysterious One?"

"We did," said Quro. His face was bruised, like someone had smashed a heavy club into it.

"But it was useless," said Malock.

"Tell us what happened," said Hana. "What did you see, exactly?"

Malock described what he and Quro saw and did in Bleak Rock, starting with their entering the island and ending with their appearing in that new hole. The tale was a tall one, but since Jenur had seen far stranger things on the southern seas, she had no trouble believing most of it.

That didn't stop her from glancing at Bleak Rock and saying, "So you guys ran into Garnal? I thought she was dead."

"She is dead, now," said Quro, nodding. "Killed by her own master. She won't be bothering any of us now, or anyone else."

"Hana, do you know what the Mysterious One meant when he said we shouldn't let our minds wander in the Void?" said Malock. "He was extremely vague and unhelpful."

"Why would I know?" said Hana. "I've never been beyond the Void before."

"Remember, Malock, he said that the Mechanical Goddess and Nimiko would understand," said Quro. "So maybe we should ask them."

"All right," said Malock. He turned to look at the highest deck and the smokestacks of the *Clockwork Heart* and shouted, "Mechanical Goddess! What did the Mysterious One mean? I know you were listening in on our conversation, so you can't ignore me if that's what you were planning to do."

Seeing Malock shout at the ship like that looked a little silly to Jenur, but it was pretty much the only way that they could communicate with the goddess who controlled it.

Without warning, the smokestacks exploded, spewing flames and smoke from within. But not together. The two smokestacks alternated, sometimes the front funnel billowing, followed by the rear funnel flaming and smoking and then the front one again. It was easily the most complicated use of the smokestacks that Jenur had seen yet.

Only Hana appeared to understand the Mechanical Goddess's noises. She had inclined her head in the Mechanical Goddess's direction, listening like she would listen to a normal person speaking.

Then the smokestacks suddenly went silent, the last wisps of smoke curling out of the funnels and into the mist that hung in the night sky above them.

"All right," said Hana, turning to face the others. "The Mechanical Goddess says that the Mysterious One is referring to an ancient process that all new gods must go through upon achieving divinity."

Quro frowned. "Are you saying that mortals can become gods?"

"Yes," said Hana in an exasperated tone. "Didn't you know that?"

"Just because I'm known as the Thinker doesn't mean I know everything," said Quro. "I'm still learning all about the difference between the northern gods and the southern gods, not helped in the least by my conversation with the Mysterious One."

"You'll catch on eventually," said Malock. "Now Hana, continue. What ancient process did the Mysterious One mean?"

"It's a form of meditation," said Hana. "At least, that's the closest equivalent that you mortals have. Whenever a godling achieves godhood, they must learn to achieve absolute control over whatever domain they have been given control over, which requires that they first gain control of their thoughts, which are the primary tool that they will use to rule their domain. It's not an easy task."

The term *godling* caused a memory to stir in Jenur's mind. "Wait, wasn't Kinker supposed to ascend to godhood? So if he hadn't died, would he have had to learn how to do that?"

"It's called 'mind-focusing,'" Hana said. "And yes, if Kinker had lived, he probably would have had to do it."

"But why?" said Malock. "Don't the gods just know how to control their domains the minute they gain control over them? I mean, they and their domains are more or less one, aren't they?"

"The original gods—like Nimiko or the Mechanical Goddess— never had to do it," Hana agreed. "But newer ones do because they aren't used to controlling the things gods usually control. Bad stuff happens whenever a god loses control of his or her domain or never even had it in the first place."

"The Godly War," Malock said, nodding. "Part of the reason it was so damaging is because so many gods died, right?"

"And the gods who slew their siblings didn't know how to control their new domains," Hana said. "So even some of the older gods, like

Kano, had to learn how to mind-focus."

"I don't get it," said Jenur. "Why do we need to learn how to do it? We're not gods or godlings."

"How am I supposed to know?" said Hana. "But if I had to guess, I'd theorize that mind-focusing might be why gods can survive in the Void and mortals cannot. Maybe there is something about the Void that destroys anyone who lacks absolute control over their own mind."

"Let me get this straight," said Quro. "If we are going to survive in the Void, we must undergo the same kind of mental training that a new god does?"

"If what the Mysterious One says is true, then it sure sounds like it," said Hana.

"How long does it usually take for a new god to learn mind-focusing?" said Malock.

The ship groaned loudly under their feet, prompting Hana to say, "The Mechanical Goddess says that it usually takes anywhere between fifty and one hundred years, though it varies depending on factors like the learning speed of the new god and who is training them."

"We don't have a century to learn how to focus our minds," said Malock. "Even if we did, we'd all be either dead or extremely old by then. There must be a quicker way to learn it."

"The Mechanical Goddess did mention that she wasn't sure if mortals could even learn it," said Hana with a shrug. "She said that she thinks that, even if it's possible, it may not take nearly as long for a mortal to do than for a god. She doesn't know, though, because no mortal has ever actually tried it."

"Can the Mechanical Goddess teach it to us?" said Malock. "I'll do whatever it takes to learn it."

Another burst of smoke from the smokestacks, but it was short and to the point, as if the Mechanical Goddess was speaking quickly.

"Uh oh," said Hana.

"Uh oh?" said Malock. "What do you mean by 'uh oh'?"

Hana began rubbing her right arm as she said, "Oh, it's nothing. The Mechanical Goddess just said that she can't teach you because she's never had to teach it to anyone before. It's one of the few subjects she doesn't know, mostly because it would uselessly take up space in her memory."

"Is there anyone who could teach us how to do it?" said Malock. "Anyone at all?"

"Well, there is one person who could," said Hana. "But there's no guarantee he will. I mean, I can't see why he would say no, but at the same time—"

"Just cut to the chase," Jenur snapped. "Who is it?"

Hana raised one finger and then pointed it down at the deck beneath their feet. "Nimiko, the God of Light."

"Say that again."

Nimiko was still in his cage, his arms and legs chained to its floor. He looked as surly as ever, but the bright glow of his body had dimmed significantly since Jenur had last seen him. Either he was conserving his energy or, for whatever reason, he was losing power. Neither option filled Jenur with much enthusiasm.

Malock stood in front of the cage, his hands folded behind his back, looking as captain-like as ever. "You heard me, Nimiko. We want you to teach us how to mind-focus."

When he said 'us,' Malock gestured to Jenur, Quro, and Rint, who all stood behind him. Hana was with them, too, but as she probably wasn't going to be coming with them beyond the Void, Jenur didn't think Malock counted her.

Nimiko's eyes flicked from face to face until they landed on Malock's again. "You kidnap me, force me to lie in the belly of one of my sisters, and now demand that I teach you a technique normally reserved for new gods. Why should I?"

"Because if you don't, then the world will end and you will die with it," Malock said. "Self-preservation seems like a great motivator to me."

"You make a good point," said Nimiko. "But I doubt you can even learn it. Mind-focusing is supposed to be about controlling your thoughts so you can control your environment. You mortals don't have any powers like that, so I can't see how learning it would help, assuming you can learn it at all, that is."

"Let us try," said Malock. "It's our best bet to surviving in the Void."

"How many days away is World's End?" said Nimiko.

"According to the Mechanical Goddess's calculations, we should reach World's End within the next five days," said Hana. "Assuming, of course, we don't run into any major troubles between now and then."

"Five days is not even a fraction of the time necessary to learn how to control your mind," said Nimiko with a snort. "Assuming I agree to teach you, I would not even be able to cover the basics unless I condensed an ancient, highly sophisticated process designed to be understood by higher minds into a tiny shell of its self. It's not worth it."

"The Mechanical Goddess thought you might not need to teach us as much," Malock pointed out. "After all, since we're not gods ourselves, there's no need to learn every tiny detail. Just enough so we can protect our minds from the Void."

Nimiko slammed his fist into the bottom of the steel cage and barked, "To blazes with the Mechanical Goddess! What does *she* presume to know about a subject that she is ignorant of? Not only does she hold me prisoner in her own body, but she also spreads misinformation about a subject in which I am a master. My southern siblings have always been idiots, but by the Powers' hundred names, this just takes the cake."

A loud groaning sound above caused Jenur and the others to start and look at the ceiling. Nimiko, too, looked up, but less out of shock and more out of annoyance.

"Is that the best insult you can come up with?" said Nimiko, apparently in response to whatever the Mechanical Goddess had said. "And I *am* aware of these mortals' plan, but haven't I already made it clear that I think it is destined to failure? I just can't believe you'd defend a bunch of mortals who have taken me, your older brother, prisoner."

More groaning, along with what sounded like steam rattling dangerously loudly through the pipes that ran along the walls of the hull. Jenur hoped that the Mechanical Goddess wouldn't somehow try to flood them all, but considering how annoyed that last groaning sounded, she didn't put much stock in that hope.

"So what if I tried to kill you during the War?" said Nimiko. "The fact is, we're both gods here. And it's even more shocking because you are a southern god. I'm surprised you haven't eaten them for lunch yet."

Some of the lights running along the ceiling started flashing on and off quickly, which combined with the moaning and groaning of the metal walls made Jenur feel like she was back in the Mechanical Goddess's castle back on Stalf.

"Oh, so now *I'm* being unreasonable around here," said Nimiko. "Just because I want to be free and not stuck in a tiny cage like a wild animal doesn't mean I'm unreasonable. I don't even want to kill these mortals."

"But she didn't say you wanted to," said Hana.

"Shut up, katabans," Nimiko growled. "This is a conversation between higher minds here. Your input is not needed or wanted."

Sounds more like a conflict between two siblings who can't get along, Jenur thought, but she kept the thought to herself because she didn't think it wise to insult both Nimiko and the Mechanical Goddess with one sentence.

The pipes along the walls rattled again, but this time less dangerously, like the Mechanical Goddess was moderating her message. They rattled for a few minutes, while Nimiko actually sat and listened. The corners of his mouth slowly rose to a line, while his eyes focused on the floor. He didn't look quite so angry or annoyed anymore, which made Jenur wonder what the Mechanical Goddess was saying to him.

Finally, the pipes ceased rattling and Nimiko looked up. "For once, sister, you make a good point, although I concede the point only reluctantly."

"So you'll teach us?" said Malock, putting his hands together excitedly.

"I suppose so," said Nimiko, in the same tone that Jenur had used as a child whenever she would do something Dad would tell her to. "But don't expect to get the full experience. I will drill down the process into a series of extremely simple lessons that you mortals might be able to wrap your minds around."

While Malock clapped his hands together in excitement, Jenur leaned to Hana and muttered, "What did the Mechanical Goddess say?"

"She said that Nimiko should teach you mortals mind-focusing because he has nothing to lose," said Hana simply.

"Seems like a pretty simple argument," said Jenur.

"That's just the gist of it," said Hana. "She used a lot of examples and arguments to make it sound much more persuasive."

Jenur nodded as Rint said, "Hold on. Are we *all* going to learn mind-focusing?"

"Why not?" said Malock, looking over his shoulder at Rint. "You want to come beyond the Void with us, yes?"

"I guess so," said Rint, though he sounded reluctant for some reason. "Is the process painful, Nimiko?"

"For gods, it isn't," said Nimiko. "But for mortals ... I can't say for sure. It has never, ever been done before; therefore, I have no idea whether it will or won't hurt you."

"Does it matter?" said Malock. "I imagine getting destroyed by the Void because we didn't bother to learn how to focus our minds will hurt a lot more."

Rint glared at Malock. "No need for the tone, young man. You may be a prince, but that doesn't mean you get to address me however you like."

"Excuse me?" said Malock, turning around to face Rint. "Are you seriously getting onto me about respecting the elderly? Do you really think this is the best time to do that?"

"Well, what do you expect me to say?" said Rint. "That I'm just fine with how you address me? That I don't care if you respect me or not? I don't think so, young man."

He said 'young man' like that was the worst insult he could come up with.

"Hey," said Jenur, "why don't you just drop it? There's no need for you two to argue if we've already come to an agreement on what we're going to do."

"I just don't see why Rint is focusing on such a tiny issue," said Malock. "It's pathetic, really. Kinker wasn't—"

"Don't you dare compare me to my brother," Rint said, raising his voice. "Or should I remind you that it was your 'girlfriend' who killed him? Jenur told me that when she told me about Kinker's death."

Malock stepped forward, his eyes focused solely on Rint, as he said, in a low, dangerous voice, "Don't bring Vashnas into this. I suppose Jenur forgot to tell you that I didn't ask Vashnas to kill

Kinker. She did it purely to spite Kano and Tinkar, a move I did not then and do not now endorse."

"Hold on," said Jenur, holding up a hand. "I didn't tell Rint that Vashnas killed Kinker because I was trying to cause trouble or anything. I just thought that he deserved to know who killed his younger brother. That's all."

Neither Malock nor Rint appeared to notice what Jenur said. They still glared at each other, like they were daring each other to say or do something they would both regret. Jenur didn't think a fight would break out, but she was still ready to intervene if necessary.

"Whether she killed him because you told her to or not, that doesn't change the fact that Kinker is dead," Rint said. His voice almost broke, but he kept it steady. "And you didn't do a thing to save him. Some captain *you* were."

"Malock, Rint," said Quro. "This isn't exactly the best time to talk about—"

Malock held up a hand to silence Quro, which worked, surprisingly enough. The Prince of Carnag still kept his gaze on Rint, however, as he said, "Do you think that I don't care about Kinker's death? That I am happy that he was killed?"

"No," said Rint. "But I do think you're responsible for it. I know enough about ships to understand that the captain is always responsible for the well-being of each member of his crew."

"Then what, pray tell, do you want me to do?" said Malock. "Kinker is dead and his body is at the bottom of the sea. I know it sucks, but—"

"I want an apology," said Rint, his tone firm. "I want you to apologize for not saving his life. I don't want any crap about having nothing to do with it."

Malock looked at in him disbelief. "An apology? Weren't you listening, you old coot? I didn't have anything to do with it. Must I repeat myself a dozen times?"

"You don't have to repeat yourself so many times because I understood your excuses the first time," said Rint. "And I don't believe a word of them. The captain of his ship refuses to apologize for failing to preserve the life of one of his crew mates. What kind of captain does that?"

"A captain who knows that he did the best he could, but that sometimes crap still happens anyway," said Malock. "Listen, Rint, I know you are hurting and obviously are still dealing with a ton of grief. That doesn't justify ranting like a fool, though."

Rint's only response to that was a solid slap to the face. Everyone else gasped, except for Nimiko, who sat watching the whole thing like it was an amusing game.

Malock rubbed the spot on his face that Rint had slapped as Jenur grabbed Rint's arm and said, "Hey! That was uncalled for. Apologize to Malock."

Rint wrenched his arm out of Jenur's grasp and said, "Tell Malock to apologize to me first. Or have you decided that he's absolved of the responsibility he has toward his former men?"

"I think that slapping him won't get that apology you want so badly," said Jenur. "That's what I think."

Rint huffed and then walked around the crates and containers that surrounded them, leaving behind everyone else. No one called him back, largely because no one knew how to comfort him or if they should even become involved in this conflict between Malock and Rint. He didn't even say where he was going, though Jenur guessed he was probably going back to his room, most likely to stew in his anger and take a nap.

Malock watched Rint go. He still rubbed the side of his face, which meant that Rint must have slapped him pretty hard, or maybe it was the heat of the Burn of Grinf flashing up again. He was frowning as well, but like Rint, he said nothing, though Jenur could only guess at what he was thinking.

"Well," said Nimiko, causing everyone to look at him. "With all of that mortal drama out of the way, how's about we schedule the first mind-focusing lesson? We should start very soon because we don't have a lot of time to waste before we get to World's End and I've already got a few ideas for how I want to teach these lessons to you mortals."

"Sounds good," said Malock, though he kept glancing in the direction that Rint had left. "Will we have to let you out of your cage so we can learn it?"

"Yes," said Nimiko, nodding. He tapped the floor of his cage as he said, "I will need freedom of movement if I am to properly teach you how to focus your minds. It will be easier for me to think that way."

"But not totally free," Jenur said. "Someone will need to hold you on your Void metal leash."

"I'll do it," Hana said. "I mean, I'm not going to be going beyond the Void with any of you, so I have no reason to learn mind-focusing with you. Someone needs to make sure Nimiko doesn't go on a rampage, right?"

"I would never rampage inside my own sister," said Nimiko. "It would be far better if you just unchained me entirely. The Void metal interferes with my powers. And seeing as I am on your side, I would never do a thing to harm any of you if I was freed."

"We can't trust that," said Malock. "We know what you really think about us. While we will let you out of the cage, you're still going to be chained up so you can't try to make an escape."

Nimiko shrugged. "All right, but I am warning you that all you're doing is pissing me off."

"We've already pissed off every other god in the Northern and Southern Pantheons," said Malock. "What does it matter if we piss off another?"

Nimiko just grumbled in an odd language Jenur didn't understand. It might have been the language of the gods, though she couldn't be sure about that.

"First lesson will be within the next hour, depending on what we need to do," said Malock. "Nimiko, is there any equipment or any special clothes or anything we might need?"

"No," said Nimiko. "Mind-focusing is a technique dependent almost wholly upon your mind. Your clothes don't matter. You could even learn it entirely in the nude, if you wished."

Malock glanced between Quro and Jenur and said, "That would be ... interesting, but I think we'll do it clothed."

A small smile flashed across Nimiko's lips. "It was a joke, Tojas Malock, but whatever suits you. Now let me free and we can start right away, if you wish."

Chapter Ten

Five days later ...

TAPPING HIS FINGERS AGAINST the wooden arms of his chair, Skimif looked up at the clock on the wall directly opposite him. It was a simple, round clock, with two hands whose position on the clock's face told the viewer what time it was. Why Skimif thought about that when he had seen hundreds of clocks like this throughout his whole life, he wasn't sure.

It must be my nerves, Skimif thought. *With the debate coming up in a mere fifteen minutes, even ordinary, everyday objects are starting to look different to me.*

At that exact moment, the door to his changing room opened and Aqur poked her head through. "You okay?"

Skimif shook his head. "I'm exactly the same way I feel every time I have to do any sort of public speaking. My stomach feels like lead."

Aqur entered the room entirely and closed the door behind her. Tonight, she was wearing a bright green jacket and matching pants, which she had explained to him earlier as her way of showing public support for the Brotherhood. That hardly made him feel better, but he had thanked her for her efforts anyway.

He himself was dressed better than usual. Rather than his sleeveless jacket and practical brown pants, he wore flowing green robes in the exact same shade as Aqur's. The silk material felt strange against his rough skin, largely because these robes had been designed for a human's body, not an aquarian's. It was the best he could get on short notice, however, having received it as a present from one of his fellow Heathens. He had learned that one of the traditions of Carnagian public debates was that both participants must wear the best clothes they could, as clothing had a very strong effect on the responses they received from the crowd.

The tips of his red shoes peeked out from under his robes, which disappeared entirely beneath his robes when he stood up and shook Aqur's hand as she came closer to him. She didn't seem at all nervous, which made sense, seeing as she was not the one who was going to debate in front of thousands tonight.

"Relax," said Aqur. "You'll do fine. You got the note cards, right? And you practiced with Kigin, who is the stubbornest pig I know. Whatever this Domaha guy has, you can take it."

Skimif nodded, but only slowly because he kept thinking about the massive Stadium in which they stood. When he had arrived hours earlier, he had seen the thousands upon thousands of seats that rose all around the playing field. Ordinarily, the Stadium was used for games of spell-cast or other popular sports, but on rare occasion it was used for public debates, as it was tonight. Skimif could just imagine the thousands of Carnagians watching his every move and listening to his every word. It didn't help his nerves much.

"I know," said Skimif. "It's just ... I'm afraid that that monster will attack."

Aqur looked up at the ceiling quickly. "You mean the flying lizard thing? That thing you said called you 'master'?"

"Yes," said Skimif. "I don't know why, but ever since I encountered it, it's like I can feel its presence. I know it's still somewhere in the city, even though the Justice Enforcers haven't been able to find it yet."

"Sure," said Aqur in a skeptical tone. "Are you sure you heard it say 'master'? Maybe its roar sounded like that word."

"I'm positive that that is what it said," said Skimif. "I can't explain how this giant dragon ... thing can speak understandable Divina, but it did. It thinks I'm its master. Why, I don't know, but it does."

"It's probably just confused," said Aqur. "As far as I know, no one has yet identified its species, so I imagine it must have somewhere wandered up here from the southern seas and just got lost."

"The southern seas are a long way away from here," said Skimif. "There is much more to this creature than meets the eye. I know it."

"Well, what else *could* it be, then?" said Aqur. "Do you think the Justice Enforcers summoned it to put the blame on us? Granted, they haven't tried to pull that kind of stupidity just yet, but given enough time and failure on their part to catch it, I'm sure they'll get around to blaming us for it."

Skimif had a brief flashback to his vision of giant flying monsters attacking the Northern Isles. He almost opened his mouth to tell Aqur about it, but hesitated. He still had not told her or any of the other Heathens about his vision of the end of the world yet. He knew he should, but the message was just too depressing for him to want to tell anyone else. Besides, with Malock on a voyage to save the world, Skimif might not need to tell anyone about the end anyway. The apocalypse might just blow over entirely.

"Maybe," said Skimif. "But so far they haven't and if we keep up our peaceful behavior then we should be fine."

Aqur gave him that same look she always did whenever he said something like that. "You still think that the Enforcers are as honest as you."

"Why wouldn't they be?" said Skimif. "Granted, they don't like us, but so far they've left us alone today, even though they have arrested a few of us in the past."

"That's because they're trying to avoid starting riots," said Aqur. "You and I both know how much the Brotherhood has grown since we came to Carnag. And that's not even counting the Heathens in the rest of the Northern Isles or aquarian cities beneath the sea."

"You make a good point," said Skimif. He looked at the clock again and started. "Oh gods! Just five minutes."

Aqur frowned and looked over her shoulder. "Five minutes? It's clearly ten. We still have plenty of time before you have to get out there."

Skimif blinked and looked more closely at the clock. "Oh, you're right. Must have been seeing things."

Aqur nodded, though she didn't seem to get his meaning the same way that he did. Ever since Ramufa had warned Skimif that a refusal on his part to throw the debate would make the gods mess with his mind, Skimif had found himself 'seeing things' more than usual.

Once, for example, on the day after his meeting with Ramufa, he had been utterly convinced that someone—who, he hadn't the faintest clue, but he knew that person was there—had broken into the Brotherhood's hideout and was hiding somewhere within it. It was only well after the sun had gone down and the Heathens had searched every inch of the place that they stopped the search, with Aqur concluding that Skimif must have heard some rats or something scurrying through the walls.

Another time, Skimif had thought he heard voices in the walls of his room. He had almost tore down the walls before remembering that the walls were made of thick brick, with no room inside them for anything larger than a mouse, if that.

Ever since then, Skimif had had to deal with sometimes 'seeing' things. And worst of all, he couldn't be sure whether it was the gods at work or his own overactive imagination tormenting him or possibly both.

"But you do realize what this debate is for, right?" said Aqur. "The King and Queen are doing this to discredit the movement. I've done some research on this Domaha guy. He's basically an extremist and well-known in the Carnagian debating circuit for winning debates."

Skimif frowned. "So he's a good debater."

"He doesn't win debates because he's a good debater, though," said Aqur. "Actually, he tends to win because he talks so fast and is a crowd pleaser. Most of the time, his logic tends to be not very well thought out."

"I can handle that," said Skimif.

"You don't understand," said Aqur. "He usually brings out argument after argument in favor of whatever position he's debating while leaving little time for his opponent to present his or her views. Isn't it obvious why he was chosen to debate with you?"

Skimif rubbed his neck as he said, "Well, yes, I can see, but even so —"

"Even so what?" said Aqur. "Listen, Skim, I know that public speech isn't your greatest skill. The Royal Family somehow knows that, too, which is why they chose the brashest debater they could find to challenge you. You'll get annihilated if you let your nerves get the best of you."

"I won't let them, then," said Skimif. He put a hand over his heart and said, "Domaha may be the better debater, but I still believe in the mission given to me by the Powers. I'll just have to up my game."

"If you say so," said Aqur. "Still, this is why I didn't want you agreeing to the debate. You might embarrass yourself, and, as a result, the entire Brotherhood."

The idea of the crowd laughing at him as he stuttered over his own words, while Domaha (who in his imagination looked like King Halock, although Skimif had never seen Domaha before) stood there smirking victoriously, made Skimif shudder.

But he shook his head and said, "Well, it's too late to back down now. And thanks for the vote of confidence, by the way."

Aqur frowned at his tone, but before she could say anything, the door cracked open again and Ower poked his head through the opening.

"Skimif?" said Ower. "The debate is five minutes away. Are you ready to do it?"

Skimif took his eyes off Aqur's face and looked at Ower. "I'm as ready as I'll ever be."

"Good," said Ower. "Because you really ought to get going. Domaha is already on stage and is working the crowd just by standing there."

"See?" said Aqur. "Domaha might be too much for you. If he's capable of working the crowd just by *standing there*—"

"What matters is who debates best," Skimif interrupted. "As long as I present my views intelligently and logically and don't screw up or let my nerves get the best of me, I should do just fine."

With that, Skimif brushed past Aqur and out of the room, following Ower down the narrow hallway that led to the stage where he and Domaha would have their debate. He didn't hear Aqur follow, but he knew she would be watching anyway. Whatever she may have said, Aqur was very much a loyal friend who would never abandon Skimif, no matter what she said.

As Skimif and Ower drew closer to the Stadium field, the sounds of people talking and screaming grew louder and louder. Skimif kept a cool face the entire time, but every time he heard the crowd go wild, his nerves jumped about ten feet. He knew that many of his fellow Heathens were going to be there, of course, watching and cheering him on, but it would be impossible to see them in the crowd of thousands that had gathered tonight. In a sense, therefore, Skimif was on his own.

They walked past a couple of Enforcers leaning against the wall, talking amongst themselves about boots, who did not bother either him or Ower as they passed. The Justice Enforcers had set up guards all over the Stadium, covering all entrances, which they had said was to make sure that no riots or anything broke out. Of course, Skimif knew that this might make it more difficult for his Heathens to leave after the debate was over, which was why he had ordered all Heathens to put away their green bandannas so they wouldn't be easily recognized as such by the guards.

Finally, after walking through the winding, well-lit stone hallway of the Stadium, Skimif and Ower arrived at the entrance to the field itself. A red curtain covered the entrance, though it did little to drown out the sounds of the cheering crowd. A couple of Enforcers stood on either side, weapons at the ready. Skimif wasn't alarmed by their appearance, as he knew that they were merely there to keep unauthorized people from entering the field. All Skimif needed to do was flash his debaters' badge at them and they would let him pass.

Skimif felt someone tugging at his sleeve, causing him to stop and look down at Ower. The young boy was smiling brightly, as if all of the problems in the world couldn't defeat his spirit.

"I know how nervous you can get, Skimif, but I know you can do it," said Ower. "You're always so inspiring. And all of us Heathens will be in the crowd rooting for you."

Skimif smiled back, even though in reality all he wanted to do was go home and hide under his blankets. "Thanks for the vote of confidence, Ower. I'll be sure to do my best. For all of us."

Ower patted Skimif on the arm and said, "Good luck, then. Hope the Powers gave you the debating skills you need."

With that, Ower dashed away, probably to go join the other Heathens in the stands. Skimif watched him go, then took a deep breath of the stale, yet slightly dusty air around him and walked up to the Enforcers.

Without saying a word, Skimif held up his debaters' badge, a small, round metal star with the Hammer of Grinf cut into it. It was a standard badge given only to participants in the Stadium games, used to allow the participants access to almost anywhere they wanted to go within the Stadium itself. It also acted as proof of identification for the participants, as only Stadium participants were given the badges or allowed to carry them.

The two guards looked at the badge, nodded when they saw it was genuine, and then stepped aside. Skimif strode between them, but as he did so, the guard on the right muttered, "I hope Domaha wipes the floor with you, you slimy Heathen."

Skimif didn't stop to look at the guard or argue with him because he didn't have any time to do that. Still, the words stung his already fragile nerves, so when he passed through the heavy red curtain and onto the Stadium field itself, he had to use all of his willpower to avoid turning around and running away (or punching out the guard who had said those words, though he thought the former action to be far more likely than the latter).

As soon as he strode out onto the field, two gigantic bright lights hit his eyes. As well, his ears were assaulted by the loud cheers of the crowd, so loud that for a moment he thought for sure he had gone deaf.

When the lights cleared, Skimif looked around the Stadium as he walked out to the middle of the field, where a stage had been set up with two podiums standing atop it. As he had imagined, thousands and thousands of dark-faced Carnagians filled the stands, cheering and booing in equal measure. In fact, their screams were so loud and confused that Skimif could not tell if most people were cheering for him or against him. The only people he could tell apart from the others were King Halock and Queen Markinia, who sat in a box well above the roaring crowd, protected by bodyguards that appeared to be elite members of the Justice Enforcers, based on their gold collars that reflected the lights.

The Stadium itself was huge. Gigantic stone walls, slanting like a dome as they rose above, towered over everyone and everything. Titanic images of Grinf had been carved into the walls and blindingly bright white lights shone from inside the Grinfian eye holes, which provided most of the lighting in the place.

The grassy field stretched out like a long carpet in both directions, smelling freshly cut and trimmed. Massive metal goalposts/nets stood on either end of the field, normally reserved for games of spell-cast but today acting only as impediments to those in the crowd who had been unfortunate enough to score seats behind them. It was all so big and made Skimif feel very small, even when he reached the stage in the center of the field and climbed upon it.

The stage was not devoid of people, however. Two other people, both humans, stood on the stage with Skimif, though not next to him. The first was a young man, perhaps in his late thirties, wearing the pale gray robes of an audimancer. A big grin splashed across the audimancer's face as Skimif stepped onto the stage, causing the mage to walk toward Skimif with his hand outstretched.

"Skimif, good to see you," said the audimancer as he grabbed Skimif's hand and gave it a hardy shake. His voice was surprisingly hoarse, though Skimif recognized it as the voice of the moderator from before. "My name is Feru Sorress and I'll be the moderator for tonight's debate."

Skimif already knew that, but he nodded anyway to show that he understood.

Then he glanced at the other man, who was already situated behind his podium. This man wore the crimson robes of a Grinfian monk, but they were fancier than the robes that Skimif had seen other Grinfian monks wore. Not a speck of dirt was to be seen on them and unless Skimif was mistaken, they smelled somewhat like smoke and new leather, a mixture that shouldn't have smelled good but did anyway.

The man himself was totally bald, with skin almost as black as night. His eyes were a deep shade of orange, which was an eye color that Skimif had never seen in any Carnagians before. He stood upright, almost arrogantly so, and was so busy waving at the crowd that Skimif thought he hadn't seen his arrival. But the man did cast a quick glance in Skimif's direction, shooting him a look filled with such venom that Skimif was almost afraid he might burst into flames from the man's evil look.

"That is Yamaru Domaha," said Sorress, nodding at the man. "I'm not supposed to take sides, being the moderator and all, but he is pretty good."

"I've heard," said Skimif; at least, he thought he said it. With the loudness of the crowd, he could barely even hear himself think.

"You're ready?" said Sorress, quickly glancing around at the thousands of cheering and screaming spectators. "Not drunk or anything, are you?"

Skimif shook his head. "Why would I be drunk?"

"No reason," said Sorress in a light voice. "Just that one time, a few years back, one of Domaha's opponents came in drunk out of his mind. Admittedly, it *was* amusing how the guy tried to argue that all of the gods were really giant cosmic boots, but the crowd didn't like it and since then we've been forced to make sure both debaters come to the debate sober."

"Oh," said Skimif. "If that's the case, then why didn't you ask me before I came on stage?"

Sorress's eyes lingered on Domaha a little too long before he snapped his attention back to Skimif. "What?"

"Never mind," Skimif muttered, though there was no need for that because the roar of the crowd undoubtedly drowned out every word he said.

"Well, it's good to see you're sober anyway," said Sorress. "Just take your place behind the podium, get your notes in order, and the debate will start very soon. And don't worry about speaking up; the crowd will be able to hear whatever you say thanks to the spell I cast on them to increase their hearing."

Skimif walked over to the second podium as Sorress retreated to the center of the stage in between the two podiums. The announcer pulled out his wand and tapped his throat lightly, though Skimif didn't pay much attention to Sorress's moves because he was currently busy shuffling through the notes he had brought with him. Each note had a basic idea he hoped to address at some point in the debate; usually just short phrase, like 'end of the gods.' He and Aqur had worked hard over the last five days to come up with all of the best arguments in favor of Heathenism, but if Domaha was truly as vicious as the rumors made him out to be, then none of it might matter. That just made Skimif shuffle through the cards a little faster while Sorress cleared his throat.

Then Sorress's voice boomed throughout the stadium, so loud that it forced the entire crowd to shut up. The sheer volume of his voice caused Skimif to cringe and cover his ears. Even Domaha leaned back from Sorress, despite the announcer facing away from the two debaters.

"Welcome, one and all, to the Thirty-Sixth Carnagian Public Debate of the year!" said Sorress. There was no hoarseness in his voice now, as if the magic he had used had also healed his voice. "Tonight's subject: The gods: Worthy of worship or worthy of scorn?"

The crowd kept surprisingly silent at the statement. Skimif did a quick glance to see if he could spot Aqur, Ower, or any of the other Heathens, but from his current position it was impossible to distinguish individuals from the crowd. So he looked back down at his notes as Sorress continued to speak.

"And tonight's debaters are: Skimif of Tunya, leader of the infamous Brotherhood of Heathens," said Sorress, gesturing at Skimif, "and Yamaru Domaha, the Grinfian Apologist and winner of one hundred public debates! Tonight's format will be simple. Each debater gets five minutes in which to respond to the opponent. As for who goes first, that was decided in a poll ran by the Justice Enforcers earlier today."

Is that normal? Skimif thought. *Who voted in that poll? How was it conducted?*

He wanted to ask all of those questions, and more, but his stomach still felt so weak every time he looked at the crowd that he didn't. He just remembered what Aqur had said, about the whole debate being done purely to discredit the movement. He now understood why she said that.

Sorress pulled out a card from his coat pocket and flipped it open. "And the winner, according to the results, is Yamaru Domaha! Monk Domaha, you may begin when you are ready."

Domaha smiled, a practiced smile that made even Skimif feel a little better. "Thank you, Sorress. Just give me a moment to collect my thoughts."

"All right," said Sorress. "But you've only got five minutes, so you don't want to waste any time."

Domaha cleared his throat, but he cleared it in a graceful way, as if he spent hours every day practicing it. Then he turned to look at Skimif and there was a kind of fanaticism in his eyes that made Skimif want to hide behind his podium.

When Domaha spoke, it was with the speed of a lightning bolt. "It's no secret that humans have always worshiped the gods, which is as it should be because the gods have guided and protected us since the beginning of time itself. But like spoiled children who don't appreciate the things that our parents have done for them, we are starting to lose our way. The Heathens claim that the gods have stifled our creativity and freedom, yet it is the gods who have granted us things like fire and magic and knowledge of the world, which has allowed us to build great civilizations far grander than anything that our puny human efforts could ever do on their own."

Although Domaha spoke fast, he spoke with a confidence and clarity that Skimif had never heard in another mortal before. A quick glance at the crowds told Skimif that everyone was spellbound by the apologist's words, even though so far he didn't seem to be saying anything new or interesting.

Then Domaha sharply pointed at Skimif, like a mage jabbing his wand at an enemy. "But I suppose life has not always been rosy for everyone. The aquarians have had a weaker relationship with the gods, at times even hostile. Heathenism has always found open arms among the aquarians, but I suppose the Heathens were not happy to spread their tasteless ideology among the fish of the sea. No, the aquarians became jealous of humanity's success and blessings by the gods, and so they sent the Brotherhood to the surface to cause us to blaspheme the gods so that the gods will punish us and destroy everything we have built."

"Hey," said Skimif, raising his voice. "That's not—"

Sorress pointed his wand at Skimif suddenly. Skimif kept talking, only to realize that his voice no longer issued from his throat.

"It is against the rules for a debater to interrupt his opponent," said Sorress, his voice losing the earlier friendliness it once had. "Please wait until it is your turn to give your response."

Skimif closed his mouth, feeling equally furious and embarrassed, while Domaha continued his ranting as if Skimif had not said a word.

"In fact, this is not the first time aquarians have attempted to undermine human society," Domaha continued. "Just twenty years ago, a member of the Heathen Society of East Yurans went to the human island of Friana and attempted to spread their toxic ideology to weaken the very foundations of Frianan society so that the East Yurans could invade it. It was only thanks to the timely and noble efforts of His Majesty King Halock that their plot was foiled and relations between Friana and Carnag strengthened, relations which continue to thrive even today."

Skimif had never heard of that, but based on the way some of the people in the crowd were nodding, he figured Domaha must be telling the truth. It also sounded like he was sucking up to King Halock, though from where Skimif currently stood it was hard to tell what King Halock was doing.

"And so, with a mere minute left, I end my turn by asking every individual in this crowd to consider my argument," Domaha said. "Let history and the gods be your guide and ask yourselves if these Heathens are really as pro-human as they say they are. For if the Heathens truly cared about us, they would be encouraging us to increase our devotion to the gods, not to abandon them."

Domaha said those last words as if the debate was over and he had won. Considering how convinced the audience already looked, Skimif had a hard time not concluding that he would do better to walk off the stage and declare defeat than lay out his side of the issue.

"Well, that was certainly a good show on Domaha's part," said Sorress. "Skimif, it is now your turn. You have five minutes."

Taking yet another deep breath, Skimif glanced at the topmost note on his pile—*Gods not great*—and decided that he would try to refute Domaha's ranting instead.

So Skimif raised his eyes and looked out into the crowd. He gathered up the courage that he always used whenever he had to give a speech, though it came far more slowly than normal due to how nervous he was.

But when he remembered that he only had five minutes—possibly less—he immediately began speaking.

"Every one of Monk Domaha's accusations are wrong. We Heathens are not spies sent by some enemy aquarian nation with the mission of upending human society. In fact, we Heathens belong to no one nation or city. There are Heathens from every nationality represented in our group: Carnagians, Shikans, Nikons, Frianans, Ruwans, and hundreds of others, including the many different aquarian peoples that populate the ocean floor. Though we recognize that societal chaos is an inevitable step toward freedom from the gods, we are not here to overthrow any governments or anything like that."

Talking to this crowd was far more difficult than any other audience Skimif had addressed. Though they were as silent for him as they had been for Domaha, he could sense the skepticism they projected, feel it like a heavy carpet thrown over his shoulders. It didn't help that even Sorress didn't seem to be paying much attention to him, nor that Domaha was looking at him with a satisfied smirk on his face.

Still, Skimif kept talking, not wanting to waste even one second of his precious five minutes. "We Heathens are spreading this message because we know that the end of the gods is near. When the gods disappear, we know that there will be chaos and fear unlike anything that has ever befallen the Northern Isles. By spreading the message as far and wide as we can, we hope to raise awareness of the issue so we can prepare for it before it destroys us."

Domaha snorted, but Sorress, the biased announcer, didn't say anything. And the audience continued to listen skeptically, making Skimif wish that he had brought a cup of water or something because his throat and skin were starting to dry out.

"None of us Heathens have ever expressed interest in overthrowing any governments or destroying any society," said Skimif. "The truth is, we Heathens see all mortals—human and aquarian—as our brothers and sisters. Unlike certain monks of Grinf, we do not try to cast suspicion on individuals because of their species. We address all arguments and accusations lodged against us with fairness and reason, not with fanaticism and—"

"Time's up," said Sorress, his voice magnified even louder than usual. "Your five minutes are up, Skimif, but good show just the same."

Skimif looked at Sorress in disbelief. "Already? But I thought I had at least two minutes left."

"Your sense of time must be off," said Sorress. "You should really pay better attention to the time. Anyway, it is now Monk Domaha's turn to respond. Remember, Monk, you only have five minutes in which to respond to Skimif's rebuttal, starting now."

Domaha launched right into it, almost as if he had memorized his response. "Notice how Skimif said that the Heathens *know* that societal chaos is inevitable? They don't even try to hide it. They are trying to destroy everything we have ever worked for, purely out of spite against the gods. And of course, Skimif continues to parrot the outrageous Heathen cliché that the gods are going to end. That is such an absurd, tired meme by now that I do not see any point in bothering to refute it."

"Not bothering to refute it?" said Skimif. "Isn't that what this debate is all—"

Once more, he lost his ability to speak. Sorress looked at him with hostile eyes, like a parent who was angry at a child that kept knowingly breaking the rules. Skimif once again closed his mouth, but just the same, he kept thinking about how unfair all this was. He started to wish that he had listened to Aqur.

"This is the true face of the Brotherhood of Heathens," said Domaha, gesturing at Skimif. "They don't care how much chaos they cause on their insane mission to blaspheme the gods. All they care about is making sure that their ideology is believed by all. They lack the proper fear of the gods which is the foundation of all valid morality. And without fear, they cannot be trusted in any way whatsoever. It is no wonder that the numbers of Heathens has plateaued. I, too, would abandon them if I had been a Heathen and learned their true nature as anarchists hellbent on destroying anyone or anything that gets in their way."

Now that was an outright lie. Last Skimif heard, the Brotherhood's numbers had been growing. Granted, it was a slow growth and most of the new Heathens didn't announce their new belief publicly, but over the past few weeks he had had several conversations with Heathens who, for various reasons, could not yet come out and be open about their beliefs. And he was certain that there were many more, but how many, he wasn't sure.

Then Domaha slammed both fists onto his podium, causing Skimif's attention to snap back to his opponent. Domaha's eyes seemed to glow with righteous fury, though to the audience's credit, it had not yet started rioting. On the other hand, it didn't look nearly as skeptical of Domaha's claims as it had of Skimif's.

"As for Skimif's talk of seeing all mortals as his brothers and sisters, that is a silly deception," said Domaha. "The truth is, the Brotherhood of Heathens doesn't see anyone outside of its little group as being part of their so-called 'family.' In fact, they often encourage new Heathens to leave their families of origin, to break ties with anyone who questions the new faith of Heathenism."

"Ridiculous," Skimif muttered, after feeling his voice return.

Sorress shot him a warning look, but Skimif didn't care. He didn't see how anyone could believe what Domaha was saying, yet the audience listened far more intently to the Monk's words than to anything Skimif had said

"And furthermore, there is evidence to suggest that the Brotherhood is not intent merely on eliminating worship of the gods," Domaha said. "Oh, no. You see, all mortals must worship something. For most of mortal history, that 'something' has been the gods, and rightfully so, for who else is worth of the honor and glory that the gods have shown to be deserving of time and again? The Brotherhood knows this, and so they are planning to take advantage of the confusion caused by the void of worship by instituting a new religion."

A new religion? Skimif thought. *That's news to me.*

"This religion will not be based in worship of the gods, but in worship of the leader of the Brotherhood," said Domaha. "To put it plainly, Skimif of Tunya, despite his claims of loving equality and wanting to lead all mortals into a new age of freedom and independence, merely wishes to replace worship of the gods with worship of himself."

That was the last straw. Skimif dropped his cards and yelled, "That is insane! How can you possibly—"

Sorress pointed his wand at Skimif again and Skimif went silent, but he still kept moving his lips. He knew it was useless, but he didn't care. He wasn't about to let these outrageous lies be passed off as facts, not if there was something he could do about them.

"Skimif," said Sorress, holding his wand like a sword. "If you interrupt ever again, I will give Domaha five more minutes in which to present his viewpoint. Sorry, but that's just how it is."

An anger like Skimif had never known rose up in his body. He still couldn't speak, but he could feel the power rising within him, that power that he had been trying to hide from everyone around him. It was rumbling within his very soul, like lava in a dormant volcano, and there was no way that he could keep it in check for much longer.

"Thank you for silencing him, Sorress," said Domaha, flashing a brilliant smile. Then he addressed the audience again. "Did you see that? Skimif is so rude that he has tried to interrupt me almost three times now. It is clear that he doesn't want me revealing all of his little group's dark secrets."

Seeing Domaha talk so smugly, watching the audience as they drank in his every word, observing Sorress's obvious bias toward the monk, and remembering all the times Aqur had warned him against this debate made something deep inside Skimif snap like a twig.

Without warning, Skimif grabbed the podium before him and ripped it straight off the stage. He performed that task with ease, causing the crowd to gasp as he lifted the heavy podium over his head, his dozens of carefully-written notes scattering in the wind.

"Skimif!" said Sorress, pointing his wand steady at the aquarian. "What do you think you're doing? Put that podium down, *now*."

Skimif still couldn't talk, so he just shook his head no.

"I would listen to Sorress if I were you, Skimif," said Domaha, a hint of warning in his voice. "You're not helping your cause one bit by acting like a savage."

Skimif wanted to tell Domaha that it was better to be an honest savage than a lying civilian, but Sorress's imposed silence made it impossible for Skimif to even grunt. He just hurled the podium at Domaha, which the monk immediately blasted out of the air with a fireball that he had conjured from nowhere. Flaming splinters fell to the stage and field as Skimif ran at Domaha, but Sorress got in between them, saying as he did so, "No fighting! That is entirely against the rules of debating."

Skimif raised his hands to smack Sorress out of the way, but he didn't get a chance because Sorress jabbed his wand in the aquarian's direction. A blunt force that Skimif couldn't see slammed into his chest, slowing him down but not stopping him. It felt like a giant hand was pressing against his chest, forcing his run to slow to a crawl, but he kept at it anyway.

By now, the audience was stirring. Several people were shouting, but with all of the noise it was impossible to tell what they were saying, though Skimif—in his rage-induced mind—thought that some of them were probably shouting aquarian slurs. He gave them little thought, however, because he was so focused on fighting this force holding him back so he could throttle Domaha.

"Sorress, why isn't he stopping?" said Domaha, his voice not nearly as confident as it once was.

"I ... don't ... know," Sorress said through gritted teeth. "He's somehow resisting my teichomancy. Granted, I'm no teichomancer, but I didn't think that any non-teichomancer could fight against it like he is."

Skimif bared his teeth. He could feel the barrier slowly collapsing under his weight. He thought Domaha was stupid for not running when he had the chance, but he supposed it didn't matter. He would go after Domaha either way, no matter what the monk chose to do. The crowd's screams roared, but for some reason they sounded distant, likely because his complete and total attention was on Sorress and Domaha.

And then the barrier 'snapped' under his pressure and he slammed Sorress out of the way and off the stage. But before Skimif could grab Domaha, the monk slashed his arm across and sent a flaming line at the aquarian. The fire cut through Skimif like a knife, which at that heat should have killed him, but somehow Skimif didn't even feel it. He just grabbed Domaha's unprotected neck, lifted the struggling monk off his feet, and then slammed him down on the stage floor.

Before Domaha could recover, Skimif slammed a foot down on the monks chest, pinning him to the stage. Domaha gasped in pain, but that didn't make Skimif feel any more merciful or sympathetic toward him.

"Hold it!" a voice shouted from somewhere nearby. "Skimif of Tunya, step off of Yamaru Domaha this instant or prepare to face the consequences."

Skimif looked up. Surrounding him on all sides were at least two dozen Justice Enforcers, clad in their distinctive crimson armor, their staffs at the ready. Standing at the head of the Enforcers was Captain Koiro, who he recognized due to the golden helmet on her head, with a sword at her side. He wasn't sure how he had missed hearing them arrive, but he supposed he had been so caught up in trying to attack Domaha that he must have missed a lot of things.

The crowd was yelling and shouting. A few people had even climbed down from the stands to try to get to the stage themselves, but they could get no farther than perhaps a couple of feet from the stands. Their progress was blocked by a barrier of some kind, which didn't bother Skimif.

"Skimif," Koiro repeated, her voice full of warning this time. "I said, step off of Yamaru Domaha. Do not make us use force."

Skimif wasn't sure if he could talk or if Sorress's magic was still in effect, so he simply pressed down harder on Domaha's chest and shook his head.

"We are warning you," Koiro said, raising her sword. "We don't want to kill or harm you. Simply step off Domaha and allow us to arrest you. This is your last warning."

A small, yet sane, voice in his mind told him to comply with Koiro's orders. After all, all of this fighting was getting him nowhere. The longer he stalled, the lower the audience's opinion became not only of him, but also of the Brotherhood as a whole.

But Skimif ignored that sane voice. When he looked at all of the Enforcers, something didn't seem quite right about them. Their bodies seem to twist and contort where they stood, like snakes. Their eyes seemed to glow like fire and the colors of their armor changed rapidly.

Skimif knew that this was probably just the gods playing tricks on his mind, as Ramufa had warned they would, but they looked so real that he hesitated. He looked down at Domaha, whose face was becoming as muddy as putty, and he started to feel sick to his stomach.

"We'll take your silence as a rejection, then," said Koiro. Then she addressed the rest of the Enforcers. "Men, prepare to fire on him. Try to avoid hitting Domaha, if you can."

The rest of the Enforcers dutifully took aim with their weapons. Flames began to swirl around the tips of their staffs and spears. Yet despite the intimidating appearance of so many Enforcers working together, with a clear intent to kill him, Skimif didn't feel at all afraid. Whether because of the gods' mind tricks or his own sanity slipping, Skimif felt a detached sense from everything around him. It was as though he was a god looking on high at the scurrying of mortals below, a thought which confirmed his 'going insane' theory.

Then a loud, ear-piercing screech echoed down from above. It was so loud that it made Skimif cringe and slam his hands over his ears. At the same time, all two dozen of the Enforcers fired blasts of fire at Skimif. It was too late for Skimif to dodge and he couldn't, anyway, because the screeching from above had stunned him.

Then something huge—like a large leather blanket—slammed down on the stage around him. The leather blanket smelled just like rotten eggs and rotting corpses, a smell which got worse when the two dozen fireballs hit home. Although the blanket blocked out Skimif's view, he heard the flames eat at the leather, heard Koiro shouting for her men to stand down, and felt the temperature inside the blanket rise immediately.

But then the blanket rose to its full height and Skimif looked up and realized that it was no blanket at all. It was the giant flying lizard creature from before, the dragon, the one which had called him 'master.' It stood up on its stubby legs, spreading out its smoking wings as it screeched in rage.

Domaha, who had been under the creature's protection with him, stuttered, "Wh-what is that?"

Skimif glanced around the Stadium. The Enforcers had retreated a short distance, almost as if they were afraid of the beast, while the crowd was now stampeding out of the Stadium. Evidently, the audience had lost the courage that had come with their righteous rage when they saw the monster. Skimif just hoped that his fellow Heathens would make it out of the Stadium without getting trampled by everyone else.

Although Skimif knew that the creature standing before him was dangerous, somehow he sensed that it was not quite as dangerous as it appeared. He reached up with one hand and stroked the creature's chin. The creature allowed him to do that, like a dog that was used to its master petting it. Its skin was warm to the touch, though whether that was because it was warm-blooded or because it had just been struck by two dozen fireballs, Skimif didn't know.

And then Skimif had another vision, but it was not like the visions the Power had given him. He sensed that this vision came from the creature before him; furthermore, he sensed that the creature was intentionally sharing this vision with him, like a messenger delivering a letter to its addressee.

In the vision, Skimif saw himself riding atop the creature, soaring above destroyed cities on countless islands. On and on they soared, flying beyond the end of the Northern Isles and into the southern seas, but they continued to fly until they reached World's End. The Void stood before them, as black and blank as ever, but something was coming out of the Void, something huge, but before he could see what it was, the vision ended and Skimif once more found himself standing in the Stadium on the stage before his steed.

Because now, he understood. This creature had been sent by the Powers as a herald of the end. It had come from beyond the Void to search for him. Why him, he still didn't know, mostly because the creature didn't know. All the creature seemed to know was that it had to get him and bring him to the Powers at all costs.

Normally, that thought would have scared Skimif, seeing as much of the creature's purpose was unknown. Additionally, he still had so much to do here. The growing Brotherhood required his leadership, now more than ever. He wasn't sure if the Brotherhood would even last without his leadership.

At the same time, somehow he knew that it didn't matter. In the long run, the survival or destruction of the Brotherhood of Heathens mattered as much as that of an ant's. He had been given a glimpse of the future, of the grand scheme that the Powers were putting into action, and he now understood that—whatever their final plan for Martir, for him, and for everyone else was—Skimif could not merely ignore it.

He now understood his own purpose better. Those destroyed cities ... as much as he did not wish to come to this conclusion, he knew that the coming destruction of civilization would be partly his responsibility. The vision had assured him that the destruction was necessary, but despite that, a small voice deep inside him told him that it was not right.

But his new-found clarity suppressed that voice. He could not ignore the Powers. This vision had shown him that the end of the world was not the last part of their plan, though it was an important first step. He would have to trust the Powers and ignore whatever apprehension or resistance he might feel.

The creature bowed low enough for him to climb on, which he did. As soon as he situated himself behind its back, sitting on a crook that was shaped like a saddle, all of his worry and anger and fear washed away, replaced by a sense of clarity that he had never quite felt before in his life. He and the creature were one now. He understood that.

Then his steed rose to its full height. Skimif didn't feel at all alarmed. He simply grabbed the bits of flesh extending from its mouth that resembled reins and held on as it rose.

"Hey!" said Domaha as he scrambled to his feet. "Where are you going? The debate isn't even over yet!"

The creature slapped Domaha with its wing, sending him staggering backward off the stage. The blow looked pretty severe to Skimif, although he did not worry, for he knew that his steed had not killed Domaha, but merely knocked him out.

Skimif quickly glanced around the Stadium. By now, most of the people had left, save for a few who had stayed to watch, though whether out of curiosity or utter horror, he didn't know.

The Enforcers, too, were still here, but they didn't look like they wanted to be. To their credit, however, they stood their ground. Skimif admired them for that, even though he knew that any attempts on their part to stop him would be useless.

"Go," said Skimif, which he had said without first finding out if he could still talk. "All of you, go and run. If you try to fight us, you will not live long enough to regret it."

The smarter Enforcers turned tail and ran, leaving about half of the Enforcers left. One of the remaining ones simply fainted, leaving only eleven Enforcers, including Captain Koiro. Her mask continued to hide her face, but Skimif sensed that she was the only Enforcer who was not afraid of him in the slightest.

"We will not run," said Koiro, raising her sword and pointing it at Skimif and his steed. "As the Justice Enforcers and followers of Grinf, it would be disgraceful for us to run like cowards."

"You don't understand, do you?" said Skimif, shaking his head. "You cannot defeat us. The Powers have chosen me to be their herald.

By standing against me, you are standing against the Powers themselves."

"Then the Powers can go and off themselves," said Koiro. "It is my duty to protect Carnag from people like you. If that means sacrificing my very life, then so be it."

A deep rumbling noise gurgled somewhere within the steed's belly. It took Skimif a moment to realize that the creature was going to attack, though he did nothing to stop it.

"Then your duty is a fraud," said Skimif. "And I pity your soul."

The dragon reared back its head and unleashed a stream of flame directly at Koiro. She didn't even try to move. The other Enforcers scattered as the flames approached, not even bothering to protect their captain. Skimif was struck by how easily frightened they were, but he soon forgot about that as the flames totally enveloped Koiro. He expected to hear her scream in pain, yet she took the fire without noise or scream, like a chicken whose head was lopped off by an expert butcher.

His steed continued to pour the flame on her until it grew tired of doing so. It closed its mouth and the flames immediately cut off. Skimif expected to see Koiro's corpse charred and smoking, but much to his surprise, Koiro was still alive. And she was not alone. A large man was crouched over her, apparently having used his massive body to protect her from the flames.

Once the fire ceased, the man stood up and turned around to face Skimif and his steed. His golden eyes shone like a forge, while his armor burned like the flames that the steed had breathed. In his right hand, he carried a huge, thick golden hammer that looked capable of shattering boulders with ease. Though Skimif had never seen this man in person before, the man's very image was carved into the walls of the Stadium and could be seen everywhere in the city. There was no mistaking his identity.

"I cannot believe it," said Skimif, rubbing his eyes. "Grinf?"

Grinf, the God of Justice, Fire, and Metal, held up his hammer. "Indeed, it is I."

"What ... what are you even doing here?" said Skimif. "I thought you gods had fled, that you were not going to confront me because it would be useless, with the Powers coming any day now and all."

"The others may have decided not to intervene, but I certainly didn't," said Grinf. "And although the Carnagians are often an arrogant and misguided people, I once fought an entire war to protect humanity, in which I slaughtered many of my own siblings just to keep them safe. I will not allow a criminal like you to make all of that for naught."

Those words were not what Skimif had expected to hear from the god. For the briefest instant, he questioned whether overthrowing the gods was such a good thing after all. If Grinf could speak so honorably and heroically, then perhaps the other gods were not so bad.

But then Skimif's mission fell upon his mind again like a steel trap. He shook his head and said, "Those are nice words, but you don't fool me. You gods are all the same. You just want the adoration and worship of us humans while giving us nothing in return for our services. You can't fool me."

Koiro was standing up now, staring up at the back of the god who had protected her. Her helmet still hid her face, but it was easy for Skimif to imagine the look of stunned disbelief that must have been on her features.

Grinf paid her no attention, however, for his focus was still on Skimif. "I do not care what my other siblings have or haven't done to mortals. What matters is that you, Skimif of Tunya, herald of the Powers, are trying to destroy my people. And I cannot allow that."

"Even though the destruction of the world is for the good of all?" said Skimif. "Grinf, you have not seen what I have seen. The Powers have given me the noble mission of cleansing the world so it may be ready for their coming."

"You sound like a deluded fool," said Grinf. "You have always sounded like a deluded fool, of course, but this is absolute proof of your insanity."

Under ordinary circumstances, Skimif might have actually agreed with Grinf's sentiments. Indeed, a small part of him felt disgust at the words he spoke, but a larger part of him—helped in no small part by his bond with his dragon—ignored the small part. His mission was clear and he was not going to give up just because Grinf told him to.

"If you will not stand down, Grinf, then I and my steed will take you down ourselves," said Skimif.

Grinf smirked. "Take me down yourselves? Please. You may have been chosen by the Powers for a special task, but you are still a mortal nonetheless. But if you insist on fighting me, then I will not deny you the opportunity to die in battle." He then tilted his head to the side and said, "By the way, what is the name of your steed? I have never seen anything like it."

Skimif looked down at his steed. To his knowledge, it had no name of its own. It had simply been created by the Powers with the express purpose of finding and uniting with him. The Powers had not bothered to name it and the creature had not bothered to name itself, mostly because it hadn't needed a name until now.

But then a good name came to Skimif's mind, a word that Princess Raya, prior to her death, had told him about once. He knew that that word would send fear into Grinf's very being if spoken aloud.

Patting his steed on the back of its neck, Skimif said, "His name is Kasrath."

Grinf's face went pale for the briefest moment, just as Skimif had thought it would. "Kasrath—? No. That cannot be the same Kasrath of legend. It doesn't look like a force that can destroy the gods."

"It's not," Skimif agreed. "But I think it is a fitting name for the creature that will help destroy all of creation, don't you agree?"

Flames burst into existence around Grinf's hammer as he said, "I suppose it is, but even the fiercest names are just words unless they have the power to back them up."

"Then I think you will find, Lord Grinf, that Kasrath here has more than enough power to live up to its name," said Skimif. "And you will find out about it the hard way, through a battle in which you shall be utterly destroyed."

"Lord Grinf," said Koiro, standing by his side. "I will fight by your side in this battle. I will not let this madman destroy my homeland."

"No, Banika Koiro," said Grinf, without looking at her. "You must run. Kill any Heathens you see, for they are his supporters."

"Kill, my lord?" said Koiro. "But what if some of them are innocent?"

Grinf glanced at her with anger. "I am the God of Justice. When I declare someone guilty, then they are guilty. Do you question my sense of justice?"

"No, no, of course not, sir," said Koiro, backing off. "I would never—"

"Then leave!" Grinf roared. "Before I make you leave."

Koiro and her Enforcers didn't even wait. They ran toward the exit. Kasrath's gaze followed them, aiming to destroy them before they could get far, but then Grinf appeared in its way once again.

"You will not bring the mortals into this fight," said Grinf. "Your conflict is with the gods, Skimif. I am a god, so let us do battle. Isn't that what you wanted?"

Skimif gritted his teeth. The Powers were supposed to be the ones who would finish the gods, but he supposed he should have known better than to believe the gods would just stand by and let him destroy everything. He had thought they would, seeing as they had done nothing to help Nimiko, but clearly they still had some fight left in them.

Redoubling his grip on Kasrath's reins, Skimif said, "Then let us battle, Grinf, although if I were you, I would not be so confident."

Chapter Eleven

THE SOUND OF NIMIKO'S chains dragging across the floor made it hard for Malock to concentrate on blocking his thoughts. The God of Light was walking around checking up on the others, most likely, but Malock wished that he would do it more quietly. Malock had always been terrible at meditation and Nimiko's inability to walk silently was not helping matters.

He cracked open his left eye just enough to look at what everyone else was doing. Jenur and Quro sat next to each other in front of him, their hands held above their heads and their legs crossed under their bodies. Rint sat next to Malock, but with his arms spread out before him and his legs stretched out, which Nimiko had claimed would be a better position for a man as old as Rint to meditate in.

Nimiko stood in front of Quro and Jenur, scrutinizing them both. Thick Void metal chains hung off his wrists and ankles, which by itself would have been enough to restrict his movement, but just to be certain, he also had a chain around his neck. Hana held the other end of the chain, like a dog's leash, and followed Nimiko whenever he moved. The God of Light hadn't been happy about having to be chained like a dog, but he had accepted the precaution and had not complained about it since they let him out of his cage.

All four of the trainees sat in the hold of the *Clockwork Heart*, which Nimiko had claimed was the best place for them to learn how to mind-focus. He said that the size of the hold gave them plenty of room to move, which he said was crucial in learning how to mind-focus, though so far they had not done much more than sit around and meditate.

Or try *to meditate, anyway,* Malock thought, shutting his left eye before Nimiko could see. *Our meditation hasn't exactly been successful.*

That was truer than he liked to admit. Since Nimiko had agreed to train them—which, as of today, had been five days ago—they had not made much progress at all. Nimiko had tried, he said, to drill down the very basics of mind-focusing into a series of lessons that mortals might be able to understand, but it seemed like all of those lessons would go to waste because none of them had progressed past the first lesson yet.

This wasn't because of Nimiko's lack of effort in training them. To Malock's surprise, the God of Light was a patient teacher. He had not yelled at any of them when they didn't understand his lessons, nor did he allow his obvious dislike of all of them to affect his teaching style. He seemed honestly interested in making sure each and every one of them understood how to mind-focus and—although Malock hated to admit it—it was mostly their own lack of understanding that was preventing him from helping them.

Nimiko's initial explanation of the nature of mind-focusing was still on Malock's mind, if only because, at the time, it hadn't made a lick of sense to him. He remembered Nimiko sitting them all down on the first day, in these same meditation positions, and explaining mind-focusing like this:

Imagine that you are standing on the bank of a massive river that flows on and on for miles. But you do not want the river to flow on forever. You want to build a massive dam to cut off the flow so you can use the water to feed your village. Your thoughts are the river and the dam is the mental barrier that you require in order to mind-focus.

Granted, when Malock thought about it now, it made more sense. But despite that, he still couldn't mind-focus at all. Nimiko had said that his metaphor was imperfect and that he usually used a different one when explaining it to new gods, but had decided upon this new one in order to help mortals wrap their minds around it. So far, it apparently hadn't worked, if their failure to mind-focus was an indication of the metaphor's effectiveness.

Every time he thought about how little progress he made, Malock got worried. The Mysterious One had said they would need to learn how to do this if they wanted to avoid being destroyed by the Void. Why this was, Malock still didn't know, but he had no reason to believe that the Mysterious One would deceive him. After all, the Mysterious One basically existed outside of the whole god/mortal conflict that everyone else seemed to be a part of, so he had no reason to harm Malock or the others at all.

Thinking about the Void made him wonder exactly what it would do to him and the others if they failed to learn how to mind-focus in time. The Mysterious One had said that the Void was 'anti-life,' but what *that* meant, Malock didn't know. Couldn't the Mysterious One have just said that the Void was death? He now wondered if the Mysterious One—like most divine beings—had a strange fetish for the dramatic and poetic.

A hand rested on Malock's shoulder, causing his eyes to snap open and his head to look up. Nimiko stood by his shoulder, a frown across his face, like he had known what Malock was thinking.

"How is your practice going, Malock?" said Nimiko. "Any progress?"

Malock shook his head. "No, Nimiko. I feel stuck."

"Your thoughts continue to stray after every little thing," Nimiko said. "And no, I did not read your mind to figure that out. It was written on your face and in the way you sat."

Malock looked down at his legs. Rather than being perfectly crossed underneath his body, the left stuck out ever-so-slightly, while his right was tucked too deeply under his behind. His arms had fallen to his sides, rather than remaining up, as they were supposed to.

Scowling, Malock said, "I didn't even notice that."

Nimiko rubbed his forehead, looking exactly like Malock's old tutor, who would do the same thing whenever Malock exasperated him. "Few do, in the beginning. If we had more time—as in, decades—then you would have eventually learn to catch yourself while doing it and correct your behavior unconsciously. As it is, you do not yet have the experience to feel your body move."

Malock looked at the others, who seemed to be doing better than him, and said, "I don't understand. Why do we need to master our bodies if we are focusing on controlling our minds?"

"Because the mind and body are linked," said Nimiko. "What affects the mind affects the body, and vice versa. It is true of gods and I imagine it is true of mortals, too. You must learn how to control both if you want to succeed."

Scowling, Malock said, "But we don't have time to do that. Hana, has the Mechanical Goddess spotted World's End yet?"

"Not yet," said Hana. "Said it should appear on the horizon any minute now. She does see the Void, however."

"Already?" said Jenur, her eyes flicking open as she looked over her shoulder. "But we haven't even gotten past the first lesson."

"And you won't, so long as you allow your worries to distract you from it," Nimiko said. "Both of you, back to meditation. Remember the river and remember the dam that you want to build."

"But—" said Malock.

"No buts," said Nimiko, holding up a stern finger. "You said you want to learn mind-focusing. And until we are on the cusp of entering the Void, you must take advantage of every spare minute you get to learn it. For all you know, you might be on the edge of grasping it and all you need to do is put a little more effort into it."

Scowling, Malock raised his arms again, crossed his legs underneath him perfectly, and closed his eyes, lowering his head as he did so. He hated to admit it, but Nimiko was right. Worrying about the Void would not help Malock focus his mind.

So Malock tried to visualize the river that Nimiko had told him about. For reference, he used the underground river in Carnag, known as Grinf's River. He imagined himself standing in the underground cavern in which Grinf's River flowed, seeing the crystal-clear water flow by him. At that precise moment, the burn on his face flared, but he ignored it in favor of focusing on the river in his mind.

As before, he tried to figure out how he could build a dam blocking it. He didn't know the first thing about building dams. He supposed it wasn't necessary for him to know that, so he decided to just imagine putting a large wall in the river's way and seeing how that .went.

There it was. A gigantic metal wall had appeared in the river's way, a wall which towered mightily over Malock. The river flowed against the wall, but didn't go around or over it, making Malock think that maybe he had done it after all.

At that exact moment, a loud, earsplitting siren shocked him out of his concentration. His eyes flew open as the pipes on the wall shook and rattled and the lights started blinking on and off rapidly. The others had also snapped out of their meditation and were looking around in shock at the sudden turn of events.

"What's going on?" said Malock, looking up at Hana and Nimiko, who appeared to have been about to talk to Rint. "Hana, what's the Mechanical Goddess saying? Did she see something bad?"

Hana's face, normally very pale, went paler than usual when she started listening. "You don't want to know."

"What do you mean?" said Jenur. Unlike everyone else, Jenur had stood up and had her hand on the handle of her knife. "Of course we want to know. Tell us."

"My sister says we've run into some ... trouble, to put it lightly," said Nimiko. "As in, an army of gods trouble."

"An army of—?" said Rint. He literally fainted just then, falling flat on his back from his meditating position.

"You can't be serious," said Quro as he got up to his feet. "You must have misheard her."

"My sister is panicking, true—which is very rare for her—but she spoke clearly," said Nimiko. "She says that it looks like nearly every god in the Northern and Southern Pantheons is there, quite unusual when you think about it, considering how much we northerners and southerners tend to hate each other."

"Every other god?" said Malock as he slowly rose from his sitting position. "You've got to be joking."

"No joke," said Nimiko. "She also says they have an army of katabans and Bird Children with them. Oh, and she mentioned that Messenger-and-Punisher is around, too."

Malock could not help but tremble in his boots, even though he didn't want to show any fear. "I still don't believe it. Not until I see it with my own eyes."

Nimiko sighed. "Well, seeing as I doubt we'll be able to get you back into the groove, I guess we might as well go top deck and see everything. I'm sure my siblings won't destroy you, however, because you have the Mechanical Goddess's protection and the Fifth Clause is still in effect."

That hardly calmed Malock's fears. He just kept imagining all of the thousands of gods that had to be there, remembering that each one had enough power to destroy whole islands if they wished, and he suddenly wished he was back in Carnag hiding under his blankets.

Stepping onto the top deck of the *Clockwork Heart*, Malock

received a shock to the system when he looked out toward the ship's bow and saw a fleet of a thousand ships—likely far more, but he felt more courageous when he downplayed the seriousness of the situation—stretching before the ship all the way to what looked like a tiny throne on the horizon, which was actually World's End. Beyond the fleet of ships and World's End was a massive, black, starless wall that marked the end of Martir and the beginning of the Void.

Not that they could get there. The fleet of ships not only stood between them and the Void, but stretched out to the east and to the west for as far as the eye could see. A dazzling variety of ships were present. Some looked like old sailing ships, except painted in extravagant colors with beautiful designs, like one ship whose main sail was designed like a peacock's tail feathers. Other ships looked nothing at all like any ship Malock had ever seen, like the 'ship' that looked like a floating castle complete with massive cannons and a set of guards standing on the high walls. Most of the ships were too far away for Malock to see their crews, but he easily spotted Messenger-and-Punisher standing amongst several battleships near the center, standing thankfully too far away for him to smell the giant's atrocious scent.

At the head of the fleet, floating directly in front of the *Clockwork Heart*, was a ship that resembled his old *Iron Wind* ship, except it was at least ten times bigger, and painted black and gray. It had a hundred cannons, with six masts. On the mainmast—which had to be at least as tall as Carnag Hall, if not taller—was a shattered clock. The ship itself towered over the *Clockwork Heart*, which itself was a large ship already, making Malock feel smaller than he normally did around the gods.

Jenur was leaning against the railing, looking at the massive ships, but she looked so close to fainting that Malock kept an eye on her to catch her if she fell. "Oh my gods."

"That's one way of putting it," said Nimiko, his expression grim as he surveyed the fleet before them. "I guess they're bringing out the big guns now."

"Are they really this scared of us?" said Quro, the disbelief in his voice reflected on his face. "So frightened of us saving the world that they would rather forget their differences and band together to stop us?"

Nimiko stroked his chin. "This is the first time since before the Godly War that we gods have ever gotten together to do anything. The Powers would be proud, I'm sure."

Even Hana looked absolutely terrified of the fleet before them. She stood squarely behind Nimiko, her hands gripping his leash so hard that her knuckles had whitened. She looked like she was about to throw up.

"But they still can't hurt us," said Malock. "Right? I mean, you said it yourself, Nimiko, that the Mechanical Goddess is protecting us and the Fifth Clause is still in effect."

"Very true," said Nimiko, nodding. "But remember, the Powers are still on their way here to destroy us all. All my brothers and sisters need to do is stall us long enough for the Powers to get here. No need to attack us when they could waste our precious time, which is just as effective as assault, if not more so."

"Those bastards," said Jenur, pulling away from the railing to look at Nimiko. "How do we get them to move?"

Nimiko seemed to give the thought deep consideration for a moment before shrugging and saying, as frankly as if he had been asked what tomorrow's weather was going to be like, "I don't know."

"You don't know?" said Jenur. "Then why the hell do we even have you around? You're the oldest god. Doesn't that give you some influence over the others?"

Nimiko laughed. "That's a wonderful joke, Jenur. Actually, although I am the oldest, the other gods don't think much of oldest brother. If they did, Grinf and I wouldn't have this ongoing feud that we've yet to resolve."

"So we just wait?" said Malock. "Sit around and hope maybe the other gods decide to do something else before the Powers destroy everything?"

"I already said I don't know," said Nimiko. "But maybe you can ask the leaders of this blockade. Looks like they're on their way here now."

Malock looked up just as a bridge of water shot out from the bow of the fleet's flagship. The bridge connected with the bow of the *Clockwork Heart* and then three gods that Malock had hoped never to see again walked down it. One was a naked woman made entirely of water, her hair flowing down her back like a waterfall before going back up and falling again. The one next to her was an elderly man, bent over and wearing robes etched with clocks in them, using a staff topped with a clock as a walking stick. And the third was a tiny green man, naked except for the leaf covering his genitals, with long hair like grass, red glowing eyes, and teeth made of wood.

"Oh no," said Malock as the three gods stepped off of the bridge and onto the deck of the *Clockwork Heart*. "You three again?"

The little green man, known as the Loner God, God of Solitude, the Jungle, and Animals, licked his lips when he saw Malock. "Hello there, mortal. Haven't seen you in a while." Then he peered more closely and grimaced. "What happened to your face? Did you happen to get on Grinf's bad side recently?"

"I talked to Grinf about that a little while ago," said the old man, who was Tinkar, the God of Fate. "Said that it was an appropriate punishment for a mortal who valued his own self so highly that he was willing to betray his friends for it."

"He used to be quite handsome for a mortal," said the woman, who was Kano, Goddess of the Sea, Sand, and Art. "But Grinf does what he does. I for one am not going to stand in Grinf's way when he wants to do something."

Malock and the others had by this time walked over to meet the three gods, though they stopped when they were about a dozen or so yards away. At the same time, the automaton Calir had appeared out of nowhere and joined them, though what he planned to do, Malock didn't know.

"Where is Grinf, by the way?" said Malock, glancing at the fleet. "Is he on one of those ships trying to keep us from saving the world?"

"Alas, brother Grinf is one of the few gods who could not be here with us today," said Kano. "He said that he had business to attend to up north, which is all you need to know."

"The other god who couldn't make it was the Historic God," said Tinkar. "He's still trapped in the Tunnel of History, thanks to that curse the Powers put on him, but he told us to give you his regards. Said he hoped you failed so he could finally finish recording history."

Malock scowled. The *Clockwork Heart* had not gone through the Tunnel of History on its way to World's End. The Mechanical Goddess had somehow managed to cross the gap between the upper half of the southern seas and the lower half without having to go through the Tunnel. She had said it was to keep the Historic God from trying to stop them or slow their progress, though how she managed it, Malock still didn't know, seeing as he and the others had been forced to stay below deck while she did it.

"For that matter, the Mysterious One is absent as well," said the Loner God. "Not that I care. Never liked that freak anyway. He's shown his true colors by helping you mortals anyway, which I assume is why he's not here."

"Why are you guys even doing this?" said Jenur. "Don't you realize what we're doing? We're trying to save the world. *This* world. You know, where all of us live? Including you idiots?"

The Loner God licked his fingers, which Malock realized with a lurch of his stomach had blood on them. "Can we be so sure that that's what you're really planning to do? I don't think we can. You mortals are so selfish. We know what you're really planning to do."

"What?" said Malock. "What do you mean, what we're *really* planning to do? We really *are* planning to save the world."

"Don't belittle our intelligence," said Tinkar, glaring at Malock with the eyes of a stern old man who was tired of disrespectful young people. "We saw right through your ploy. You want to find the Powers, not to convince them to save the world, but to convince them to spare *your* lives over everyone else's."

"Now that is a lie, Tinkar, and you know it," said Nimiko. "These mortals may be dim, limited, and disrespectful, but they aren't selfish. They truly do have the world's interests at heart."

"I'm sure they do," said Tinkar. "But in all of my years as the watcher of fate, I have seen more than a few 'selfless' mortals succumb to their own impulses. I am not interested in handing over the fate of the world to a bunch of mortals, especially mortals I already dislike."

"As fatalistic as ever, brother," said Nimiko. "I bet the only reason you stand against us is because you think it's fate, right?"

"Correct, oldest brother," said Tinkar. "With the end of days just around the corner, I have now seen the ultimate fate of Martir, which until now I have never been privy to knowing. The end is near and there is nothing we can do about it."

"You fools," said Jenur. "Each one of you—and each one of those other gods out there on those ships—are fools."

"It takes one to know one, mortal female," said the Loner God. "Or have you forgotten just how foolish you mortals are?"

"But we're not the only ones doing this," said Quro. "Nimiko and the Mechanical Goddess are on our side."

"Nimiko has always been an idiot," said Kano. "I'm sorry, brother, but it's true. You may be the oldest, but you've also been very slow, never quite as quick as some of us youngsters."

Nimiko's hands balled into fists, but he didn't step forward or even threaten to attack her. His body did glow more brightly, though it was a threatening brightness.

"And the Mechanical Goddess is a pragmatist," said Tinkar. "In fact, I'd say she ought to be the Goddess of Pragmatism rather than the Goddess of Machines. By winning your favor, she hopes to preserve her own life at the expense of ours."

At that moment, the smokestacks exploded, almost literally, spewing out so much smoke and ash that Malock almost thought that the ship's engine had exploded.

The gods, however, seemed to understand what she was saying, because the Loner God said, "Don't deny it, sister. We all know how you've always looked out for number one. Even during the Godly War, you would sacrifice your siblings just to survive. We're not stupid, unlike Nimiko here."

"Stupid?" said Nimiko. He pointed sharply at his siblings and said, "I think that it is stupid—no, beyond stupid, downright suicidal —to stand in the way of the only beings in this world who care about it. For once, I am ashamed to be a god. If this is how we react when faced with our possible, perhaps inevitable, extinction, then we truly deserve our destruction."

"We are simply ensuring that all of us perish together," said Tinkar. "If there is one thing I have learned in my long days, it is that you cannot fight fate. And it is our fate to be destroyed. The Powers have shown me this."

"If we are going to die anyway, then what does it matter if we try to stop them or not?" said Malock. "You all sound like fatalistic idiots."

"We're not fatalists," said Tinkar. "Merely realists. The Powers are a step above even our understanding. How can you humans, who are below us, even hope to comprehend them, much less communicate with them?"

"I don't know," Malock said. "But it's better to try and fail than to never try at all."

"Spoken like a true mortal," said the Loner God with a sarcastic chuckle. "Blindly optimistic, ignorant, and extremely naïve."

"There is nothing you can do to make us move," said Kano. "Although we cannot assault our sister or any of you, neither can she attack us. For you see, we have all invoked the Fifth Clause. You cannot convince any of us to move."

Malock looked out over the massive fleet. There had to be thousands of ships, each one captained by a different god, most likely manned with a large crew of katabans. And even worse, he sensed that Kano's words were correct. There was nothing that he or any of the other people on board the ship could do to get past them. No ideas occurred to him, and none of the others seemed to have any ideas about it, either.

"Even if we did let you go, did you forget that the Void destroys all mortal life within it?" said the Loner God. "Not that I care about your safety or anything, but I am merely pointing out that no matter what happens, no matter what you do, you lose. Like you mortals always do."

"You will die," Tinkar said. "Though the Mechanical Goddess's protection prevents me from seeing your fates, I am confident in saying that you will all die, seeing as the world is going to end, after all. Just like Vashnas."

Anger shot up through Malock's body like a firework. He pointed sharply at Tinkar and said, "Don't. Say. Her. Name."

"Or you'll do what?" said Tinkar. "Get angry? Make empty threats?"

"Don't stop him," said the Loner God. "This is good entertainment. Mortals always get angry when they're trapped in a corner like this. It's highly amusing, though not as good as actually sinking my teeth into their flesh and chewing it up."

Malock looked at his friends. Jenur looked at least as angry as he did, if not more so, and in fact had drawn her knife, though there was nothing she could do with it. Quro stared at the army of gods and their ships. It was easy to see the hope in his eyes leaking away, almost like watching a ship with a leak sinking into the ocean.

Hana was literally sweating now and even shaking in her boots. She had actually let go of Nimiko's chain, but the God of Light didn't bother to run. Like Jenur, Nimiko looked more angry than anything. He was muttering curses under his breath, alternating between Divina and another language that Malock didn't recognize.

Only Calir appeared at all calm, and that was because he was an automaton and was completely incapable of showing or feeling any emotion whatsoever. He just stared at Tinkar, Kano, and the Loner God, then glanced briefly out at the fleet, then looked at Malock and the others. The automaton appeared to be thinking hard, but Malock wasn't sure what good it could do. Like the rest of the world, Calir would be destroyed once the Powers arrived. Likely the only reason the automaton hadn't stopped functioning was because it had been programmed to never be afraid or hesitant, no matter how hopeless the situation appeared.

Then Calir began to walk away. It did so at a slow pace, but gradually sped up until it was running faster than the wind. The *clang, clang,* of its metal feet against the deck echoed through the still air until Calir reached starboard. Then it leaped off the railings and dove into the water. A *splash* was the only confirmation they received that it had made it.

"Wow," said the Loner God, after seeing Calir jump ship. "Even the automatons are realizing that suicide is their only option. Your children aren't very brave, sister."

Another column of smoke shot out of the frontal smokestack, followed by a briefer one from the back one.

The Loner God folded his stubby arms across his chest. "I don't have any children, sister. Unlike some gods I know, I happen to be just fine with solitude, thank you very much."

"Hana," said Malock in a low voice, leaning toward her as he did so. "Why did Calir jump ship?"

Hana, who looked more like a dying patient in a medical ward than anything, shook her head. "No idea. Maybe it's like the Loner God said; Calir just realized that we can't win and decided to end it all on his own terms, rather than let the Powers finish him off."

The Loner God chuckled. "See, sister? I'd advise you to do the same, but then I remembered that the Treaty specifically prohibits godly suicide. That just means we'll all die together."

"Which is appropriate," said Tinkar, nodding. "Though we may have our differences in opinion, we are all still gods and thus it is only fitting that we will all go down together."

While the Loner God smirked, Kano looked a little worried. She was looking down at the deck, like she could see right through it.

Malock didn't know what she saw, or what she thought she saw, but whatever it was, she was frowning and her brow was furrowed.

"I can still sense Calir in the ocean," said Kano. "He's swimming fast, almost as fast as a singing leaper. He's using some sort of propulsion system in his legs to help him go deeper."

"Maybe our sister dropped something and Calir is being a good little boy and fetching it," the Loner God suggested. "While I have no use for servants or followers or children, I have to admit that having other beings do your dirty work is appealing."

"I don't think so," said Kano. "If the Mechanical Goddess had dropped something, then I would have felt it. No, Calir is looking for something else."

"Maybe *he* dropped something," the Loner God said. "I don't know if sister ever gives her children any presents, but maybe she gave him a toy or something and he somehow dropped it and is going to retrieve it."

"No," said Kano, shaking her head. "Because he's picking up speed, going so fast now that even I can barely keep up with him. He seems to be trying to reach the sea floor. But I still don't know what he wants."

"Then maybe he's not trying to kill himself at all," said the Loner God, his tone annoyed. "Maybe he thinks he'll be safe from the Powers' wrath on the ocean floor. Like *that* will work."

Malock didn't know what Calir was trying to do, but he found it interesting that the Mechanical Goddess had said nothing about one of her own children jumping into the sea seemingly for no reason. He had been told that she was fiercely protective of her children and that she would go to great lengths to protect them.

If that was true—and based on his experience with the Mechanical Goddess, he believe it was—then her complete disinterest in her child's safety made no sense at all. Either she hated Calir for some reason ... or she had ordered him to do this.

But what could possibly be on the ocean floor? Malock thought. *There's nothing more than a bunch of fish down there. Certainly, there is nothing that could help us get past this blockade. Otherwise, I think Kano and the others wouldn't seem so confident.*

Then a week-old memory stirred in his mind. He remembered Hana telling him something about the southern seas once. So much had happened since then that he had not thought about it, and even though the conversation had been a mere week ago, he found himself struggling to remember the details. Best he could remember was that there was something on the sea floor that the gods didn't like, but what, he could not recall, even though it was on the tip of his tongue.

Then Kano gasped. "He isn't."

"What?" said Tinkar, throwing a sharp look at Kano. "Calir?"

"What's he doing?" said the Loner God. "Trying to sabotage the ships?"

"No," said Kano. She looked up at all of them. There was actual fear in her eyes; real, genuine fear. "He's awakening the Sleeping Beast."

The Loner God's hair stood on end, while Tinkar immediately looked out over the sea as if he thought the Sleeping Beast might already be there. Even Nimiko looked terrified, as if Kano had just said that they were all going to die.

"No way," said the Loner God. "He wouldn't be *that* stupid. No one is."

"I sense him down there," Kano said. "Unless you happen to be the God of the Sea—which you aren't—you have to trust me. He's poking it, trying to enrage it."

"Then stop him," said Tinkar, his voice full of undisguised panic. "Send a water spout at him or have a current rip him to shreds or send some sea creatures to kill him or whatever. Just stop him."

Kano shook her head. "Too late. The Sleeping Beast is awakening."

"Impossible," said the Loner God. "Your powers must be wonky. Or maybe the Beast is just turning over in its sleep. Ever thought of that?"

"No, it's stirring," said Kano. "This isn't just a brief awakening, either. It's actually standing. I can sense the fluctuations in the ocean where it's shaking its head. It's even sneezing due to the mud in its nose."

"Why would that automaton ever ..." Tinkar's voice trailed off as he looked up at the Mechanical Goddess's smokestacks. "Oh. I get it now."

"Get it?" said the Loner God. "I'm confused. What—"

"Our sister ordered Calir to do that," said Tinkar. "She must have been aware that we would do whatever we could to stop these mortals from going beyond the Void. So of course, she came up with a backup plan: She decided to fight one apocalypse by starting another."

The Mechanical Goddess's smokestacks blew more smoke and

flames. This time, based purely on the looks that her siblings wore, Malock understood that she had confirmed Tinkar's theory.

"I always knew she was a bitch," said the Loner God. "But *this* takes the cake."

"All may not be lost just yet," said Tinkar, scratching his chin as he looked out at the fleet. "It's not like the Beast has started to actually rise, correct?"

Kano's expression wasn't encouraging. "Actually, brother, it's chasing Calir. Who, not-so-coincidentally, is heading directly for the surface."

"I'm out of here," said the Loner God, taking a step back. "The world's about to end anyway. No need to stick around while *that* thing is around. Good bye."

With that, the Loner God turned and ran back up the water bridge connecting the flagship to the *Clockwork Heart*. Tinkar followed, but not before glaring at the smokestacks. Kano scowled at Malock and the others, like she blamed them for the Mechanical Goddess's plans, and then crossed the bridge.

"How long has she been planning to do this?" Jenur asked Hana, as soon as Kano had left.

Hana shook her head helplessly. "I don't know. This is the first time I even knew about it. She must have wanted to keep this a secret to ensure that the other gods wouldn't find out about it before she put it into action."

"Just like my sister," Nimiko sighed. "Well, we might as well head below deck. I don't think any of us want to be top deck when the Sleeping Beast—"

Without warning, the *Clockwork Heart* shook under their feet. It was not a huge tremor, not enough to throw anyone off their feet, but it was enough to alarm Malock.

"It's coming," said Nimiko, who now looked as sick as Hana. "We've got to get below deck before it surfaces."

No one voiced any disagreement, so the group turned and began making their way to the hatch when Jenur stopped, looked over her shoulder, and gasped. "Look at the fleet!"

Though Malock wanted to run, he nonetheless stopped and looked at the fleet. News of the Sleeping Beast's arrival must have already spread throughout the fleet because the thousands and thousands of ships were attempting to flee, but it was no use. They were all so packed together so closely that they ended up crashing into each other accidentally, in one case even causing a couple of ships to catch flame. Amid the crashing of ships, the yells and curses of katabans sailors could be heard, while Messenger-and-Punisher did his best to make sure none of the ships collided into his legs.

But then the center of the fleet started to rise on top of a massive wave. The wave rose higher and higher, the ships on the peripheral falling off the sides and into the ocean below, until finally the water flowed off the creature that had arisen from the depths of the ocean.

The Sleeping Beast was easily the largest creature that Malock had ever seen in his life. Hana had said it was as big as an island, but looking at it now, Malock could have been forgiven for thinking it was as big as a continent. Its head was large, flat, and hippo-like, its massive snout caked with muddy sand. Its skin glistened in the sun, slimy and wet and covered in mud and seaweed and barnacles. Its legs were thick and tall, like massive trees growing from the bottom of the ocean floor. Its eyes had to be as big as the skyscrapers of World's End, but they were only partially opened, as if the Sleeping Beast was not yet fully awake.

When the Sleeping Beast opened its mouth to yawn, it revealed row upon row of huge, blunt teeth that looked more than capable of tearing an island in half. Its mouth was so wide and so huge that it looked like it could swallow an entire armada of Carnagian Navy battleships in one gulp. It shook its head slowly, but that slow movement sent several ships that had gotten caught on its flat head flying. One of the ships—a blocky, metal one that resembled a floating fortress—crashed near the *Clockwork Heart*, splashing water onto everyone on the ship's top deck.

"How the hell are we supposed to get past *that*?" Jenur asked, wiping her wet hair off her forehead. "It's huge!"

"The Mechanical Goddess said she's going to take advantage of the confusion and sail around it," said Hana as she squeeze water out of her jacket. "Said she's going to go at full speed directly toward the Void. Said it's our only chance at getting to it."

"What?" said Malock, shivering from the cold water. "But none of us have even—"

His voice was cut off by a loud sonic boom that almost knocked him flat to his feet. In fact, the blast of sound was so loud that for a moment he temporarily lost the ability to hear. He looked around in alarm, noticing how the others had covered their ears, and then looked back to the Sleeping Beast and saw that it had its mouth open. It looked like it was roaring and as soon as it closed its mouth,

Malock's hearing returned in full force.

"What was that?" said Malock, rubbing his aching ears.

"The Sleeping Beast's roar," said Nimiko. Unlike the others, he looked more shaken than harmed. "The legends said it could destroy mortal ears, but I guess you must have gotten lucky, or maybe the legends were wrong."

"The Mechanical Goddess says she has a plan to help you mortals survive in the Void, but we've got to go below deck for it to work," said Hana. "Just trust her. This is the only chance we've got."

Though his ears still rang, Malock had to look out at the Sleeping Beast, mostly because it was impossible not to. It looked fully awake now, its massive eyes taking in the environment around it. The smashed fleet at its feet looked like a bunch of toy ships that had been thrown about by a careless young child. Malock didn't see any of the gods or katabans, but he had a feeling they would be showing up soon enough to attack that creature, unless they were all as brave as the Loner God, that is.

"We don't have much choice in the matter," said Quro. "It's either get killed by that thing or survive."

"Or die in the Void," Malock said. "Hasn't that ever occurred to you as a possibility?"

"Well, what else should we do?" said Jenur. "Do you have any better plans? The Powers could be here any minute. We don't have all the time in the world to put this off or learn how to mind-focus, you know."

Malock gritted his teeth, but he said, "All right. Let's go below deck. And quickly, before the Beast notices us."

The five of them dashed to the hatch as fast as they could. They didn't stop even when the sound of thunder overhead exploded, nor did they stop when the deck shook from the Sleeping Beast's stomping feet shaking the ocean.

Almost as soon as Quro, who was in the back of the group, made it into the hatch, the hatch door slammed shut behind them without any work on their part. They all gathered in the dining room, which was currently empty, and took seats around the table just as the *Clockwork Heart* began moving. Through the steel walls and ceiling, the sounds of the Sleeping Beast growling and the sounds of the other gods attacking the monster could be heard almost as if the walls and ceiling weren't there at all.

Then an automaton appeared from the doorway at the end of the room. It immediately spoke in that strange language that the automatons spoke in, addressing Hana, and then disappeared back into the doorway from which it came.

"What did it say?" said Jenur, looking at Hana.

"Said we should hold on tight because the Mechanical Goddess is going to go faster than usual," said Hana. "Something about super speed, though to be honest, he spoke so fast that I couldn't quite catch—"

Without warning, the *Clockwork Heart* jerked forward, almost throwing Malock off his seat. He grabbed the table just in time, however, and held on tightly as the ship picked up speed. The others also grasped the table, particularly Jenur, who held onto it so tightly that Malock doubted she would ever let go even if it slowed down to a more reasonable speed.

It was impossible to tell for sure what was going on outside. The sounds of battle roared through the walls, getting louder and louder the closer they got to the Sleeping Beast. A massive *boom* somewhere above them almost made Malock jump, but he kept his self-control and tried not to dwell too much on the fact that they were soon going to be passing by an island-sized monster that the gods were afraid of. For that matter, he tried not to think too much about the fact that he and the others were, in all likelihood, going to die anyway once they passed through the Void.

How much time passed, neither Malock nor any of his friends knew, though they did not dare speak or move to find out. The Mechanical Goddess was still moving at full speed, the sounds of battle continued to rage, and more than once the ship lurched to the right or left for reasons unknown, making Malock's stomach lurch with it. He could just imagine them passing by the Sleeping Beast's legs, hopefully unnoticed, but if the creature did take notice of them and decided that they were a threat ...

Then a series of groans and rattles from the ship itself, followed by the lights overhead blinking on and off several times in rapid succession, occurred. None of the mortals understood what any of it meant, but a look at Hana and Nimiko's alarmed expressions told Malock that something bad was about to happen.

"Uh oh," said Hana. "Guys, hang on! The Mechanical Goddess says that a giant wave is heading her way and she can't dodge it."

"She says that, if it hits, it'll probably knock her over," said Nimiko. "So we'd better—"

Then, without warning, the sound of something huge slamming

against the side of the ship echoed like a gunshot throughout the dining room. At the same time, the entire room lurched to the right, throwing everyone off their seats as the ship tumbled over.

Malock, having sat on the left side of the table, was sent flying. He slammed headfirst into the metal wall directly opposite him, knocking him out instantly.

Chapter Twelve

SKIMIF AND KASRATH FLEW through the skies over Port Blasan, their eyes scanning the destruction below. Countless buildings were little more than rubble. Countless more were on fire. The Fountain of Justice had been smashed, water trickling out of its pipes into the streets. There was no screaming or movement from the people, as most of the inhabitants of Port Blasan had already been evacuated once the situation became known to the rest of the Justice Enforcers. The only building that had managed to escape destruction so far was Carnag Hall, thanks in no small part to the Protection that surrounded it, a massive, clear magical barrier maintained by the city's teichomancers. To Skimif's knowledge, the King and Queen of Carnag were still in there. Sooner or later he would have to destroy the Protection, but for now he had to find Grinf.

The God of Justice, Fire, and Metal was nowhere to be seen. Their fight had started in the Stadium, but Skimif and Kasrath had taken it out into the rest of the city, despite Grinf's best attempts to confine it to the Stadium. Skimif didn't want to battle on Grinf's terms, however, which is why he had taken it to the city itself. That, and he was supposed to destroy Carnag anyway. Might as well kill two birds with one stone, the way he saw it.

After taking their battle to the city streets, Skimif and Kasrath had battled for at least half an hour with Grinf, during which they had caused most of the destruction that lay beneath him now. Grinf had clearly been holding back, however, perhaps because he didn't want to harm his people. Whatever the god's reason, Skimif had taken full advantage of Grinf's restraint to pummel him with everything he had.

Then an opening had shown itself, which Skimif took advantage of. He and Kasrath knocked Grinf out of the sky, sending him crashing into a group of apartments below. When Skimif and Kasrath had gone to finish him, the god's body was nowhere to be seen.

That was why they had taken to the skies again. Though Skimif was not a big fan of flying, he found that he didn't mind this much, even though he was several hundred feet above the ground. He supposed this feeling of safety was coming from Kasrath, who soared through the skies as easily as an aquarian swam through water. His steed had suffered some terrible burns from Grinf, even a direct blow to the face from the god's hammer that almost smashed his lower jaw, but Kasrath still hung in there. If ever there was a finer creation of the Powers than Kasrath, Skimif didn't know about it.

As he and Kasrath did another circuit around the area, Skimif could not help but feel that he was wasting time. Though he had already destroyed a good portion of the city, the rest of it still stood unharmed from his and Grinf's battle. His eyesight was not as good as Kasrath's from the sky, but occasionally he caught glimpses of the rest of the city's inhabitants evacuating. Some were heading farther inland, toward the cities and boot factories in the northern and western regions; others, largely foreign merchants and tourists from what he could tell, were taking their ships and fleeing to the Crystal Sea. He was tempted to chase those fleeing via the sea and burn their ships, but he knew that would be a waste of time. Besides, once he finished with Grinf, he would go on and destroy the rest of the Northern Isles one island at a time. There was nowhere anyone could run now that was safe.

Kasrath raised its head, sniffing the air with its tiny nostrils. Through his connection with the steed, Skimif smelled the same thing as Kasrath, a familiar scent, one that was somehow still distinct in spite of all of the fire and smoke that burned away at the city below. Without thinking, Skimif urged Kasrath down, and the steed soared down to the streets.

As Kasrath came to a landing in one of the backstreets, Skimif looked at the area in which they had landed. The roof of a nearby building had caved in, while the building next to it was slowly burning away. A burned corpse—blackened to the point where Skimif couldn't even tell if it was human or aquarian—lay underneath a pile of rubble, while the streets themselves were cracked or covered with burning debris. The temperature was hotter down here, almost like standing inside an oven, but Skimif was used to the heat by now. Normally, his skin should have dried out due to the lack of moisture, but ever since bonding with Kasrath, Skimif had noticed that his skin seemed impervious to changes in temperature and climate. He was not sure why, but he wasn't complaining.

Kasrath's nose was pointed to the building on their right. Even a cursory glance of the place told Skimif that it was the old hideout of the Brotherhood. The windows had been burned out, the door was smashed in, a fire had somehow started in one of the second story rooms; nonetheless, he had no trouble recognizing the building that had acted as the home base of his movement for the last month or so.

Despite himself, Skimif had to hold back tears when he saw it. It had not been a very good building; in fact, its decrepit, rundown appearance had been exactly the reason why Skimif had chosen it as the Brotherhood's hideout. Nonetheless, the building had served as his refuge whenever things got dicey with the Enforcers. Just looking at it brought back memories, such as when he first learned that the mysterious Hood was in fact Prince Malock or when he informed Malock and the late Princess Raya Kabadi that the world was going to end.

Skimif had to chuckle bitterly at that. *Here I was, afraid that I would die with everyone else. Yet the Powers decided to spare me out of every other mortal on Martir. 'Bout as funny as thinking you're gonna get bitten by a water snake only to find out that it was your father who had actually gotten bitten.*

He wondered if any of the other Heathens were still inside the building. He doubted it. Likely they had fled with everyone else. Still, a part of him—the part of him that was still the leader of the Brotherhood instead of the part of him that was the herald of the Powers—was concerned for the lives of his former siblings. He had not seen any of his fellow Heathens since the start of his fight with Grinf.

If I've killed any of them, then it's all my fault, Skimif thought. *None of them deserved to die. I should have found a way to spare them.*

Then again, what good would it have been? No matter whether he spared them or not, death was to be their fate sooner or later. He was going to destroy all of Martir, or at least prepare it for the Powers to do it themselves. That included his former fellow Heathens, but he didn't feel at all happy about that knowledge. It just made him want to get this over with quickly so he would not have to be stuck with these dark thoughts anymore.

"Skimif of Tunya," came a voice behind him, snapping him out of his thoughts. "Turn and face me like a true warrior. Or are you too proud to grant me even that much?"

Skimif turned, tugging on Kasrath's reins as he did so. The voice belonged to Grinf, who stood in the center of the street not very far from where Skimif and Kasrath were. A terrible, thick scar ran along the right side of Grinf's face, going through his right eye, which had been the work of Kasrath's sharp wingtips. His face was stained with the gold blood of the gods, which had came from the scar when it was first inflicted. The god's armor, too, was dented and beaten, like scrap metal, but despite the blows he had taken, Grinf looked as ready for battle as ever.

Skimif frowned as Kasrath snarled. "You had the perfect opportunity to brain me with your hammer because until you spoke, I didn't even know you were there."

"It would have done nothing except enrage your pet," said Grinf. "And I hate dealing with angry animals. Animals don't understand justice."

"I see nothing just about braining someone from behind," said Skimif. "Anyway, have you decided to give up? I'll understand if you have. I and Kasrath still have a ton of energy left for battle. You, however, get weaker with every blow we deal to you."

Grinf's chest rose and fell as he stood there. "Don't be so stupid. Justice never gives up. It hounds the guilty to the very ends of the earth, and beyond if necessary. As justice incarnate, giving up is not an option for me."

Skimif yawned. "Then why did you give up the perfect opportunity to take me out? Just want to brag?"

Grinf shook his head. "No. I've realized that, somehow, despite your status as mortal, you are my equal in combat. Battling you does nothing except destroy the city dedicated to me and harm the people who have spent their whole lives praising my name and living by my ideals. I may not have chosen their Royal Family, as they like to believe, but I do not let good behavior go unrewarded."

Skimif scoffed. "So that's why you melted Malock's face, yes?"

"Prince Malock is a guilty criminal," said Grinf. "He betrayed one of his fellow crew mates for the sole purpose of making himself look good. There is a saying among my judges that is very true: 'Criminality is the fruit of haste.'"

"Whatever," said Skimif. "Kasrath here is getting tired of standing around. He likes to be on the move. So, unless you've said all you've wanted to—"

"But I haven't," said Grinf. He held his right hand out to his right side and snapped his fingers. "Enforcers?"

Two Justice Enforcers—one Captain Koiro, the other the huge man Skimif remembered seeing a week ago, when he first got the invitation for the public debate—stepped out of the ruins of one of the few buildings that had yet to suffer from the battle. They were not alone, however. They carried with them two beings that Skimif had not expected to see were still in the city.

"Aqur? Ower?" said Skimif, his voice almost choking as he said their names. "No, it can't be."

But it was. Koiro held one of Aqur's arms twisted behind her back; am impressive feat, as Aqur had a slimy body. Aqur's face was bloodied and swollen on one side, like she had been beaten with a mace. Her clothes, too, had been burned, going from the bright green of seaweed to the darkened blackness of a fire-swept field. Skimif did not know if her clothes had been burned by him or by Grinf accidentally.

The huge Enforcer from before held Ower. Poor Ower looked even worse than Aqur. He'd clearly tried to fight, based on the bloody scars on the Enforcer's face, but Ower's left eye was swollen and he appeared to be missing some teeth. His shirt had been nearly torn off, its tatters just barely hanging off his tiny body. The Enforcer held a gun to Ower's head while holding Ower's left arm similar to how Koiro held Aqur's.

Grinf was not smiling. "I know that these two are your friends, Skimif, or were. The other Heathens—curse them to the heavens and back—managed to escape, but these two were trapped in the Stadium when a chunk of the ceiling fell on the female. When you knocked me out of the sky, I found Koiro and Byki here and told them to bring them here."

"Let them go," said Skimif. His voice had deepened now, without any conscious effort on his part. "Now."

Grinf shook his head. "No. Not until you agree to stand down and cease your unjust destruction of my city."

"Unjust?" said Skimif. "Who cares about justice? The Powers will be here soon. You think that my actions were bad? Trust me, I am like a light breeze in comparison to the tornado that is the Powers."

"That may be true," said Grinf. "But I know that you still remember them. You may currently be a high and mighty herald of the Powers, but you were once still mortal and, like most mortals, you are hesitant to sacrifice your friends even if it would help you advance your goals."

Skimif growled deeply, or maybe it was Kasrath who had growled (the longer they stayed together, the harder it became for him to distinguish himself from his steed). Either way, he knew that Grinf was right. As much as Kasrath's anger urged him to strike down that god, regardless of the consequences of that action, Skimif could not forget Aqur and Ower. Though Grinf hadn't said what Koiro and Byki would do if Skimif did not give up, it clearly was not going to be pretty.

"Skim, don't let him win," said Aqur, speaking up suddenly. "No matter what he threatens to do to us, you can't give up."

"Are you honestly that stupid?" said Grinf, looking at Aqur with disgust. "He is going to destroy the entire world. That includes *you*. By urging him to attack, you are guaranteeing your own demise."

Aqur shrugged as best as she could with Koiro still twisting her arm. "So what? We're all going to die anyway. I am still a Heathen through and through. I would rather see you get your backside handed to you by Skimif than live long enough to see him die at your hands. Right, Ower?"

Ower didn't seem capable of speaking anymore. The little boy was whimpering, probably from the pain of Byki holding him the way he was. To Skimif's fury, Byki didn't look at all apologetic for harming the boy. If anything, the Enforcer seemed to enjoy it, although that may have just been Skimif's imagination.

"You Heathens truly are pathetic," said Grinf, shaking his head again, except this time with more disgust. "Willing to sacrifice a small child—an innocent child—just to satisfy your own ideological agendas. What other kind of monstrosities would you do, if you thought it would help you strike a blow against me and my siblings?"

"Says the god who is using said child as blackmail," said Aqur. "Don't play all high and mighty with me, Mr. God of 'Justice.'"

"Regardless, you still have a choice to make, Skimif," said Grinf, turning his attention back to Skimif. "Either stand down and I will order my Enforcers to set your friends free, or attack me and I will order them to kill your friends. The choice is yours."

"Does it matter?" said Skimif. "Whether my friends live or die, the Powers will destroy us all. This does nothing except make you gods out to be as bad as I always said you were."

"You may be correct in saying that the Powers are coming whether we want them to or not," said Grinf. "But that doesn't mean I must stand by and watch while one of their servants destroys the most just mortal city on the planet. Better to go out, knowing I have defended my honor, than to die trying to hide from that which no living thing can hide from."

Skimif's stomach seemed to twist in his body whenever he looked at Aqur and Ower. Grinf wasn't lying. Koiro and Byki looked more than capable of killing his friends, if ordered to by the god whom they had sworn their lives to.

Part of Skimif simply wanted to attack Grinf, consequences be damned. As he had already said, it didn't matter, in the end, whether Aqur and Ower lived or died right now. Once the Powers came—and Skimif could sense them drawing closer and closer every minute—everything and everyone on Martir would be annihilated. And anyway, he could avenge Aqur and Ower if he had to. As strong as Koiro and Byki may have been, neither of them were a match for Skimif, especially with Kasrath on his side.

But the other half of him—the part that still saw all mortals as his siblings—resisted. There was no reason to attack Grinf, who might very well win in battle, and guarantee the deaths of his friends. Skimif had been through much with Aqur and greatly cared for Ower, who he had always seen as the future of mortals on Martir, an example of what people might be like after the gods. To sacrifice them for short term gain, just to satisfy his bloodlust, would be wrong. He realized that he would have to abandon the title of leader of the Brotherhood of Heathens if he dared do such a thing.

But the end of the world is going to happen anyway, Skimif thought. *You were chosen by the Powers to herald it. You can't stand here in indecision forever.*

Almost as if he had read Skimif's thoughts, Grinf said, "Every minute you waste is another minute that I grow weary of waiting. Make a decision. Or is this how the herald of the end intends to bring about the end, holding out as long as he can until the Powers arrive and do his job for him?"

Kasrath hissed, tiny flames spitting from its mouth, but Skimif pulled back on the reins, causing it to close its mouth. He understood Kasrath's hatred toward Grinf, but he now knew what he wanted to do. Grinf's rhetorical question had given him an idea, though whether it would work, he didn't know.

"All right," said Skimif. "I've made my decision."

"Finally," said Grinf with a sigh. "What is it?"

Skimif looked at Aqur and Ower again before he said, "I will not attack you. In exchange for the lives of my friends, I will spare Carnag."

A smile passed over Grinf's lips like a flame. "I did not expect you to make that choice. Very well. Koiro? Byki?"

The two Enforcers let go of Aqur and Ower. To Skimif's surprise, Aqur and Ower were fit enough to run over to him. They ran past Grinf, who merely watched them pass with contempt in his eyes, until they reached Kasrath. They then clung to Kasrath's legs like a child grabbing its parents' legs for safety.

"Are you two okay?" Skimif asked, looking down at them from his seat on Kasrath. "Are you hurt?"

"Yes," said Aqur, nodding. "But I think we'll be okay."

Ower, however, looked up at Kasrath with fear in his eyes. "Skimif, is it true that you're supposed to destroy the world? Why? Why do the Powers want you to do it?"

"I don't know why," said Skimif. "But I do know this: I am going to go to the Powers and convince them to spare your lives—and the lives of every other Heathen in the Brotherhood—when they come to destroy everything."

For once, Grinf laughed. "You are going to go and reason with the Powers? The Powers cannot be reasoned with. Trust me. When the Powers declare that they will do something, they do it. They are not ones to negotiate, especially with their own creations."

"I know that the Powers are not easily moved by pleas of mercy," said Skimif. "But I must try. And as their specially-chosen herald, who knows? Maybe they will make an exception and listen to me."

Grinf looked disapproving, but he said nonetheless, "Fine. Do as you will. I presume that means you are going to leave Carnag. That means my people will last a little while longer."

"That is true," said Skimif, nodding. "But it won't be for very long. I doubt I'm the only one here who senses the closeness of the Powers."

Grinf turned his gaze south, as if he could see the Void and what lay beyond it. "Indeed."

"Are you going to leave us here, Skimif?" said Ower.

Skimif gripped the reins tighter. He didn't want to bring Aqur and Ower with him, but he didn't want to leave them here with Grinf and his Enforcers, either. He had no idea what they might do to Aqur and Ower if he left them alone with them, so he forced himself to come up with an idea.

A solution to the problem occurred to him immediately. He said to Aqur and Ower, "I'll take you two out of Port Blasan. Meet up with whichever members of the Brotherhood survived my battle with Grinf and don't let anyone find or catch you."

"But I want to come with you," said Aqur.

"Me, too," said Ower. "I want to help you."

"Neither of you can help me where I am going," said Skimif, shaking his head. "It is too dangerous. You must stay on Carnag, where you will be safe."

"Safe?" said Aqur, the word slightly slurred through her swollen lips. "We're not going to be safe anywhere, Skim. You know that."

"Just trust me," said Skimif. "You heard what I said. Find the other Heathens and stick with them until I return."

"*If* you return," said Grinf. "The Powers may not take your defiance very kindly. They may just decide to eliminate you and replace you with someone else if you resist their plans."

There was no concern in Grinf's voice. The god was simply telling Skimif the facts; or what he believed to be the facts, anyway.

"It doesn't matter what they do to me," said Skimif. "I'll take that chance. Right, Kasrath?"

He could sense that Kasrath didn't agree at all. A cloud of confusion existed in the dragon's mind, mostly because it did not see how going to the Powers to convince them to spare a handful of mortal lives had anything to do with their mission of preparing the world for the Powers' arrival.

But Kasrath didn't resist. It deeply trusted Skimif and would go wherever he told it to go. He sensed that.

"All right, you two," said Skimif to Aqur and Ower. "Climb on. I'll take you to the borders of Port Blasan. Then I will travel south to

TIMOTHY L. CEREPAKA

World's End."

Chapter Thirteen

Jenur's head hurt. It felt like someone had slammed a massive hammer against it a couple hundred times and then placed a ton of rock on it for a few days.

As a result, she didn't want to get up. She just wanted to lie there forever, her eyes closed, and let the pain continue to ache, but then she remembered that the end of the world was just around the corner and that if she didn't get up now and do something, then she'd die.

Slowly opening her eyes, Jenur was confused. Right in front of her face was one of the light fixtures, long and thin, that was supposed to be on the ceiling. Her first thought was that the fixture had fallen, but it didn't look like it had. The fixture was stuck inside the floor, like it had been built there, though she could not recall ever seeing that light fixture on the floor. Its light was dimmer than before, too.

Something wet and hot was running down her forehead. Jenur reached up and touched it. She raised her fingers in front of her face and discovered that it was blood, slightly shining in the glow from the light fixture. She tried to sit up, but then one of her legs burned with pain and she had to stop. She looked down at her legs and her heart failed her when she saw how her left leg was bent an an unnatural angle.

Then Jenur looked up at the ceiling and started. The table and chairs—which had been bolted the floor—hung from the ceiling. Even the white tablecloth still clung to the table itself, even though gravity ought to have taken it off.

What the hell happened? Jenur thought. *It's like the whole world was flipped upside down or something.*

Jenur heard movement nearby and looked directly ahead of her. Quro was lying near her, on the other side of the light fixture. Whereas she was lying on her belly, her father had somehow ended up with his head on the floor and his back against the wall. His legs hung over his head like overhanging tree branches, but none of his limbs seemed bent unnaturally.

Just beyond Quro lay Nimiko. Unlike Quro, Nimiko wasn't moving at all. He lay face down on the floor, like he was taking a nap. His Void metal chain was wrapped around his neck, although it didn't seem to impede his breathing. No blood, but he was clearly out for the count.

Another sound of movement and Jenur looked to her left. Malock and Hana lay on top of each other awkwardly, looking like a couple of dolls that had been tossed around. Both of them were still breathing, however, so Jenur wasn't too worried, although she did take note of Hana's left arm, which appeared to be dislocated.

Aside from the occasional movement from the others and the sounds of her own breathing, the entire ship was utterly silent. Jenur didn't hear the engine of the *Clockwork Heart*, that ever-present hum that would even invade her dreams at night; nor did she hear the familiar smokestacks as they billowed smoke and ash into the air. The steam pipes were quiet, as if someone had shut them off.

The pain in her leg made her gasp, but she didn't focus on it too much. She had learned that the best way to avoid giving an injury too much power is to ignore it, at least until you could find someone to give it the medical attention it deserved. Right now, she just needed to find out what had happened and if the others were awake.

She then realized that Rint was nowhere to be seen. She remembered that they had taken his unconscious body up to his room and left it there while they went to see the army of gods that the Mechanical Goddess had told them about. Was he still okay? Was he in any condition to come over and help them? Was he even still alive?

Then it all came back to her like a deluge of ice-cold water.

A wave smashed into the Clockwork Heart, Jenur thought. *Then we were all sent flying out of our seats and then ... what?*

The silence of the ship made Jenur feel like a trapped animal. She crawled over to Quro—slowly, because her twisted leg still hurt like hell—and tapped him on the shoulder.

"Dad?" she said, speaking in a whisper for reasons she could not entirely be sure of. "Are you awake?"

Quro's eyes flickered open. For a moment, he just stared blankly at Jenur, as if he did not recognize her face.

Then recognition dawned in his eyes and he sad, "Jenur? What happened?"

"I don't know," said Jenur. "Everyone is knocked out and my left leg is broken."

Quro leaned to the side and his body fell over with an audible *bang* that was much louder than it should have been in the stillness of the ship. He then slowly moved to an upright position, but based on the sluggishness with which he moved, he clearly was in pain.

"Ow," said Quro, rubbing his back. "I think that my back took the brunt of the pain. Otherwise, I'll be okay."

"That's good," said Jenur. She looked around at the others and said, "Let's wake everyone up. Maybe one of the others know what happened."

"I'll do it," said Quro. "You just sit here and rest your leg. No sudden movements or you'll just make it worse."

Jenur nodded and just watched as Quro crawled carefully around the room. He first woke Nimiko, who took a fairly long time—at least five minutes—before he even stirred. Then he went over to Malock and Hana, first dragging Hana off Malock and then awaking the two separately.

Soon all five of them were awake. Nimiko sat up, his chain hanging off his neck, looking drowsy and confused, while Malock was rubbing his head and muttering curses under his breath. Hana had relocated her own shoulder with a *pop* that made Jenur shudder, although she had to admit that she admired the katabans' unflinching expression in the face of what surely must have been serious pain.

Swinging her relocated arm back and forth, Hana looked around at the others and said, "Is everyone all right?"

"No," said Malock. "My head feels like a cracked egg."

"Good," said Hana. "No injuries or anything?"

"My leg," said Jenur, pointing at her left leg. "Somehow it got bent weirdly."

Hana crawl over to Jenur and put her hands on Jenur's broken leg. They were cold, almost as cold as a corpse's hands, but then a warmth spread through them into Jenur's leg. Before Jenur's eyes, her leg adjusted itself until it was back to normal. Then Hana removed her hands from Jenur's leg and went back to her position by Malock.

Moving her stiff leg to make sure it worked, Jenur looked up at Hana and said, "Thanks."

"No problem," said Hana. "So, does anyone remember what happened? All I remember is getting thrown out of my seat."

"I do," said Malock. "We were trying to get past the Sleeping Beast, but then a tidal wave struck the ship. After that ... I don't know."

"How come the Mechanical Goddess hasn't talked to us yet?" said Quro, looking around the room. "And why are the chairs and table on the ceiling?"

"Can't you feel the pressure?" Nimiko said. "Feels like we're being crushed like tin cans."

Now that Nimiko mentioned it, Jenur did notice a powerful pressure exerting itself over them that she hadn't noticed before. It was not quite as powerful as it could have been, but it was impossible to ignore now. Like being inside a can that was slowly being crushed underneath a giant's foot.

Hana tapped her chin, like she was thinking hard. "None of this makes any sense. The Mechanical Goddess would have told us what was happening by now. She's *never* this silent in emergencies. Not ever."

"And what about Rint?" said Malock. "Do you think he's okay?"

"I don't know," said Hana. "I don't know ... what's ... happening
..."

Hana's voice trailed off as if someone had just lit a candle in her head. "I think I know what happened."

"Do tell," said Nimiko. "We're dying to know here."

"You won't like it," said Hana. "Just promise not to panic if I tell you, okay?"

"Sure," said Malock. "Just tell us already."

"I think ..." Hana grimaced, like she was about to deliver some bad news. "I think we're underwater. On the bottom of the ocean."

Jenur, Malock, and Quro looked at her in alarm, while Nimiko nodded and said, "Makes sense."

"Makes sense?" said Malock, staring at Nimiko in disbelief. "Tell me, God of Light, how does this make sense?"

"It explains so many strange things that I've noticed about our current situation," said Nimiko. "Here's probably what happened: While the Sleeping Beast thrashed about, it sent a gigantic tidal wave at us. Not intentionally; it probably didn't even know we were there. My sister couldn't dodge the tidal wave in time, so it hit her directly. The tidal wave knocked her beneath the waves, perhaps knocking out her engines in the process, and dragged her down below the surface until she landed on the ocean floor."

"My mistress is probably unconscious," said Hana. "Maybe even dead. I doubt any of the automatons are active."

"Dead?" said Malock. "But the gods—"

"Can't be killed except by other gods," said Hana. "Yes, I know. But the Sleeping Beast has always been theorized to be stronger than the gods. Who's to say that it couldn't kill a god, if it wanted to? That's why the gods have always feared it."

"Let me get this straight," said Quro. "We are trapped hundreds of feet below the surface in the body of an unconscious goddess. How come we haven't drowned yet?"

"Easy," said Hana. "The *Clockwork Heart* must have been dragged underwater quickly. With the hatch door closed, an air bubble must have been caught in this room and it's lasted for as long as it has because we were unconscious for most of the time and therefore did not breathe as much air as we normally do."

"Uh oh," said Malock, his face turning pale. "Doesn't that mean that every time we talk, we use up more air?"

"Exactly," said Hana, nodding. "Since we don't know how much air we have left, it would be wise for us to conserve as much as we can."

Panic began to rise in Jenur's chest, but she tried to ignore it and keep calm. "Do you know how long have we been out?"

"No idea," said Hana. "I doubt it's been more than a couple of hours, if even that, considering we haven't drowned yet."

"This situation is not quite as grim as it appears," Nimiko chimed in. "As a god, I do not require air to breathe. Nor does Hana, who as a katabans can go without air if necessary. And Quro here is an aquarian, making him amphibious, so if necessary, he could swim back to the surface without fear of drowning."

"Which pretty much means that Malock and I are the only two

who will die for sure," said Jenur. "Thanks for the confirmation." She looked at Malock and said, "How do you think we're gonna die? Drown when the water breaks through the hatch? Or run out of air?"

"Neither, I hope," said Malock. He seemed remarkably calm about all of this. "We'll find a way to make sure everyone survives."

"I doubt it," said Nimiko. "The ship has likely been flipped completely upside down. That means that the only exits are blocked by tons of sand. And as far as I know, there are no exits through the bottom of the ship."

"Even if there were other exits, we'd still have to drag you and Jenur out ourselves," Hana pointed out. "Considering we're hundreds of feet underwater, that means you two would have to hold your breaths long enough for us to reach the surface. *And* avoid getting crushed by the pressure."

"You two are just a barrel of sunshine and rainbows, aren't you?" said Jenur, glaring at both of them.

"We're just being realistic," said Nimiko. "I see no way for all of us to make it out of here alive. Me, Hana, and Quro, yes. But you and Malock?"

"Can't forget Rint," said Malock. He looked toward the door that led out of the room. "He's probably still in his room."

Hana laughed bitterly. "You think that he's even still alive? He's so old and frail, I bet he was killed the minute that the tidal wave hit the ship."

"You don't know that," said Jenur. "Destanians are a lot tougher than they look."

Hana shrugged. "Does it matter? Even if Rint, by some miracle of miracles, is still alive, he can't escape. He's probably lying, with broken bones, on the ceiling of his room, unable to reach his door, which is probably above his head. If he's not dead, then he's probably dying even as we speak."

At that, Jenur tried to stand up, though it was difficult thanks to her stiff leg. "Then we've got to go save him."

"Are you for real?" said Hana. "Weren't you just listening to what I said? Why do you even care about saving him, anyway? I always thought you hated the old coot."

Jenur glared at Hana, glared at her so hard that for the first time in Jenur's memory, Hana actually looked a little apprehensive, maybe even afraid, of her. "Because I couldn't save Kinker when he died. I made a promise to myself to save Rint. So long as Rint's life is in danger, then that promise remains unfulfilled. And until I know he's dead, I can't just sit around and worry only about myself."

The others were looking at her with surprise. Of course they would. She had never told any of them about her promise. Mostly because she felt that it was a promise only she needed to know about. Only Quro seemed unsurprised at her revelation, which made sense, seeing as she had made similar proclamations to him before, when she had been a member of the Dark Tigers. He had most likely figured it out on his own.

"And I'll save Rint myself, alone if I have to," said Jenur. "I won't ask any of you to go with me."

Malock held out a hand. "But Jen, what if the sinking caused a hole in the bottom of the ship? The hallways might be flooded with water and Rint might be dead."

"Quro, she's your daughter, is she not?" said Nimiko, looking at him. "Tell her to stay put. For all of our sakes."

Quro simply sat there, his expression revealing that he was deep in thought. Jenur had seen him act like this before. It was the expression that had earned him the nickname of Thinker from his fellow Dark Tigers, as fitting a nickname as any.

Then Quro looked up and said, "Jenur can do what she wants. I'd rather she stay here, but in all of my years knowing her, I've never been able to stop her from doing something that she wants to do. Nor would I try."

Jenur smiled. "Thanks, Dad."

But Quro was still speaking. "Having said that, we really don't know what conditions outside of this room are. We have no idea if the rest of the ship is flooded or not. Therefore, it may not be entirely wise for her to go and look for Rint, at least until we find out more about the ship's current situation."

"None of the doors look dented," Malock observed, gesturing at the doors on both ends of the room. "If the ship is upside down, then that means it's impossible for any water to enter, at least right now."

"You were the one who said that there could be a hole in the hull," said Hana. "You know what I think we need to do? We need to awaken the Mechanical Goddess."

Nimiko looked down at the ceiling underneath his legs, a frown on his face. "I barely sense her life force. I think she's in some kind of coma. It might not be safe to awaken her."

"If we awaken her, then we can ask her to help us," said Hana. "She'll know what to do. She has contingencies for every situation."

Jenur raised an eyebrow. "Including getting dragged underwater to the bottom of the sea?"

"Probably," said Hana. "Even more importantly, only the Mechanical Goddess has access to the automatons. If we can awake her, she can get the automatons to work on digging her out of the sand. They might even be able to push the ship up to the surface."

"It's our best shot," said Nimiko. "Even I must admit that. The only question is, how do we awaken her?"

"Use your light powers," Malock suggested. "Send a spark of light energy through the light fixtures. It might go to wherever the power source of the ship is, which might be just enough to awaken the Mechanical Goddess."

Nimiko tugged at his collar, an uncertain look on his face. "I've never done something like that before. There's no guarantee it will work."

"It's either that or we wait until the pressure crushes us and we all drown," said Hana. "Your choice."

"Fine," said Nimiko. "I will try as Malock suggested. But don't expect it to work."

So Nimiko crawled over to the nearest light fixture and placed one hand on top of it. He ran his hand up and down the thin fixture before suddenly tightening his grip on it somewhere around the middle.

Then he closed his eyes and a bright light—shining so brightly that it illuminated the entire room like the rays of the sun—crawled down his arm down into the light fixture. The light disappeared into the fixture and the room's lighting returned to normal.

Looking exhausted, Nimiko sat back and sighed. "There. It should go through her system until it reaches the ship's power source. Not sure how long that will take, but it shouldn't take any longer than a few minutes at most."

"Just a few minutes?" said Malock. "That's not too bad. We can last for a few more minutes, I should think. But in silence. We need to conserve air."

So they sat there for a few minutes in total silence. As time passed and there was still no communication from the Mechanical Goddess, Jenur thought about Rint. Even if the Mechanical Goddess awoke, would it be in time to save Rint?

Then, without waiting, the light fixture flickered slightly. Jenur almost dismissed it as the electricity acting up, but the light kept flickering regularly, in a consistent pattern. One flick, followed by two more flicks in rapid succession.

She wasn't the only one who noticed. Nimiko and Hana were staring at the light fixture as though they were reading a book.

"What're you two looking at?" said Malock, looking between the two of them in annoyance. "So the light is flickering. What does that —"

"It's the Mechanical Goddess," said Nimiko. "She's awake."

"Just barely," said Hana. "Look at that light. And she's speaking very confusedly. Don't think she really knows what's going on."

Malock leaned forward, looking at the light, which still flickered. "Who cares? As long as she's awake, everything should be just fine, right?"

Then the fixture went out, briefly plunging the room into

darkness before Nimiko's natural glow illuminated the place.

"She fell back unconscious," said Hana, her voice full of disappointment. "Oh joy."

Malock slammed his fist against the wall. "Nimiko, can you wake her up again?"

"It would be incredibly risky," said Nimiko. "Based on what little she said, she's in no condition at all to move right now. Her motors are out, the engine is damaged and could explode if she's not careful, and most of the automatons are in pieces or too damaged to operate correctly."

"So we're back at square one," said Jenur. She lowered her face into her hands. "Great. Just great."

"Then ... how do we get out of here alive?" said Malock with a gulp.

No one answered that question, perhaps because everyone knew what the answer was and no one wanted to make it real by saying it aloud.

Chapter Fourteen

AFTER DROPPING OFF AQUR and Ower just outside of Port Blasan, Skimif and Kasrath began to make their way south.

They were not actually going to fly all the way there. Although Kasrath was a swift flier and could move at astonishing speeds, it would have taken them days, perhaps even a whole week, to reach World's End at their current speed. That would not have bothered Skimif if they had had a week to spare, but he sensed that the Powers were just around the corner and that if he wanted to meet them before they started destroying the world, he had to get there much faster.

Thankfully, Kasrath carried a secret travel method in its memories that it had initially used to get to Carnag. Using his connection with Kasrath, Skimif learned that the dragon had originally emerged from the Void, but rather than fly from the southern seas to the Northern Isles, it had traveled via something called 'the ethereal.' Exactly what that was, Kasrath's memories were not clear, but Skimif decided that if it could use the ethereal to travel from the southern seas to the Northern Isles in less than a day, then surely the reverse was possible.

So, once they were so high up in the sky that they skirted the edges of the clouds, Skimif and Kasrath dove into the ethereal. 'Dove' was the best word Skimif could use to describe the sensation of entering the ethereal, although in reality, one moment he was in the blue skies above Carnag and the next he found himself in a strange black, starry sky that seemed to stretch on forever.

While Kasrath shot forward through the air at an astonishing speed, Skimif took the time to look at where they had ended up. Aside from the thousands of stars that shone in the darkness above, below them was what appeared to be a shining, white road, paved with a type of stone that Skimif had never seen before in his life. Upon the road traveled a bunch of slightly transparent, shimmery figures, many of whom looked up in surprise as Kasrath zoomed by. All of them were heading in the direction that he and Kasrath were coming from, like a nation of refugees fleeing war.

Occasionally, they would pass over what appeared to be shining white islands—made of the same stone as the paved roads—upon which the weary travelers below rested. Sometimes they would fly close enough that Skimif would try to get a closer glimpse of the spirits, but they always fled whenever Kasrath flew by, as if afraid they would killed.

Their time in the ethereal lasted only for a brief period, however, and soon Skimif and Kasrath 'fell' out of it and back into the open blue skies of Martir. It took Skimif's eyes a moment to get used to the sudden change in lighting, but when they did, he saw a scene below that he had never expected to see.

A hulking monster—at least as big as an island, maybe even bigger

—was rampaging through the waters around World's End. Every stomp of its massive feet sent gigantic tidal waves in every direction, while its roar was so loud that it might as well have been a sonic boom. Bright lights flashed around it, like a group of beings was attacking it, but whoever they were, they were little more than minor annoyances to the beast, which growled and thrashed about as it tried to knock them out of the air. Furthermore, he saw hundreds of ships around it, firing cannonballs and other projectiles at it, with hundreds more smashed into pieces around its feet.

What in the names of the Powers is that thing? Skimif thought as he and Kasrath flew in a circle overhead. *Have the Powers already started their destruction of the world?*

Kasrath growled. He could sense that Kasrath had shot down that idea. No; whatever this monster was, it had nothing to do with the Powers. It was a native creature of Martir, though that didn't explain where it had come from or who was fighting it.

Seeing as Skimif was not interested in getting involved in a conflict that he wasn't sure he could win (he was actually more afraid of that monster than he had been of Grinf), he urged Kasrath on toward an island in the distance. It had to be World's End because just beyond it was a massive, black, starless wall that signaled the end of Martir and the beginning of the Void.

As they flew, Skimif tried to think of the best arguments he could use to persuade the Powers to spare his Heathens. The only problem was that he didn't know the Powers well enough to know what kind of arguments worked best against them, and based on Kasrath's thoughts, Kasrath knew as much about negotiating as he did. He would have to come up with something to say, however, because the Powers were not big fans of negotiation.

In just a few minutes, Skimif and Kasrath reached World's End's shores and soon passed the city's walls. Skimif looked down as they flew, temporarily distracted from his own thoughts. Though they flew by fast, it was obvious that the Throne of the Gods had been abandoned by its original inhabitants, whoever they were. Not a single soul could be seen in the streets and most of the buildings—massive and mountain-like as they were—looked abandoned now. In some ways, World's End reminded Skimif of the abandoned aquarian city known as the City of Ghosts, a place he had only visited once as a child but had vowed to never return to ever again.

Thus, he was surprised when a couple dozen vines leaped out of the windows of a nearby building and constricted around Skimif and Kasrath. Before either of them could act, they were pulled into the side of the building, smashing through the windows and landing on top of a desk, which exploded into pieces when they fell on it. Dazed from the attack, Skimif shook his head and tried to get up, only to discover that the vines had wrapped his arms and legs together, as well as tying him securely to Kasrath's back. Additionally, Kasrath's wings had been tied down, too, along with its legs, making it impossible for it to do much more than wriggle and growl, although even that movement was limited by the sheer amount of vines holding him down.

"Look what we have here," said a voice behind Skimif. "A tasty mortal. And a tasty flying lizard dragon thing that I don't know the name of. The world may be about to end, but that doesn't mean I can't enjoy a good meal before it's lights out."

Skimif twisted his head as much as he could to see who had spoken. A small, stout green human stood on top of a large plant, his red eyes glowing through the curtain of grass that made up his hair.

"Who are you?" said Skimif as he struggled to break free of the vines, though it was a useless effort, as the vines were thick and tied securely around his body. Also, tiny thorns running along the vines' surface cut into his skin.

"Call me the Loner God," said the man as he reached out with one stubby hand. "But right now, I'm more like the Hungry God."

"You can't eat me," said Skimif. "I'm the herald of the Powers, chosen by them to prepare the world for its destruction at their hands."

"Do you think I give a damn?" said the Loner God. "I know all that. Doesn't mean I have to let you go free."

"But the Powers will be angry if they find out what you're doing," said Skimif.

"Again, I don't care," said the Loner God. "The world is already falling apart all around us. The gods are scattered and afraid, the Sleeping Beast has arisen and will sooner or later make its way here— by which time I will be long gone—and the Powers will be here any minute. About the only good thing that has happened so far is that that idiot mortal Malock and his friends are dead."

Skimif stopped struggling for a moment. "Malock and the others ... they're dead?"

"Oh, not my idiotic older brother and equally idiotic sister," said the Loner God, shaking his head. "They're at the bottom of the sea.

But yes, the mortals died. Their ship was dragged to the bottom of the ocean a few hours ago and they haven't been seen since. I imagine the mortals on board drowned, while my brother and sister are just stuck."

"No way," said Skimif. "If you haven't found a body—"

"I don't need to see a body to know if someone is dead," said the Loner God. "But who cares? I'm still going to eat you either way. I'd suggest closing your eyes, though I suppose that would be useless as those are the first things I intend to eat."

As the Loner God's plant platform moved toward him, Skimif could not believe the Loner God's words. Malock and the others ... dead? It could not be so. Yet if the Loner God's story was true, then there was no way they could have survived being dragged down to the bottom of the ocean inside a massive metal ship. Even if Skimif went down there right now, he would probably only find their corpses.

Anger flooded Skimif's veins just then. He didn't know where it came from all of a sudden, but he didn't question it. Something about hearing that Malock and the others were dead gave him strength unlike any he had ever known before.

He flexed his muscles and the vines snapped as easily as string. The Loner God halted in midair, his eyes widening in shock as Skimif and Kasrath stood up, though they could not stand up very high due to the ceiling above their heads.

"How did you do that?" said the Loner God, disbelief coloring his voice. Then he shook his head. "Doesn't matter. I'll kill you anyway."

The Loner God thrust a hand forward and a dozen more vines shot from underneath the pad he stood on. The barbs on these vines looked even sharper than the barbs on the previous ones, but Skimif wasn't afraid of them.

He raised a hand and the vines stopped just inches from Kasrath's face.

"No way," said the Loner God. "How did you do that? I'm the God of the Jungle. These plants obey my orders. Not yours."

"I'm not sure," said Skimif, his hand never wavering. "All I know is that the Powers granted me many abilities even I am not aware of yet. Including ones that you will likely never know."

Skimif flicked his wrist and the vines immediately twisted around and flew at the Loner God. The Loner God tried to move, but the vines stabbed straight through his body, piercing his muddy skin and appearing on the other side of his body. The Loner God opened his mouth, perhaps to hurl a curse at Skimif, but then Skimif pulled his hand back and the vines wrapped themselves around the Loner God's mouth and body, twirling around and around until he was entirely cocooned in the vines.

The cocooned god wriggled inside the vines, but then Skimif closed his fist and the vines constricted. The cocoon ceased struggling immediately and gold blood seeped through the cracks. Then the pad beneath it fell out from underneath the Loner God's feet and the cocoon fell to the floor with a mild *thump*. It twitched every now and then, but it was obvious that the Loner God wasn't going anywhere any time soon.

Skimif looked down at his hand in amazement. He had been telling the truth when he said he didn't know how he could do that. He suspected that the Powers must have given him the power to override a god's control over their own domain, probably to give Skimif an edge over any gods who tried to stop him from destroying the world.

With the Loner God dealt with, Skimif urged Kasrath toward the smashed open window behind them. Though Kasrath was still slightly dazed from being dragged through the window, it had nonetheless recovered enough by now to run toward the window and leap out. Its windows extended with a *snap* and they were once again soaring toward the Void.

Which they would have passed straight through ... had not the Powers emerged from it at that moment.

Chapter Fifteen

THE SILENCE IN THE upside down dining room in the sunken *Clockwork Heart* was stifling. Not a single person in the room said even one word, although all of them probably had a lot to say. Conserving air was the highest priority for everyone at the moment, mostly for the sake of Malock, Jenur, and Quro. None of them knew how much air was left, so until they could find a way to escape, they had to speak as little as possible.

Unless Malock was mistaken, he thought he could feel the air being used up even as he sat there next to Hana. His face continued to burn, but for once he didn't reach up and rub it, as he usually did whenever he felt it. Breathing was becoming a feat in itself and he could not afford to be distracted from this precious task for too long, although his pessimistic side was telling him that it didn't matter what he did because, either way, he would die.

Death might not be so bad, Malock thought. *Sure, my parents will miss me, and probably the rest of the Carnagians, too. But I'll finally be reunited with Vashnas. And with Raya, too, even. I won't even die alone.*

He thought that while looking at Jenur. Like him, she seemed to be having increasing trouble with breathing. Quro didn't look much better, but Malock figured that if they had to, they could get him out into the water, where he would recover. And of course, Nimiko and Hana would be all right no matter what happened.

Well, they'll be all right until the Powers come and destroy everything, of course, Malock thought. *Then they, too, will die.*

His air-deprived mind wandered to Skimif and the Brotherhood. He wondered how Skimif was doing. Had he made any progress in converting people to Heathenism? Had the gods finally decided to do something about the Brotherhood? Had Skimif told everyone about the inevitable end of the world?

Not like any of it really matters, Malock thought. *We've lost. The Powers will come and destroy everything they created. It won't matter whether we mortals worship or don't worship the gods because there will be no mortals to worship any gods. Nor will there be any gods to worship.*

With death looming before him, Malock oddly did not regret much in his life. Sure, he'd made a lot of mistakes—just looking at Jenur reminded him of the time he'd thought her a spy and tried to hand her over to a servant of the gods to be punished for her imaginary crimes—but he realized that he'd lived more or less the way he had wanted to. That knowledge made death seem a little less scary, but only a little.

Just as Malock wondered what death, exactly, would feel like, Nimiko raised his head. He looked around the room, as if he had heard something and was looking for the source of the noise. Malock didn't even bother to ask what he had heard, partly because it would waste more precious air, partly because he did not care. Nimiko had probably just heard some sea creature scraping against the outside hull, or maybe it was the stomping of the Sleeping Beast causing tremors in the ground. Either way, it was not like knowing the sound's source would help them survive.

Then Rint stepped through the walls and said, "I hope I am not too late."

That caused everyone's heads to turn and look at him. Jenur's mouth fell open, Quro wore a mild look of surprise on his face, Hana didn't seem to quite believe her eyes, while Nimiko simply looked like he had expected this to happen. Malock himself had a hard time maintaining an expression of surprise, mostly because the lack of air was getting to him.

"What?" said Jenur. Her voice was brittle, like she was on her last legs. "Rint, how—"

"Oh, I'm not actually the mortal you call Rint," said Rint, his voice vaguely familiar. He patted his chest and said, "This is his body, which I have commandeered for this purpose, but I am not actually him."

"Then ... who are ... you?" said Malock. His own voice didn't sound much better than Jenur's.

Rint's eyes started to glow the same shade of blue as the lights back on Bleak Rock. "You don't recognize me? It is I, the Mysterious One."

"The Mysterious One?" said Nimiko. "How did you find us?"

The Mysterious One shrugged. "It was an accident, more or less. I was at World's End, about to go through the Void to escape the coming apocalypse, when I sensed that your ship had sunk. I debated whether to save you or not, but I decided that, although the end is just around the corner, it would not inconvenience me much to rescue all of you."

"But ... how?" said Malock. "The ship is upside down on the bottom of the ocean."

The Mysterious One nodded. "Not much of a problem. I found some willing help; as a matter of fact, the ship is already heading up to the surface even as we speak."

Malock was about to say that he disagreed, but then Nimiko said, "I thought I felt the ship move, but I wasn't sure."

"It won't be long now before we reach the surface," said the Mysterious One. "After that, you will all be safe. Or as safe as anyone can be in the twilight of the apocalypse, anyway."

"Rint," said Jenur. "Is he—?"

The Mysterious One patted his chest again. "The old mortal was near death when I came down here to check up on you. My possession of his body certainly hasn't helped matters, but he might survive, if that's what you're asking. It all depends on whether we can heal him or not before he breathes his last."

"I cannot believe it," said Quro. Like Malock and Jenur, his voice was weak, though now it was full of joy. "How can we ever repay you for your help?"

"By convincing the Powers to spare this world," said the Mysterious One. "I do not believe ants can reason with a giant, but I've seen your tenacity and belief in your own self. It is not my role to keep you from saving the world."

Before Malock could thank the Mysterious One, the room began to tilt. Startled, Malock and Hana rolled onto the wall behind them as the ship's position changed, while Nimiko, Jenur, and Quro had to crawl forward to avoid rolling toward them. Only the Mysterious One retained his original position, though he eventually moved to be on the same level as everyone else.

Then a loud creaking noise, followed by a shuddering *boom*, caused everyone to start, save for the Mysterious One, who simply smiled.

"Looks like we've reached the surface," said the Mysterious One. "That was faster than I expected. I will lead you out. There's not much time left."

When Malock and the others emerged from the *Clockwork Heart*, they discovered that the ship had been deposited on its side on the beaches of World's End. The ship looked absolutely terrible. Both of the smokestacks had been snapped off, with muddy sand and water filling the spots where they had once stood. The top deck had been smashed almost entirely, hanging on by only a tiny thread of metal, while the lower deck was covered in the muck that lay on the ocean floor. It looked less like the imposing flagship and body of a goddess and more like a forgotten wreck.

Standing behind the ship, leaning against its hull, was a being Malock had never thought he'd see again: Messenger-and-Punisher. The giant's body continued to leak that same foul-smelling ooze from before, but now its massive form was covered with dripping wet seaweed. Through the black thunder cloud around its face, its red eyes gleamed like rubies.

"You have done your job, Messenger-and-Punisher," said the Mysterious One, actually giving the servant of the gods a thumbs up. "You are now dismissed."

Looking grateful, Messenger-and-Punisher pushed itself off the hull of the *Clockwork Heart* and walked away toward the Throne of the Gods. He didn't even say anything, though perhaps that was intentional, as he walked at a fast pace. It took Malock a moment to realize that Messenger-and-Punisher must have known about the end of the world, which explained why he was running away, though where he could run to, Malock didn't know.

Nor did Malock particularly care. At the moment, he was breathing in as much fresh air as he could. He had forgotten how good air tasted. All he wanted to do was keep breathing in as much air as he could. Jenur, too, seemed to enjoy the air as much as he did, but she seemed to get enough air because she soon stopped and then turned to look at the Mysterious One.

"Rint," she said. "Are you going to give up his body?"

The Mysterious One bowed. "A deal is a deal. I imagine he won't be conscious when I let him go, however, so do not be surprised if he doesn't awake immediately."

Nimiko stepped forward at that moment. "Before you leave, Mysterious One, I just wanted to thank you for your help. I've never known you before this, but I am now convinced of your godhood. I will be sure to tell the others about your deeds and to get you a statue and throne in the Temple of the Gods, should we succeed in our mission."

The Mysterious One flashed Nimiko a chilling smile. "When did I ever say I was a god?"

Then Rint's eyes ceased glowing and he collapsed onto the sand, but not before Jenur rushed forward and caught him. She slowly lowered his body to the sand and then put her hand on his chest.

"He's still breathing," Jenur said, looking up at the others. "But he's unconscious, just like the Mysterious One said he would be."

Malock gave a sigh of relief. "That's good."

Quro nodded in agreement and then looked out over the sea. "Uh oh."

"What?" said Malock, following Quro's gaze. When he saw what Quro was looking at, all he could say was, "Uh oh."

Not far from the shore—and drawing closer every minute—was the Sleeping Beast. Though it did not have a human face, it wore a clear expression of annoyance and tiredness. Its eyes were fixated on the skyscrapers of the Throne of the Gods. So intent on its goal was it that it outright ignored the various gods and goddesses zooming around it, attacking its rough skin with bursts of light and energy that resembled flickering fireflies from Malock's current position.

"That thing isn't coming this way, right?" said Malock, looking at the others nervously. "It's just a trick of the eyes, isn't it?"

Nimiko shook his head. "No. The Sleeping Beast is heading this way, likely to destroy World's End. It must be smarter than it looks. It somehow must have figured out that this is the gods' home and that destroying it would deal a serious blow to us."

"But it's just a city," said Jenur. "Isn't it? Sure, its destruction would be pretty serious, but—"

"You don't quite understand," said Nimiko. "When the Powers ended the Godly War and divided the gods into northern and southern, they tied our essence to this island. It was their way of keeping us from becoming too separate. By giving us a common ground on which to meet and discuss important matters, it was supposed to help us get over the dislike and distrust of each other that we had developed during the War."

"Did it work?" Quro asked.

"Obviously not," said Nimiko. "But it is, most likely, why the Powers will destroy World's End before any other island. It will get rid of us, thus making it easier for the Powers to destroy everything else."

"Then we have no time to lose," said Malock. His head was still slightly airy, but he felt good enough to walk now. "We should find another ship that we can use to get to the Void. And then—"

A sudden change in the atmosphere of the world made Malock stop talking. He looked at the others. It was obvious that all of them felt it. The feeling was difficult to describe, as Malock had never felt anything quite like it before, but when he gave it some thought, he realized that it felt like the world was dying.

Then a massive tendril made of light hurled over the tops of the skyscrapers of World's End and struck the Sleeping Beast. The Sleeping Beast had time only to give one last roar of surprise before the light totally evaporated it in an instant, leaving only a slightly bluish cloud of vapor where the once mighty beast had once stood.

"What was that?" said Jenur, looking up in the direction that the tendril had come from. "Did one of the gods do that?"

Nimiko fell to his knees as he looked up at the skyscrapers. He looked utterly defeated.

"That, Jenur, had nothing to do with the gods," said Nimiko. "That was the Powers. They are here. We have lost."

Chapter Sixteen

SKIMIF HAD ALWAYS KNOWN that the Powers were alien creatures, their power and understanding beyond even that of the gods. Few legends existed about the Powers among mortals, mostly due to how unknown they were to most mortals. Skimif did remember one tale—a scary story his grandfather had told him once as punishment for some offense Skimif had committed when he was little but which he could not recall—about an aquarian who tried to find the Powers, but ended up completely losing his sanity and killing himself and his family once he actually found out what the Powers were.

Until today, Skimif had not believed that a very believable reaction to seeing the Powers. After all, the Powers had created Martir and everything within it. Surely they must be understandable to mortals, shouldn't they?

But now that Skimif lay eyes on the Powers' true form for himself, all he wanted to do was run. Run and hide anywhere. He would have been far gladder to fight all of the gods of Martir, with his legs broken and one of his arms ripped off, than gaze upon the

Powers.

Understanding the Powers' appearance was a feat in itself. He saw tendrils made of light; strange glowing orbs that flashed different colors at an unpredictable and irregular rate; black, slimy tongues that darted in and out of what might have been mouths; with what appeared to be teeth made of flame instead of bone; and shapeless heads that resembled globs of mud; and bodies made of shining crystal. He could not think of any creature in Martir that came even close to resembling the Powers, making him wonder at first if these creatures were not the Powers at all but were in fact some strange monsters from beyond the Void that had come in their place.

But as he and Kasrath flew in their view, Skimif felt something enter his mind, a presence he had felt twice before. The first was when he received his first vision from the Powers so many months ago; the second was a week ago, when he first learned of the Powers' ultimate plan to destroy everything. Until now, of course, he had never actually seen them, which was why he found it hard to believe what he was looking at.

Even stranger, they did not walk or swim through the sea. They floated, like clouds, through the air with about as much effort put into it as Skimif put into walking. It was like they were being pushed along by a gust of wind, which made them look even weirder than normal.

The most horrific part about them, however, was not their appearance or the eerie, otherworldly presence they gave off. It was how every time their tendrils touched the surface of the ocean below, the water would completely evaporate. That particular action was soon topped, however, when one of the Powers extended its tendril over World's End to attack something on the other side of the island, though what it was reaching for, Skimif didn't know. They soon retracted the tendril, however, like they had accomplished their goal.

While Skimif was apprehensive, Kasrath seemed perfectly at ease in their presence. In fact, it was Kasrath who urged Skimif to move closer to the Powers, as if it felt comforted by their appearance, though Skimif reined in his steed in order to keep their distance.

From what Skimif could understand—not see, but understand, as he had a feeling that his eyes were not telling him the whole story about the Powers' appearance—there were six of the Powers, all of them identical in appearance. They had no distinguishing characteristics, no way of telling one apart from the other. They even moved as one, like a collective hive mind. It was unnerving to watch their tendrils wave through the air, for they moved erratically and unnaturally, as if reality itself could not properly contain them.

Nonetheless, Skimif could not simply fly there and stare at them. The Powers, although they moved at a leisurely pace, were not stopping. Their first target was World's End, which would turn to rubble the minute they touched its shores. And while Skimif was no fan of the gods, he didn't want the Powers destroying anything just yet, not until he could convince them to spare his fellow Heathens at least.

So Skimif urged Kasrath to fly directly into the Powers' path. This Kasrath did happily and without complaint, soaring down into the Powers' path before they could get very far. Skimif could feel the Powers' eyes following them as he and Kasrath got before them, and despite knowing that they probably wouldn't destroy him, he still felt nervous and did not look them directly in their faces.

As Kasrath flapped its wings up and down to stay airborne, Skimif stood up on his steed's back. The collective eyes of the Powers fell upon him, a powerful gaze that felt like the universe itself staring down at him. He could sense that the Powers were not to be trifled with, a fact he had always known but had never truly understood until now.

"Welcome, Great Powers that Be," said Skimif. "Do you recognize me? I am Skimif of Tunya, the aquarian you chose to be your herald. I have not done my job quite as well as I should have, but rest assured that I will return to my destruction of the world and the gods as soon as I make one request of you."

The Powers said nothing; in fact, now that Skimif thought about it, he wondered if the Powers actually could speak Divina or Aqua or any other Martirian language at all. They had only ever communicated with him via dreams and visions, after all. Was it possible that the creators of the whole world had never mastered verbal language? It was a strange thought.

Then one of the Powers raised a tendril and gestured at him, a seemingly harmless move. Then Skimif felt a sharp stab of pain in his head that almost caused him to fall off Kasrath, but his steed maneuvered to help steady him. Skimif looked up at the Powers again, rubbing the back of his head as he did so.

"What ... what was that for?" said Skimif.

Unless his eyes were mistaken, the same Power that had gestured at him looked supremely irritated. The others' expressions changed to reflect the irritation of that one, although it took him a moment to understand that at first, seeing as their faces were not easy to read.

"Am I misunderstanding your intent?" said Skimif. "What are you trying to tell me?"

This time, the Powers didn't even move and Skimif still felt a sharp stab of pain in his head, far worse than the one before. He forced himself to sit down on Kasrath's constantly rising and falling form to avoid falling off into the ocean below. It was like someone had tried to smash in his head with a sledge hammer.

"I don't understand," said Skimif. "Are you telling me to leave?"

Then Skimif heard a voice—no, six voices, all speaking as one—in his head: *You are not very bright.*

That one sentence seemed to fill Skimif's entire mind. For a moment, he forgot all else except guilt, guilt at unnecessarily delaying his masters, who were supremely displeased with his getting in their way. He sensed they could go around him, if they wished, but that at the moment they were more interested in showing him the consequences of his actions than in doing what they had come to do.

"My masters, I understand your impatience," said Skimif. He had to say each word carefully, mostly because his head still hurt. "But it's just one request. Could you not take even five minutes to listen and consider it?"

The Powers' tendrils curled around their bodies, but this time, Skimif felt no impatience or annoyance from them. He took that as a cue to go ahead and ask.

"Although I understand that you wish to destroy your entire creation, I wish for you to spare the lives of a handful of mortals," said

Skimif. "These mortals are my friends and stood by me in good times and bad, well before you ever chose me to be your herald. I do not think it would be right if they were to be destroyed alongside everything else. They deserve to live."

For a long moment, the Powers just stared at Skimif. They probably understood his request, but something about their blank stares made Skimif feel anxious. He didn't know what they were thinking or feeling. They might have been internally debating with one another about what they should do or say to him. It didn't seem like a terribly complicated request to him, but it was obvious that they had not expected him to ask them of it.

Then a thousand different thoughts entered Skimif's head at once, coming in rapid fire one after the other, like an archer firing arrows at a wall.

Why? Who are these mortals? Where did you get this idea? Why do you value their lives? You will get so much better soon. Why even ask? Their lives will be replaceable. Your duty is to destroy the world, not save it. All must go. Everything is imperfect. Everything is flawed beyond repair. Not even one part of it can be allowed to survive. Except you. You and only you may live. All else must die. All else must die to make way for the New World. The New World will be better than the Old World. You will see it and you will agree. Our best work yet. If you will not do as we say then we must put you away.

Putting his hand on his head, Skimif said, "Wait, wait, hold on a moment. What New World? What do you mean, 'must put me away'? What are you talking about?"

But the Powers' thousand thoughts had ceased streaming into his head. They seemed to think they had answered enough of his questions, for one of their tendrils rose up and wrapped itself around him and Kasrath. He had expected to be turned to vapor, but to his surprise, the tendril only felt like a soft, warm glove. The Powers then carefully moved Skimif and Kasrath over their heads, bringing them closer and closer to the Void.

"Hey, wait," said Skimif as he struggled to break free, but it was no use. "Let go of me. I don't want to go into the Void. I want to know if you will spare my friends."

The Powers said nothing to him and their grip on him and Kasrath did not lessen. The two of them drew closer and closer to the darkness of the Void, a darkness that Skimif didn't want to go beyond at all. At least, not until he could convince the Powers to spare his friends.

Then, without warning, something small but blindingly bright flew up from the shores of World's End and struck the tendril holding Skimif and Kasrath. The Powers let go of Skimif, though more out of shock than pain, causing Skimif to spur Kasrath to fly away.

With a screech, Kasrath flew up high above the Powers. The Powers tried to catch him, but Kasrath expertly dodged their tendrils. Kasrath then banked to the left and soared down to World's End as more tendrils grabbed for him, but Kasrath moved too fast for them to catch up. Skimif looked over his shoulder at the Powers as they retracted their tendrils and began slowly making their way across the open waters. Skimif realized that he and Kasrath would make it to World's End before the Powers, but they would likely only get there first by mere minutes.

He turned his attention back to World's End. He knew he couldn't beat the Powers; in fact, he knew that nothing in Martir could beat the Powers. But he was curious to know who had saved him anyway, because he couldn't think of anyone who would dare to attack the Powers.

Attacking the Powers is a suicidal move, Skimif thought. *Only a great idiot or someone who really wants to die would dare to even try it.*

As Skimif drew closer to World's End's back shores, he saw five beings standing on the sands. At first, he didn't know who they were, but the closer he got, the clearer their forms became, and when he recognized them, he at first thought that his eyes were acting up again. There was no way that that man with the burned face could be Malock, but he could never mistake that face for anyone else's. He didn't recognize any of the others, but he figured they must have been Malock's friends and at least one of them had to be Nimiko, the God of Light.

When he and Kasrath flew over those five, they looked up at him in surprise. He urged Kasrath to land on the beach, a difficult thing to do because Kasrath wanted to keep flying from the Powers now, despite its earlier desire to be with them. Still, Kasrath listened to his urgings and it soon landed lightly on the sand, near a grove of trees that grew near the city's walls.

As Skimif climbed off Kasrath, Malock and the others ran to meet him.

"Skimif?" said Malock, stopping several dozen feet away from Kasrath. "Is that you? What are you doing here? And where did you get the dragon?"

"Better question is, how are you still alive?" said Skimif, looking at Malock and the others. "The Loner God told me you were dead."

One of Malock's friends—a young human woman with short dark hair—laughed. "Yeah, I'm sure he would have liked it if we had died."

"We nearly did," said another of Malock's companions, an older male aquarian wearing dark robes. "But thanks to a miracle, we survived and made it here just in time to stop the Powers."

"Or *try* to stop them, at any rate," said a short, older man, whose constant glow told Skimif that he had to be Nimiko. "That was my light I hurled at them, by the way. The only reason I did that was because Malock thought he recognized you and convinced me to do it." He looked out over the sea at the Powers, frowning. "I am pretty sure I am going to regret that very soon."

"But seriously," said Malock, glancing at Kasrath apprehensively, "how did you get here? And where did you get the dragon from?"

Seeing no use in lying, Skimif briefly recapped what had happened back on Carnag, starting with Kasrath's first appearance to his battle with Grinf. He fully expected them to run when they heard what his role was, but to his surprise, only Nimiko looked worried, perhaps because Skimif had just proven that he could take on a god in a fight.

When Skimif finished his tale by telling them what the Powers had said to him, Malock said, "A New World? What does that mean?"

"I have no idea," said Skimif, shaking his head. "But what were you guys up to while I was on Carnag?"

Malock gave him an extremely condensed version of the events they had experienced since leaving the Northern Isles about two weeks ago. He also introduced Skimif to Jenur, Quro, and Hanarova, so Skimif now knew who everyone was. There was no need for Skimif to be introduced to Nimiko, for the god's identity was obvious.

After Malock finished, Skimif said, "It sounds like we've both been through a lot. I'm surprised any of you are still alive."

"We won't be in just a few minutes," said Nimiko, looking at the Powers, who were now closer than ever before. "Once they get here, not even all of the combined powers of the gods will be able to save us."

"Skimif, you're their servant," said Jenur. "You can convince them to not destroy the world, can't you?"

Skimif kicked the sand. "I tried to convince them to spare just a few people and look at what happened. The Powers decided to end the world long ago. And once they've got an idea in their minds, they won't budge on it no matter what."

"Nimiko, then," said Jenur, turning to the God of Light. "You're the first god, right? That means you've got a connection to the Powers that the rest don't, right?"

Nimiko chuckled bitterly. "If only it were so simple. No. Say what you will about the Powers, but they've never been one to play favorites." Then he looked at Skimif. "Except, perhaps, in your case. I still don't understand why they chose you to be their herald."

"Neither do I," said Skimif. "All I know is that they are intent on carrying out their ultimate goal of destruction. I and Kasrath here will probably survive, but the rest of you ... I'm sorry to say, but the rest of you will not."

"There's gotta be *something* we can do," said Jenur. She kept glancing over her shoulder at the Powers, whose progress had not slowed in the slightest. "Anything. Anything at all. Doesn't anyone have any ideas?"

"None of us do, Jenur," said Nimiko. "You cannot reason with beings who exist on a higher plane of reality than you do. The Powers will wipe us all out, no matter what we think about it. Perhaps the best we can do is sit here and await our deaths."

"That will accomplish nothing," said Malock. "We have to do *something* to save the world. There must be some argument we can come up with, something we can say that will make the Powers change their minds."

"I wish there was, but you heard Skimif," said Nimiko, shaking his head. "When the Powers decide to do something, there is no convincing them to give up. Believe me, I tried to negotiate with them to alter the terms of the Treaty, but they laid it down like the law and did not appreciate my attempts at negotiation."

Hana scratched the back of her neck. "Well ... if this is truly the end ... then I guess Nimiko is right. Sitting here and awaiting our deaths is our only option."

Malock bit his lower lip, looked at the Powers, who were so close that Skimif could feel the energy radiating off their bodies like the heat of the sun, and then said, "No. This is not the end. This is not how it all ends."

"What's your plan, then?" said Hana. "Going to try to use dense philosophical arguments to convict the Powers' conscience? Maybe get on your knees and beg for them to spare you?"

"Nope," said Malock. He looked at Skimif and said, "Skim, can you take me up to the Powers?"

"What?" said Skimif. "Why?"

"Because I want to try to reason with them," said Malock. "That's why."

"But if I do that, you will probably be killed," said Skimif. "Remember, the Powers want to destroy everyone and everything. Your status as royalty will not persuade them to spare you."

"I don't care," said Malock. "Just take me up there. I'm sure an idea will occur to me."

Skimif didn't like the idea at all, but when no one else objected, he nodded and said, "All right. Hop on Kasrath. It will be a bumpy ride and I can't assure you that you will survive, but I will do my best to help you however I can."

"That's all I need to know," said Malock. "Now let's go."

"Hold it," said Jenur, stepping forward before either Malock or Skimif could move. "You aren't going anywhere, Mal. Do you want to die?"

"Do you have any better ideas?" said Malock. "Whether I go up there or not, the Powers will still kill us. I just think I have a better chance of going up there and talking to them face-to-face than sitting down here like a duck."

Jenur's fists shook, but she kept a level voice. "All right. It's just … I don't want to lose you, too. Not after everyone else."

"You won't," Malock said. "Because I'll make sure to send the

Powers home."

Then Malock looked at the others, who had not said a word. "Any objections?"

"None here," said Quro. "Good luck."

"It's suicidal, but I guess it's our best bet," said Hana. "Do your best."

Nimiko said nothing. He merely looked toward the Powers again, probably thinking about how they were all going to die.

Seeing as no one objected, Malock turned back to Skimif again and said, "Now let's go. We don't have much time."

Chapter Seventeen

MALOCK'S HAIR BILLOWED IN the wind as he and Skimif soared through the air on Kasrath. The wind was cold, but it felt good against his burning face, which seemed to burn even worse the closer they got to the Powers.

Though Malock tried not to show it, he was desperately afraid. He held on tightly to Skimif's waist, under the pretense that he was trying to keep from falling off, but really, he was more terrified of coming face to face with the Powers than anything. Deep down, he just wanted to run from them, but he knew that running would be useless.

The only way we can save the world is by confronting those who would wish to destroy it, Malock thought, peeking over Skimif's shoulder at the Powers. *I just wish that there was another way.*

They soared high over the ocean's stormy surface, heading directly toward the Powers. Skimif's muscles were tight and he held the reins with unusual intensity, while Kasrath made low whimpering noises, as if it was afraid. Malock understood.

"Have a plan yet?" Skimif yelled over the wind as they drew closer and closer to the Powers.

Malock shook his head. "Not yet. Still thinking."

"Better come up with one fast," said Skimif. "Because the Powers will notice us soon, and when they do, I can't guarantee your safety."

Malock nodded. It was impossible for him to think clearly, however, because the sheer, primal fear overwhelming his mind basically made deep thinking as impossible for him as sprouting wings and flying away. His mind kept returning to this very simple, very easy to understand thought: *Run. Stop going towards danger. Run all the way back to the Northern Isles. Hide. Hide anywhere. Doesn't matter where. Just run and hide.*

Just then, one of the Powers' tendrils lashed out at Malock and Skimif. Skimif pulled hard on Kasrath's reins and the dragon soared up and over the tendril, but then another tendril came out of nowhere directly in front of them. Kasrath managed to dodge that one by banking to the right, but just barely. The Powers were now looking up at them and, although their faces were far from human, Malock had no trouble telling that they were out for blood.

"Still don't have a plan?" Skimif asked as they turned to the right to avoid yet another flying tendril of light.

Malock didn't respond because he was now looking at the Powers. He didn't see how he could possibly communicate with them. There was no way he or Skimif could convince them to calm down long enough to listen to him. Indeed, now that he was actually up close to the Powers, he realized just how foolish and futile this whole plan—if it could even be called that—was.

He almost asked Skimif to turn Kasrath around and head home, but before he could, two tendrils came at them, one from the bottom, one from the right. Kasrath successfully dodged the bottom one, but the one from the right sliced straight through its right wing, causing Kasrath to roar in pure agony as it plummeted from the sky like a rock.

They tumbled through the sky head over heels for what felt like forever. The entire world was a confused mess to Malock. The sky ... the Powers ... World's End ... the sky again ... the Powers ... World's End ... the sky once more ...

And then they landed on top of the Powers. It was like falling into a vat of pure flame. Every molecule in Malock's body shrieked with pain, but he felt the pain only for a little while because in a moment he sunk straight into the head of the Power that he had fallen on and everything went dark. His last vision was of his own right hand reaching for the sky.

Then Malock awoke. He gasped, like he had been holding his breath, and his mind was a confusing mess of feelings and memories and thoughts. He didn't know where he was or how he got here, could barely see anything, even didn't know if his name was actually Malock or not. His body continued to burn in pain, but the pain was rapidly subsiding, like a piece of burning metal dunked into a bucket of ice cold water.

When the pain cleared, so did Malock's vision. He sat up and rubbed his eyes to clear out the last of the dots from his eyes and then looked around at his surroundings. He could not believe what he saw.

He sat in the middle of a wide-open, empty field of wheat that stretched on in every direction for as far as the eye could see. He saw no sign of the sea, didn't smell any sea salt or fish, and didn't hear the crashing of the waves against the shore. There were no paths, either, or houses or any signs of civilization at all. The sky was as clear and blue as a summer afternoon, with nary a cloud to be seen anywhere. The air was still; there was not even a light breeze to blow through his hair.

How did I get here? Malock thought. *For that matter, where is here?*

The last thing Malock remembered (and he had to struggle to remember this, as his mind seemed intent on forgetting it) was falling onto the Powers and sinking into their heads. He recalled believing that he was about to die, that he was the first casualty of the apocalypse. But as far as he could tell, he was alive, as not only did he continue to feel pain, but the rest of his senses seemed to be in working condition, too.

A groan to his right caused Malock to look in that direction. Skimif and Kasrath lay not far from him. Skimif looked unconscious, while Kasrath appeared to be awake, but it was moaning softly, for its wing still had a large, bloody hole in it. Malock didn't know how to fix its wing, so he merely got up and walked over to Skimif.

"Hey, Skim, wake up," said Malock, nudging his friend's unconscious form with his foot. "Get up. How do you feel?"

Skimif's eyes flickered open. He then sat up abruptly, causing Malock to jump back in surprise, and he whipped his head back and forth, his eyes bugging out.

"What happened?" said Skimif. "Where are we? Are we dead?"

"I don't know the answer to those first two questions," said Malock. "But I do know the answer to the third, which is no, we are not dead."

Skimif got to his feet, looking quite harried, and then noticed Kasrath's wing. "Oh, Kasrath. Hang on. I'll heal that for you."

Malock was about to say that, while that was a nice thought, it didn't mean much due to Skimif's lack of expertise or skill in panamancy, when Skimif walked over to Kasrath and waved his hand over the wounded wing. Within seconds, the wound had closed completely. Kasrath experimentally flapped its wing twice and then stopped when it was satisfied that it had healed well. It then rubbed its head against Skimif's leg affectionately, a bizarre—though harmless—sight if Malock had ever seen one.

"Skimif," said Malock, looking at Kasrath's healed wing, "when did you become a panamancer?"

Skimif scratched the back of his neck. Now that Malock got a better look at him, Skimif looked a lot stronger than he had back on Carnag. There seemed to be an aura of power around the former farmer, almost like the aura that the gods gave off.

"Oh, I'm no panamancer," said Skimif, shaking his head sheepishly. "I'm ... well, when the Powers first gave me a vision of the end, they also granted me many strange and unique powers. I don't even know what all of them are yet, but so far, I've found that I can control plant life, heal beings, take more pain than the average mortal, and even bring new life into existence."

Malock looked at Skimif skeptically. "That last one sounds very hard to believe."

"But it's true," said Skimif. "Watch."

Skimif held out his right hand. He focused intensely on it, so intensely that he appeared to be trying to set it aflame with his mind. His right arm shook, but not enough to change much.

Then, right before Malock's startled eyes, something small and black appeared in Skimif's hands. The small, black thing expanded and stretched, however, until it became about the length and width of a water snake. The snake raised its head and hissed at Malock, before Skimif dropped it. The water snake hit the grass, hissed again as though annoyed at having been dropped, and tried to slither away before Kasrath snapped it up and gulped it down in one bite.

"Amazing," said Malock. "Can you bring anything else into existence?"

Skimif shook his head. "I don't know. I haven't practiced much because the ability still frightens me."

"What is so frightening about being able to bring life into existence?" said Malock. "I mean, you can bring life into existence through sheer force of will. That's a better miracle than all of the hundreds of so-called 'miracles' I've seen court entertainers perform in front of me and my parents over the years."

Skimif shrugged, as if to say it wasn't a big deal. "Do you know where we are?"

Malock looked up at the wide, blue sky above them. "I have no idea. Last I remember, we had fallen on top of the Powers. Then somehow, we sank into their heads."

"I would not have believed a word you said if I had not experienced it myself," said Skimif. "But it still doesn't explain any of this. How does a wide-open, wheat plain exist inside their heads? Granted, the Powers are massive, but they're not *that* big."

Malock tapped his chin. "I don't know. Maybe our bodies were actually destroyed when we fell into them and our souls passed on to the afterlife."

Skimif frowned and looked around the area once more. "This does not look like the Beautiful Blue that my grandfather told me awaited every good aquarian who died."

"The Beautiful what?" said Malock.

"The Beautiful Blue," said Skimif. "It's basically the most popular version of the afterlife, believed by lots of poor aquarians. Legends say that beyond death exists a sea that is bluer than any sea on Martir. It is stocked with fish of every kind, with enough space and room for all aquarians to swim in peace. It is said that the gods do not travel there, either, but that it is sustained instead by the Powers themselves."

"I've never heard of that," said Malock. "I suppose there is much more to aquarian culture I have to learn."

"Either way, this still doesn't look like it to me," said Skimif. "And seeing as Kasrath's wing was still wounded, I think it's safe to say that we are still alive and probably are inside the Powers' minds."

"Then why are their minds so empty?" said Malock. "Surely the Powers—being the creators of all existence—would have minds bursting at the brim with ideas and thoughts that neither of us can even imagine, right?"

"But we do," said a voice. "You simply cannot comprehend any of it."

The voice was coming from behind Malock, causing Malock to

whirl around to see who was speaking. A strange, red-skinned creature stood not far from them. Though its upper body was humanoid, it lacked normal legs, instead being supported by a snake-like tail with barbed hooks running its length. Its features were androgynous; at least, that was the conclusion Malock was forced to come to, for its face would sometimes look male, other times look female, and then look like both.

It wore no clothes and had no hair. But its eyes gleamed with intelligence and it radiated the same kind of power and energy that the Powers had. Its fingers—indeed its whole hands—appeared entirely mechanical, as if it had cut off its old organic ones and replaced them with superior mechanical ones.

"Who are you?" said Malock, taking a step back and wishing he had some kind of weapon with which to defend himself.

The being smiled, revealing a wild mishmash of teeth. Some were sharp and jagged, almost like daggers, while others were blunt and short, like the head of a hammer. About half of the teeth were rotting away, while the other half gleamed pearly white in the sunshine.

"Call me Spark," said the being. "Short for Spark of Creativity."

"Spark of Creativity?" said Skimif. "That's an odd name."

"It is also quite appropriate," said Spark. "For you see, I am the cause of the Powers' creativity. It is the ideas I generate that causes the Powers to create ... or destroy." He squinted at them, like he needed glasses. "You two, though ... yes, a human and an aquarian. It has been years since I came up with you two, yes it has. You don't look much different from my original blueprints, which is fine because you two were perfect just the way you were."

"Hold on," said Malock. "Are you saying that you are basically the reason we even exist?"

Spark nodded. "Of course. Your world—imperfect little Martir—and all that lives in it, would never have come into existence if I had not inspired the Powers to create you."

"So let me get this straight," said Skimif. "There is a little ... whatever you are, living inside the Powers' heads, telling them what to create?"

"That is a crude description of it, but you got the major details right," said Spark.

"And all of this ..." Skimif gestured at the wheat field. "This is also inside their heads?"

"It is inside *your* heads, actually," said Spark. "You see, when you three first fell into the Powers' heads, your minds simply could not comprehend all of the vast and wonderful things you saw. To keep your heads from exploding, your minds conjured up this field. In actuality, you are floating within the Powers' minds, surviving only because it has been so long since I last saw some of my creations up close like this."

"Our minds did this?" said Malock.

"Yes, indeed," said Spark. "To be honest, I didn't know what your minds would do when they entered the Powers' minds, so it was fascinating to see them come up with this defense mechanism. Sadly, it's not fascinating enough to make me want to keep you around much longer."

Malock still didn't quite understand everything Spark had said, or even exactly what Spark was, but he did understand that Spark was the being who was behind it all, which meant that, if Malock was to save the world, he would need to convince Spark to spare it.

So Malock stepped forward, looking as confident as he could, and said, "Spark of Creativity, I am Prince Tojas Malock of Carnag, and this is my friend, Skimif of Tunya."

Spark did not look particularly impressed. "I already knew that, but go on."

Malock didn't let that crush his spirit. "We want you to tell the Powers to spare Martir and all who live within it. At the very least, spare the mortals. We can do without the gods."

Spark stroked his chin, brushing flakes of skin off it as it did so. "Spare Martir, hmm, an interesting thought, but not an *inspiring* one, you know what I mean? It's not particularly creative. So I'm afraid the answer is no. The Old World's time has come and begging won't change my mind."

Malock grit his teeth, but tried to keep a level tone to avoid offending Spark. "But there are millions of innocent people on that world, people who have not done anything bad enough to warrant dying. It's unjust."

"Who said this had anything to do with justice?" said Spark, spreading its arms. "It is art. It is experimentation. It is inspiration."

"Please, Spark," said Skimif, putting his hands together in supplication. "Please listen to Malock. I know the Powers have always done what they want, but just this once, can't you spare our world? What use is there in destroying it?"

"You have no right to be asking me for that," said Spark. "If I recall correctly, Skimif of Tunya, your job was to prepare the world for the Powers' arrival. And I see you haven't done a very good job about that, but no worries, seeing as the Powers will destroy the world anyway, no matter what its current condition is."

"I know," said Skimif, bowing his head. "But if doing a 'very good job' means destroying all of my friends, I would rather do a very bad job, thank you very much."

"What is so artistic about apocalypse?" said Malock. "The deaths of millions, the destruction of so much natural beauty ... do you even understand what it is that you are advocating here?"

Spark frowned, like it was confused. "You say all of that like I haven't considered it. Or like I am not going to make something better from the remains."

Now it was Malock's turn to frown in confusion. "What? What do you mean, 'make something better'? I don't understand."

Spark crossed his arms and said, "I'm surprised. I thought you *would* have asked me why we're destroying Martir at all. I suppose you didn't think you'd get an answer, so you didn't even bother to ask the question."

"Then why are you destroying Martir?" said Malock. "All your said to justify your actions is 'art,' that you're going to 'make something better.' What does that even mean?"

Spark sighed. His sigh came out like a powerful gust of wind, like a cool breeze on a summer day. "Where do I start? I suppose at the beginning. The very beginning. Before the beginning, actually."

Spark slithered past them until he reached Kasrath. He reached over and began petting Kasrath's head, which the dragon seemed to enjoy because it closed its eyes and began wagging its tail back and forth.

"I assume you both know that the Powers created Martir eons ago, at the beginning of time itself," said Spark. "Well, technically, that was the beginning of *Martir's* time, but we needn't talk about what happened before Martir or what existed before it. Useless exposition, you understand."

In reality, Malock wanted to know what happened before Martir, but it was clear that Spark was in no mood to give them a history lesson of prehistory, so he and Skimif simply nodded.

"Martir was first created when an idea came to me," said Spark. He tapped the side of his head. "A wonderful idea. A world in which a huge variety of creatures—ranging from small insects to gigantic sea beasts and everything in between—existed. This world would be the finest creation I had made yet, so I urged the Powers to get to work on it immediately."

Spark held up his free hand. A tiny, flat blue model—with a bunch of green, brown, and white landmasses on it—appeared in his palm. A massive continent dominated the center, although as far as Malock knew, there were no continents that big anywhere on Martir.

"It was the most daring project we had made yet," said Spark. "In fact, it was much larger than I had envisioned it. Therefore, in order to aid with the creation of the world, the Powers created a set of lesser powers, which you two know as the gods and goddesses of Martir. Each deity specialized in one realm or power and each was given a specific part of the world to work on. They were highly efficient; so efficient, in fact, that when the world was finished, we gave them control over it. We believed they were responsible enough to rule the world and all who lived within it wisely, seeing as they had been so helpful in helping us create Martir."

Then Spark scowled, a scowl that seemed older than the stars. "But as it turned out, we made a mistake in trusting the gods. Almost as soon as we left to work on other things, the gods went to war with each other. Half wanted to eat you mortals, the other half didn't. The war was so terrible and violent that Martir itself was on the verge of utter destruction. Think about the irony; our creations—whose sole job was to rule and protect Martir—almost destroyed it."

"We know this," said Skimif. "We've already heard about the Godly War and what happened in it and after it."

"Then you know that we Powers learned of the War and hurried back to Martir to end it before it got ugly," said Spark. "By the time we got back, many gods had been slain, countless mortals and animals had lost their lives, and much of the original climate of Martir had been irrevocably changed."

The tiny display in Spark's hand changed. The large continent in the middle suddenly disintegrated, turning into hundreds if not thousands of smaller islands, while the sea's color slowly changed from a bright crystal to a dull blue.

"Oh, were we angry," said Spark. "But we did not think to destroy the gods. Instead, we separated them. We gave the northern half of the world to those gods who wanted to preserve mortal life and gave the southern half to those who didn't. We came up with a very complicated Treaty, which the gods still abide by to this day. At the time, we thought it enough to govern their actions and keep them from causing any more trouble or damage to our finest creation. But we were wrong."

Spark closed his fist around the display, shattering it into a million pieces. The shards fell to the ground, disappearing into the blades of grass.

"The gods never went to war again, mostly because they had failed to recover from the first one," said Spark. "For years, we received reports from our agent about all the various and sundry ways that the gods fought against each other, the ways in which the gods manipulated innocent mortals into striking petty blows against each other, how they used their intelligent minds to find all sorts of loopholes in the Treaty. As the years passed, it became increasingly obvious to me that making the gods had been a mistake right from the start."

Malock nodded. "I agree."

"So our first thought was that we would just destroy the gods," said Spark. "And their destruction, by the way, is still on our list. But then it became clearer that it was not just the gods, but the whole of Martir, that needed to be rethought and redone."

"Rethought and redone?" said Malock. "Is that what you call destroying millions of innocent lives?"

"It doesn't matter if they're innocent or not," said Spark. "The mortals have basically failed as well, seeing as most of them spend their whole lives groveling at the gods' feet. It is why we originally had Skimif start a movement to convince as many mortals as possible to give up worship of the gods. We didn't want to destroy the mortals, but when it became clear that most mortals did not want to live independent of the gods, then we folded them into the plan, too."

"You mean us," said Malock. "Me and Skimif."

"Skimif?" said Spark. "Skimif will survive. He is the only mortal we have deemed worthy of being spared. His honesty and sense of fairness has earned him our admiration. He will be better than the gods, that is for sure."

"Thank you, Spark," said Skimif. Then he frowned. "But what do you mean that I will be better than the gods?"

Spark smiled again. "Here is the best part of the plan. Once all of Martir is reduced to nothing, we will start over again. We will build a New World, one better than the old one. There will be no quarreling gods, nor sniveling mortals too afraid to stand up to said gods. All in that world shall be one. All will be efficient."

"No gods at all?" said Malock. "Now that doesn't sound like such a bad thing to me, but it's hard to imagine."

"Oh, it won't be entirely god-less," said Spark. "We Powers will not rule it, seeing as we have many other projects we wish to attend to. It shall have but one god, who shall rule the world by himself. He will bring life into existence, create the forests and jungles and plant life, sustain the New World, and make sure to protect it from all harm."

"Who is this one god?" said Malock.

Spark raised one hand and pointed at Skimif. "You, Skimif of Tunya, shall be that god. You will be far greater and stronger than all of the gods of Martir combined. Whereas the gods of Martir spend their days quarreling and thinking of the best ways to get back at each other for wrongs done long ago, you shall stride forward into the future, your step confident and your purpose clear. You will not need to wait for the approval of others before instituting the necessary changes to make the world a better place because the only approval you will need is your own."

Skimif put his hand over his heart. "Me? A god?"

"Of course," said Spark. "Wasn't it clear from the start? We gave you the same powers as the gods so you could practice and prepare for your eventual role. We thought about destroying you and simply making a brand new god altogether, but we decided that it made more sense to work with what we had than to start over anew."

Malock could not believe his ears. It was like learning that Kinker was going to become a god all over again, although this time Malock was not nearly as angry, mostly because he didn't want to become a god himself.

"But I don't feel prepared for godhood," said Skimif. "I mean, not to offend you, Spark, but even as a farmer, I was not much to speak of. My little farm didn't make much money and I only barely scraped by. I am the last guy you would want to run a whole world."

"We shall provide you with the knowledge and experience you need," said Spark. "You won't go wrong, unlike the gods of Martir. We will ensure it."

"Listen, that's great for Skimif and all, I guess, but it still doesn't solve the problem of Martir," said Malock. "You are still going to try to destroy it."

"Not *try* to," said Spark. "*Going* to. It is our only choice. It is the only logical choice."

"No, it's not," said Malock. "There's a lot of stuff you could do. Like let us fix our world."

"We have given you thousands of years in which to do that," said Spark. "Thousands of years in which the gods have ruled Martir, and yet they are still as petty, selfish, and quarrelsome as ever. They rarely agree much on anything and must go through all sorts of agreements and deceptions simply to keep the world running day to day. A New World, with only one god to rule it, would be far more efficient."

"It's not about efficiency," said Malock. "It's about lives. Real, innocent lives, that *you* are trying to destroy because what, we're not perfect? Because we don't fit your idea of artistic perfection or whatever excuse you've come up with?"

Spark stopped petting Kasrath. It put its arms behind its back, tilted its head to the side, and said, "Have you ever, in your life, created something that you later came to regret? Have you ever had high hopes for your creation, only to see it miserably smash those hopes into pieces again and again, over and over, with no chance of ever changing? Of ever learning from its mistakes?"

"No," said Malock, shaking his head. "But—"

Spark pointed at Malock. "Because that is what we see whenever we look at you mortals and your gods. We see gods who abuse their power to get back at each other, rather than work with each other. We see mortals who are too stupid—yes, I said stupid, because that is what you all are—and frightened and ignorant to stand up to them. It is why we wish to make a New World, except with one god rather than many and with mortals who hopefully have more backbone in their little finger than you mortals have in your whole bodies."

Malock, at first, didn't know what to say to that. Every word Spark had said was true. The gods *had* been largely petty and selfish.

The mortals had not been much better. When he looked at it from the Powers' point of view, he understood why they were so eager to wipe everyone out and start anew.

Still, Malock said, "But why do you have to destroy this world? Can't you just create your New World somewhere else and leave all of this be?"

Spark began rubbing his temples with his fingers. "And leave this ... this *mess* as an example of our creative work, for anyone to see? I mean, yes, we *could* find another place to create our New World, but it is not quite as simple a task as you make it out to be. It is much easier, simpler, and more practical to destroy what we've built and to use its remains to build a better world."

"Who else is out there to see this?" said Malock. "I mean, it's not like there are any other beings beyond the Void than the Powers, right?"

"Foolish, naïve mortal," said Spark. "Then again, I suppose it makes sense that you would know nothing about what exists beyond the Void. No mortal has ever gone beyond it and returned, nor will any. And seeing as there is no reason for you to know, I will not tell you, especially since you will not live long enough to see it."

"Why don't we make a deal?" said Malock. "You can destroy the world, but spare the mortals. Let us live in this New World under Skimif's rule. How does that sound?"

"No," said Spark. "Deals don't inspire me much. I feel a dead sense of artistic boredom at the very thought. Besides, you mortals already messed up this world. Why should I think that you mortals will not mess up the next?"

"Excuse me, Spark," said Skimif. "But the reason the mortals of Martir 'messed up' this world is because of the gods. For our own survival, we've had to worship the gods. I wouldn't make the mortals do anything or worship me if they don't want to, so I doubt they will mess anything up in your New World, if you choose to spare them."

"A reasonable argument, but not a convincing one," said Spark. "As I said, we want to start from scratch. Well, *almost* from scratch, seeing as we will still use Skimif, but he's an exception to the rule."

"Don't you have a shred of compassion in your souls?" said Malock. "What artist destroys their creation, even if it didn't quite come out the way they wanted it to?"

"Many artists do," said Spark. "Many artists are embarrassed by some of their work. Please don't lecture me, the Spark of Creativity, about what artists do. I know very well how creativity works, much better than either of you will ever understand. I know what I am talking about here."

"But destruction isn't art," Malock said. "Destruction is the exact opposite of creativity."

"Destruction is a necessary part of art," said Spark with a laugh. "Martir would not even exist if we had not first destroyed the world that had existed in its place."

"What?" said Malock. "You mean you've done this before?"

"It wasn't a very inspiring world," Spark said. "Lacked any real intelligent beings, partly due to some global conflict that led to the decimation of the world's primary civilization at some point in that world's history. Since no one was using it, we felt free to use its materials to create our own world. And now the time has come for this world to end."

"Not unless we stop you," said Malock. "Right, Skimif? Skimif?"

Skimif was looking down at his feet, as if lost in thought. Then he looked up at Malock. His brown eyes were defeated and resigned.

"I'm sorry, Malock, but ... I think Spark is right," said Skimif. "I don't see how anything we say will convince him to spare Martir. I mean, when someone is inspired—truly inspired—it's almost impossible to stop them. Especially if that someone is the Powers."

"I am glad to see you are starting to see reason, Skimif," said Spark. "It is why we chose you. You will be a wise and just ruler of the New World, much better than the old gods."

Now Malock's mind raced, looking for any argument—any at all —that could possibly help him convince Spark. Yet every argument that came to mind, he had already used and Spark had already debunked. The main problem, he realized, was that each argument rested on the assumption that Spark had humanitarian interests at heart, when it was plainly, painfully obvious that Spark—and by extension, the Powers—only cared about 'art' and 'efficiency.'

Therefore, I must somehow convince Spark that destroying the world is neither artistic nor efficient, Malock thought. *The only question is, how do I do that?*

"I see you have no more arguments," said Spark with a smirk. "Which is good. We have already wasted enough time here, talking to you and explaining far more than either of you ever really needed to know. It is time that we continue our destruction of Martir. I am already getting bored of it and wish to move onto the new thing, so I hope to get this over with quickly."

"Wait, please," said Malock, holding up a hand. "Just give me a few more minutes. Just a few more. Can't you grant me that much, at least?"

Spark didn't look at all happy about the request, but with a nod of its head it said, "Fine. Five minutes. Five minutes in which you try to come up with the best argument to convince me not to destroy your world. Those five minutes start now."

It was times like this that Malock wished he had been a more diligent student as a teenager. His tutor had taught him some debating and logical skills, but Malock had never been much interested in them and had always figured out how to get by using the least possible effort. He wished Raya was still alive because her intellectual mind could probably have come up with a good argument quickly.

With his mind racing, Malock once again reviewed each argument he had used so far. Of course, it was to no effect. He came up with nothing new, no new angle at which he could approach the subject. Skimif wasn't helping, either. The soon-to-be-god of the New World just stood there, looking down at his feet, like he was too ashamed to show his face.

Malock almost gave up in despair. Then he remembered Jenur, Nimiko, Hana, Quro, and Rint were all waiting for him and Skimif back on World's End. His own parents, although probably unaware of his current location, no doubt awaited him as well. There was the rest of the Brotherhood, too, and although he didn't know most of them, he knew that their lives were in his hands as well. Not to mention there was the entire population of Carnag, his own people, who he could not give up on no matter what. Everyone was waiting for him and Skimif to save them.

But how? Malock thought. *Just wanting to save people isn't good enough. I need an argument good enough to convince the embodiment of creativity not to destroy one of its own creations. How do you do that?*

He didn't know, mostly because he found it hard to argue with Spark's arguments. Maybe Martir really was a terrible world, beyond saving. Maybe it really would be better if the Powers destroyed it all and started again. Skimif could be a much better god of the New World than any of the gods could. He was kind, honest, and just. It wasn't like the Powers' idea of a New World was worse than Martir, after all.

Just as Malock almost gave up, a new idea occurred to him. He had no idea if it would work, but seeing as he had no other options, he had to take it.

"Consider this, Spark," said Malock. "Artists grow, don't they? They grow in their skills and abilities. I don't know much about the Powers, but they, surely, didn't start out as perfect world creators, did they? At least at first?"

Spark pursed his lips. "That is ... true. The Powers have not always been the best. There was a period of awkward practice and leaning, but we are past that point now. What is your point?"

"My point is simple," said Malock. He gestured at himself and Skimif. "When the Powers first created Martir, they no doubt did the very best they could at the time. If you are afraid of others—I don't know who they could be, but I know they're out there because you mentioned them—seeing it, of seeing us, then is that not showing that you lack faith in your own work? That you were lazy and did not do your best? That you are afraid others will look at your work and think it a halfhearted effort, and think you, by extension, are halfhearted creators?"

"But it has all gone horribly wrong," said Spark. "The gods and the mortals ... none of you came out the way we wanted. This whole world was a serious mistake on our part. And mistakes must be fixed."

"Just because something didn't come out the way you wanted it to doesn't mean it must be 'fixed,'" said Malock. "Because while there has been a lot of trouble and tragedy in the world you created, there's also been a lot of good things and good people."

He was thinking of his friends as he said that. All of the good times he had shared with them, all of the good things they had done for each other. He didn't know if Spark could read his mind or not, but he knew that whether Spark could or couldn't, these thoughts gave him the strength he needed anyway.

"Good things? Good people?" said Spark with a snort. "Like what?"

Much to Malock's surprise, Skimif stepped forward and said, "Like the Brotherhood of Heathens. We are like one large family, looking out for each other when the gods have shown themselves not to care about us."

"A while ago, I was the Captain of the greatest crew that has ever sailed the Crystal Sea," said Malock. "We weren't perfect—far from it —but my men stuck with me through thick and thin. I don't know what most of them are doing nowadays, but I am certain they are living honorable lives, lives that you want to cut short for no reason other than they are not perfect."

"How many times must I say this?" said Spark, throwing his hands into the air. "We. Don't. Care. Our art didn't come out the way we wanted it to and so it must be destroyed."

Malock shook his head. "Maybe, rather than returning to your old mistakes, you should have just gone forward and made your New World without ever looking back. Maybe you should put more faith in your own art, rather than destroying it and starting again under the false idea of making it 'better.'"

Spark cracked its knuckles, but for once, it didn't respond. It appeared to be thinking, as if seriously considering what Malock had just said. There was no guarantee that it would actually agree with him, but its continued silence gave him hope.

Then Spark sighed deeply. It moved away from Kasrath, folding its arms behind its back, its head bowed as if it didn't want to look at anyone else.

"Prince Tojas Malock," said Spark, its voice lower than usual. "You have made ... a good point. A point I cannot argue. I must concede that you have won the argument."

Malock leaned forward, his mouth gaping. "Do you mean to say that you're going to spare our world?"

Spark nodded, still without looking at either of them. "Yes. Because you are right. When we Powers saw how terribly our creation turned out, we acted hastily and without thought. Our instinct was to tear it all down and start again. It is what we have done before when our creations have not turned out the way we like. And yet ... it has never occurred to us before to think of it the way you suggested."

"Never?" said Malock.

"Not once," said Spark. "But it makes sense. Destroying Martir would make us feel better, but when I look at it from an artistic perspective, it is incredibly rash and crude. What's done is done, and we cannot grow as artists if we are stuck in the past."

Spark raised its head. "Do not get us wrong. We will still build our New World, but elsewhere now. We will leave Martir in peace, to evolve and change as the times demand. To be a testament to our ability as artists at the time we created it."

"What about the gods?" said Skimif. "Are you going to spare them, too?"

Spark sighed again. "The gods will continue to live, but we will once more have to give them new boundaries. They have too much power now, too much freedom. It must be restricted."

"How so?" said Skimif. "Are you going to take their powers away?"

"No," said Spark, shaking its head. It pointed at Skimif and said, "It will be you who will become their new ruler and leader. Although we would like to make you the god of the New World, it has occurred to me that you would be far more efficient here, in your home that you know, than in a New World that you do not."

Skimif pointed at himself. "You mean, I'm going to become the leader of the gods? But—"

"Do not argue," said Spark, its tone sharper than a knife. "We think you will do a fine job leading the gods and making sure they learn to work together, rather than constantly fighting and bickering. You have already proven yourself a good leader of the mortals. It is time you take on new powers and responsibilities as the God of Martir."

While Skimif looked astonished, Malock said, "What about me? I'm not interested in ascending to godhood, to be sure, but are you going to let me leave here alive?"

"Might as well," said Spark. "You have nothing to offer us. Unless, of course, you'd like to come with us to the New World?"

Malock brushed his bangs off his forehead. "Sorry, but I still have a lot of friends here on Martir. I'm not interested in going to some kind of New World, even if you would make me the god of it."

"It was not a genuine offer," said Spark, "but that is fine. We would rather start from scratch anyway, to prevent your flaws and imperfections from affecting the New World right from the start."

Malock figured he should feel insulted by that, but frankly he was just so glad that Martir was not going to be destroyed that he just nodded in agreement. He didn't want to make Spark think twice about its decision to spare their world.

Then Spark put its hands together. "Now that we have come to our agreement, I believe it is time to say good bye."

"You mean you are leaving?" said Skimif. "For good?"

"For now," said Spark. "We will be so busy building and maintaining the New World that we will likely never have time to come back and check up on things. But our agent will make sure to keep us informed of goings on, we are sure."

"Who is your agent?" Malock asked.

"Their identity is not important," said Spark. "They are no threat to you or anyone else on this world, so you need not worry about them. Anyway, it is time for us to leave. Good bye, Malock, Skimif. You two have made me think about my art differently. And that is always a valuable gift, but especially from some of our own creations."

With that, a huge burst of light exploded from Spark. The light struck Malock head on, feeling more like a powerful gust of wind than a burst of light. It hit him so hard that Malock almost went flying, but he stood. His consciousness rapidly slipping from his grasp, Malock turned to look at Skimif one last time, but to his astonishment, his friend was nowhere to be seen.

Yet when the darkness finally claimed Malock, he realized that he was not worried, not even one bit.

Chapter Eighteen

MALOCK FELT COLD AND soaked through. His hair clung to his head like seaweed and his clothes felt heavier than usual, like they carried extra weight. Not only that, but he felt something rough and wet underneath him, like wet sand. He heard the waves of the ocean crashing nearby, but with his eyes closed, he could not tell where he was. For that matter, he could barely remember how he had gotten there or what had happened before he got there.

He heard voices nearby, familiar voices, but his ears were so waterlogged that he couldn't understand most of what they were saying, at least initially. Then he felt a sharp poke in his side and his eyes flew open as he gasped in pain.

"You're awake," said a familiar feminine voice. "You're not dead after all. Which is both good and disappointing, all at the same time."

Malock coughed up a lot of salt water and looked to his right. Hana was standing above him, carrying a large stick, which he realized she must have poked him with. She no longer wore her Monmouth cap; instead, her hair flowed freely down her shoulders, swaying gently in a breeze that picked up just then.

"What ... where am I?" said Malock between coughs.

Hana stabbed the stick into the sand and said, "Still on World's End. You washed up on the beach ten minutes ago. I volunteered to keep an eye on you while everyone else went to get Rint."

Malock tried to sit up, only to discover that his boat cloak—which was heavy with water—was weighing him down. With his joints aching, Malock slipped out of his boat cloak. Though the rest of his clothes were still sopping wet, he found it easier to sit up now that he didn't have the weight of his boat cloak on his shoulders.

Shaking his head, Malock looked out over the sea. It was calm and quiet, very unlike how it had been when the Powers had been here. The Powers themselves were nowhere to be seen, but the entrance to the Void continued to stand at the edge of the world, as dark and threatening as it ever was.

"Where did the Powers go?" Malock asked, looking up at Hana. "Did they leave?"

"Yep," said Hana. "About five or ten minutes after you and Skimif fell inside their heads, the Powers turned and left. A few minutes after that, you washed up on shore and we dragged you out of the surf to make sure you didn't get dragged back in."

"Did the Powers say or do anything before they left?" said Malock.

"Nope," said Hana. "Just turned and left, like they had forgotten something back wherever they came from. Not that I miss them, but it was curious how they just went and did that."

Malock rubbed the back of his head, which hurt for some reason.

"It's a long story, but suffice to say, Skimif and I succeeded in convincing the Powers to spare Martir and everyone who lives within it."

"Really?" said Hana, crossing her arms. "You two? All by yourselves? How did you manage that?"

Oddly, Malock's memories of his conversation with Spark were foggy and vague. It was almost like someone had tried to erase them, but why anyone would attempt that, he didn't know.

So he just said, "As I said, it's a long story. I'll tell you about it some other time, perhaps."

Hana frowned, as if disappointed. Then she glanced at the sea and said, "Where *is* Skimif, anyway? His body didn't wash up on shore. Do you know what happened to him?"

Malock looked up at the sky. His memories of Skimif's fate were as clear as the sky above, so he said, "He's fine. More than fine, actually; he's the God of Martir now."

Hana tilted her head to the side. "God of ... Martir? I've never heard of a God of Martir. What does that mean?"

Malock stretched his arms and legs as he said, "Means he's the boss now. Every other god in Martir must now answer to him. It's part of the agreement we made with the Powers."

"Hold on," said Hana. "You mean he's like, the leader of the gods now or something?"

"That's what I said," said Malock. "Like I said, it's a long story, but the gods, I think, will be a lot less divided from now on."

"Now *that* is hard to imagine," said Hana.

At that moment, four beings appeared at the far end of the beach.

As they drew closer, Malock recognized them as Jenur, Quro, Rint, and Nimiko. Rint was leaning on Nimiko, who supported the old man without complaint, but despite that, Rint didn't seem terribly injured.

Jenur must have been the first to notice Malock because she suddenly pointed and said, "Hey, look. Malock's awake. He's alive!"

Malock slowly rose to his feet as the others approached. Jenur, however, ran ahead of the others and actually hugged Malock. She was far stronger than she looked, a fact Malock had always known from his observations of her but which he was now learning firsthand from her crushing hug.

"Oh, I thought you were dead," said Jenur. "You looked like drift wood for a while. So glad you're alive."

"Yes, Jen, that's nice," said Malock, his voice strained. "Can you let go of me now? I'm still not entirely better."

"Oh, sorry," said Jenur as she let go of him, looking slightly sheepish. "It's just if you died ... well, never mind. You know how I feel."

Malock nodded as Quro, Rint, and Nimiko finally reached them. Quro shook Malock's hand, while Rint said, "Good to see you survived, young man. I guess the world is going to keep going after all."

"It is indeed, old man," said Malock. "But it won't be exactly the same as it was before."

Everyone else looked confused at that, except for Hana (who already knew what he was talking about) and Nimiko, whose expression said that he somehow already knew about Skimif's fate.

So as briefly as he could, Malock explained just what he and Skimif had done when they fell inside the Powers. Due to his fuzzy memory, he had to skip over some of the details, but he was surprised at just how much he remembered. The others listened with interest, although Nimiko kept glancing at the sky like he expected to see the Powers again.

When Malock finished, Quro was the first to respond. He said, "My. Now *that* is one tale."

"Skimif is going to be a god?" said Jenur. "Kind of ironic, isn't it, considering he was the leader of the Brotherhood of Heathens?"

"It is," said Malock. "But it's better than the end of the world, isn't it?"

Rint opened his mouth to say something, but Malock never found out what it was because at that moment, all of their surroundings shifted and changed. For a long moment—which only lasted a few seconds, but it felt much longer—Malock feared that maybe the Powers had changed their minds and had decided to come back and destroy everything anyway because he could not see or hear anything.

But then his surroundings stabilized and Malock found himself and his friends standing in a very familiar place, a place Malock recognized instantly despite having visited it only once: The Throne Room of the Temple of the Gods.

Like before, the Throne Room was a massive, wide open chamber, its center like an arena battleground complete with sandpit. Above them, a massive, clear dome acted as the ceiling, giving them a perfect view of the sky above.

And all around them stood hundreds, if not thousands, of thrones of various heights. The first time Malock had been here, there had been only two gods present, but today, all of the thrones were occupied. It seemed like all of the gods of Martir, both northern and southern, were there. Kano, Tinkar, Grinf, and all of the others, most of whom Malock couldn't identify. The Loner God was there, too, but with the hole in his chest, the dried golden blood covering his skin, and the bits and pieces of plant hanging off his shoulder, he was not recognizable as himself at first. The Temple of the Gods already gave off a powerful aura, but with the combined presence of all of the Martirian gods, Malock found it hard—almost impossible, really—to stand. It was like the will of every god in that room was trying to crush him, but he stood strong anyway, and so did the others with him.

In spite of so many gods, the room was eerily silent. The eyes of each god fell on Malock, Jenur, and the rest. With so many beings looking at them, it was impossible for Malock to tell what they were thinking. Some of the gods looked annoyed, as if wondering why a bunch of filthy mortals were standing in their Throne Room. Others looked intrigued, as if they had never seen a mortal before in their life. And still others looked hungry, as if imagining what the mortals might taste like.

Malock turned to ask Nimiko how they got here, but to his surprise, the God of Light was nowhere to be seen. He then scanned the thrones until he spotted Nimiko sitting in a throne about halfway up, between Kano and the Rain God. He looked as astonished by all of this as Malock was.

"What happened?" said Rint, who in Nimiko's absence now leaned on Quro for support. "How did we ... where are we?"

"The Throne Room of the Gods," said Malock. "It's the main chamber of the Temple of the Gods. We're still on World's End."

Rint looked around the place nervously. "Does that mean the gods summoned us here? Are they going to kill us?"

"I don't know," said Malock. "But I doubt it. If they had wanted us dead, they would have already killed us by now."

"Then what are we—" said Jenur, before a sudden bright light above them burst into existence.

Malock had to shield his eyes to avoid getting blinded by the light, while the eyes of every god in the room locked onto the light, but few of them looked surprised. In fact, as Malock turned to avoid the light, he noticed how many of the gods looked as if they had been expecting this to happen.

The blindingly bright light soon faded, allowing Malock to turn and see who had caused it.

Floating in the air—in the very center of the Throne Room, just above Malock and the others—was Skimif. But he didn't look quite like Skimif anymore. His body was larger, with thicker muscles on both his arms and legs. His bright green robes had been replaced with robes of pure white. His skin shone like silver and his eyes held such authority in them that Malock felt a need to bow down before him, like royalty.

Skimif was not alone, however. He sat on top of Kasrath, but the dragon didn't look exactly the same, either. Its scales flashed like gold, while the insides of its wings shined like brilliant crystal. Its teeth looked like perfectly forged knives, and its tail snapped through the air like a whip.

The two floated in the air for a moment, all eyes on them. Then they flew toward the back of the room, toward a new throne that Malock had not noticed before. It was much larger than the other thrones, large enough to fit at least three or four full-grown humans side-by-side. Kasrath landed on it with perfect ease, turned around, and crouched down, bringing Skimif closer to the rest of the gods, though the elevation of the massive throne still put him at least a head above the nearest gods and several heads above the farthest.

"I am glad to see that you all could make it," said Skimif, reclining on Kasrath like it was a comfortable chair. "Because this will be the most important meeting among the gods of Martir since the day the Treaty was signed. Today will be the start of a new era, one much better than the last."

Skimif held up his right hand and a long scepter—made of purest gold—appeared inside it. He raised the scepter and said, "To make certain that everyone knows who I am, I am Skimif, formerly of Tunya, but current God of Martir."

Mutterings—some in disbelief, some angry—spread through the gods. Malock, personally, was surprised at how confident Skimif seemed in his new position. It was almost like he had been meant for this all along, as if from birth he had been destined to take this role.

"I know that many of you—probably most—do not approve of this," said Skimif. "After all, when have you gods ever been ruled by anyone? For as long as you have existed, you gods have been equals in every way. You could not fight each other, at least not directly, and could not kill each other. There has never been anyone to unify you because you gods have lost your original purpose, which is to keep Martir running exactly as the Powers intended."

More muttering, although Malock detected more anger this time, as if most of the gods were starting to move from disbelief to anger now.

"I know how most of you feel, but trust me, this is far better than the alternative," said Skimif. "Which, as you all know very well, was that *all* of you gods would be destroyed. The Powers were quite serious in their desire to destroy you all like a disease-infected blanket. I would think you would be grateful that the Powers chose to spare you. They had nothing but harsh words for every last one of you."

"Grateful that we've lost our freedom?" spoke up one god. It took Malock a moment to realize that it was the Historic God, who clung to his throne with his tentacles. "The freedom under which we lived for so many centuries?"

A lot of the gods were nodding in agreement, including Kano among them.

Skimif did not, however, look disturbed by the question. "The gods gave you a purpose, which was to maintain Martir. You were never supposed to have free rein of the place. My job is to keep all of you on the straight and narrow. No more petty conflicts. No more manipulating mortals to do your will." Skimif smirked. "Besides, Historic God, you have your freedom now, do you not? You out of all the gods have the least to complain about, seeing as I lifted off the Powers' curse off you so you could be present for this meeting."

"This is not much of an improvement," said the Historic God.

"Unless you are going to nullify the Treaty and let me and the other southern gods take up human-hunting again, that is."

"And if Skimif does that," said Nimiko, before Skimif could say anything, "then I and the other northern gods will oppose you, as we always have. We are perfectly willing to fight another Godly War if we have to."

A bunch of gods nodded in agreement with Nimiko's words. They must have been northern gods, for most of them looked at least vaguely human. By contrast, most of the gods glaring at Nimiko looked more like animals or forces of nature, which made it easier for Malock to tell that they were southern gods.

"The Treaty and its clauses are still in effect," said Skimif. "While the Treaty has many loopholes, it has so far managed to prevent another Godly War, which is what it was designed to do. I will add my own laws in addition to it, however, to ensure that unity among the gods is achieved."

The Historic God immediately started cursing and grumbling, while some of the southern gods near him leaned together and started discussing something Malock couldn't hear. Meanwhile, on the other side of the room, Nimiko reclined in his chair, putting his hands over his belly, looking quite pleased with Skimif's words, as did some of the other northern gods who sat near him.

"Things will be different from now on," said Skimif. "I have many ideas in mind that, if put into effect, will hopefully make the world a better place than it currently is."

"Oh?" said the Historic God. "And what might those changes be?"

"I'm glad you asked," said Skimif. "Firstly, I will have the northern gods put more effort into maintaining the world instead of spending so much time worrying about what the mortals think of them."

"What?" said Grinf, looking at Skimif with more than a hint of disbelief. "But the mortals—"

"It doesn't matter what the mortals think of you or how they choose to worship you," said Skimif in a firm voice. "Or whether they choose to worship any gods at all. Remember, I said I am trying to return you gods to your original purpose. The Powers did not make you to be worshiped by mortals, but to maintain and defend this world."

Grinf sat back in his throne, looking more than a bit put off by being bossed around by the very person who he had tried to kill not long ago. Malock liked seeing Grinf put down, but he didn't voice it or show it in any way because he wasn't interested in getting on Grinf's bad side again. Just looking at Grinf was enough to make his face burn.

"As for the southern gods, they, too, will have to change some of their habits," said Skimif. "They will learn to work more closely with their northern siblings when it comes to making sure that Martir runs as intended. While they will not be allowed to hunt mortals—remember, the Treaty is still in effect—they will be allowed to venture into the Northern Isles more often than they have, although under strict conditions that limits how they may interact with mortals."

None of the southern gods looked particularly happy about that. The Loner God in particular looked furious, but all he did was sit there and fume silently, as if imagining all of the things he would do to Skimif, if given the chance.

"I know these all sound hard, but they are necessary," said Skimif. "I promised the Powers that I would put this world back on track. They would have destroyed it otherwise."

"Then what are these ... these mortals doing here?" said the Historic God, pointing one accusatory tentacle at Malock and the others below. "Do you have special instructions for the mortals? If we're not going to eat them, then why do we even have them?"

"Because I wanted them to be the first mortals to know," said Skimif, his eyes on Malock and the others. "These changes will be known throughout the whole world. All mortals will know of them."

"All mortals?" said Kano. "Do you mean that the mortals will even know about the southern gods?"

"Yes," said Skimif, nodding. "The southern gods will no longer be a secret to most mortals."

"Now that is insane," said Kano. "I am sorry, Skimif, but it just is. Think of the utter chaos that will ensue when the mortals find out that there is an entire pantheon of gods that would like nothing more than to eat them. Even if we tell them about the Treaty, even if we assure them that they are safe from harm, the consequences for informing them of their existence could be catastrophic."

"For once, I agree with my sister," said the Loner God. He pointed sharply at Malock and the others below and said, "For different reasons. I don't want mortals to know about us because it would take away from the fun of seeing the horror on their faces when, after wandering into the southern seas, they first learn about us."

He said that while looking directly at Malock, although he was obviously addressing Skimif. Malock returned the gaze, as he was not going to be afraid of the Loner God anymore, until the Loner God broke away and looked at Skimif again.

"I understand your reasoning, but my answer is still the same," said Skimif. "If the reveal of the southern gods causes harm, I will take full responsibility for it. Yet even if it does, I doubt it will cause any long term, lasting damage. Mortals can adapt to anything, no matter how dire or grim. It is simply the way we are."

"We?" said Kano. "You sound like you still think of yourself as a mortal."

Skimif froze for a moment as if that realization had just hit him. Then he relaxed and said, "Well, I *did* just ascend ten or fifteen minutes ago. I'm still not used to thinking of myself as a god, much less the God of Martir itself. But that doesn't change a thing. My plans are set and we will go through with them, whether you want to or not."

He spoke his words with such authority that none of the gods responded. A few of the gods—such as the Loner God, who was mumbling under his breath, and Kano, who had crossed her arms across her chest and scowled—clearly didn't approve, but it seemed like all debate had ceased. That amazed Malock. He had always known Skimif could be a strong leader when he needed to be, but to see Skimif shut up all of the gods was another thing entirely.

"Now that we've established all of this, you gods may go in peace," said Skimif, gesturing at both sides of the Throne Room. "I will make sure each one of you gains the specific instructions you need to fulfill your new duties, once I have it all figured out."

As soon as the words left Skimif's mouth, the gods began to leave one by one. Some flew through the domed ceiling above, which apparently had some openings Malock couldn't see. Others got up from their seats and walked to the nearest exit, while others simply vanished into thin air. None of them seemed keen to stick around, probably because so many of them disliked Skimif.

Soon every throne was vacant, including Nimiko's throne. Which Malock found strange because he had thought Nimiko might want to stick around, though perhaps Nimiko had something more important to attend to.

Then Skimif stood up on Kasrath and jumped off the dragon. He flew through the air with ease until he landed on the sandy floor of the center of the room, directly in front of Malock and the others. When he stood up to his full height, Malock was shocked to see that Skimif had actually physically grown. While he had always been slightly taller than Malock, he now stood at least a head above him, which made him seem even more godlike than before. He even gave off the presence of a god, but it was clear he was holding back his presence, perhaps so it wouldn't crush everyone else.

"Wow, Skim," said Malock, looking up at his friend in amazement. "Making the gods listen to and obey you ... that's impressive."

Skimif shrugged sheepishly. "It's nothing. Even though the gods tend to hate being bossed around, most of them are smart enough to know that arguing with me won't get them anywhere. Nothing to do with my own leadership abilities, as much as I'd like to take credit for it."

"They sure didn't look happy about it, though," said Jenur, glancing up at the thrones all around them. "And unhappy gods generally don't sit around and whine about it."

"I doubt there's much they can do," said Skimif. "Granted, I am still learning what being the God of Martir actually entails—where my control ends and the gods' begin and vice versa—but I can't see any of the gods causing that much trouble, to be honest. This actually isn't even my true form."

"It's not?" said Jenur. "But it looks so much like your old body, just bigger and shinier."

"I took on this form so I could communicate with everyone in a nonthreatening way," said Skimif, patting his chest. "My true form is basically incomprehensible to mortal eyes. Much like how the other gods' true forms are, actually."

"I see," said Malock, stroking his chin. "So ... is this the last time we'll ever see you?"

Skimif put his hands on his hips and said, "I doubt it. It's not like I'm going anywhere. I'm the God of Martir, after all. I'll always be here, in one form or another. I may not always be able to come down and have a chat with all of you, but I'll still be here."

"Are you going to be watching us at all times?" said Hana.

"I'm not sure what the extent of my powers is, to be honest," said Skimif. "I'm still testing my abilities. The Powers told me I would learn what I need to know when I need to know it. Seeing as I am basically immortal now, I have plenty of time to figure it all out."

"It will be interesting to see how that works out," said Malock.

"It will indeed," said Skimif. "Anyway, do you guys need help going home? I can take all of you back to the Northern Isles, if need be."

"I certainly do miss Carnag," said Malock. "You didn't trash it too badly when you fought Grinf, did you?"

Skimif looked down at his feet. "Oh, well, just a few buildings here and there, nothing too serious. I bet they're in the rebuilding phase already. If not, you should probably get back so you can supervise it."

Malock nodded. "Right."

Avoiding looking at Malock, Skimif glanced at Jenur, Quro, and Rint. "What about you three? Do you want to go home, too?"

Jenur and Quro exchanged uneasy looks. Malock didn't know the full details of their lives, but from what Malock knew, none of them really had any homes to go back to.

"We still need to talk about that," said Jenur to Skimif. "It's a topic we've been thinking of and something we still haven't agreed on."

"Actually," said Rint, holding up one hand. "I have come to my own decision about where I want to go."

"Oh?" said Jenur, looking at him in surprise. "When did you do that?"

Rint waved at the Throne Room all around him. "When I first saw World's End up close. I only kept quiet about it because of everything that was happening earlier, even though I knew that sooner or later I would have to tell everyone about my decision."

"So where do you want to go?" said Skimif. "Back to Destan?"

"Nope," said Rint. He pointed at the floor. "I want to live here, on World's End, by myself, if necessary."

"What?" said Jenur. "But why?"

"I have nowhere else to go," said Rint. "If I went back to Destan, the Priestly Guard would likely execute me for my role in Deber's assassination. I have no family or friends on any other island back up north. I have always been a devout follower of the gods—even now, when I've seen everything they've done and learned so many horrible things about them—and I would like to stay here in this city of the gods, even if that means finding a new home for myself."

"I suppose that can be arranged," said Skimif. "To keep you safe from the southern gods, however, I'll have to cast my protection over you. Remember, World's End is still in the south, which means that this is the southern gods' territory."

"I understand," said Rint. He hesitated, then said, "Besides, this is the island—the very room, in fact—where my brother Kinker died, yes? I know his body isn't here anymore, but maybe his spirit is still around here somewhere. Maybe I will see his spirit again. Who knows?"

That seemed unlikely to Malock, but he didn't want to rain on Rint's parade. Besides, for all he knew, Kinker's spirit really *could* be here. It's not like Malock was some expert on World's End and all of its mysteries or quirks. That Skimif didn't shoot down the idea immediately either meant that there was some truth to Rint's theory or that Skimif didn't know the answer himself.

"I'm going back to Stalf, probably," said Hana, speaking up

suddenly. "Not that anyone asked, but I should probably go back to the *Clockwork Heart* and make sure that the Mechanical Goddess isn't dead."

"She's not," Skimif said. "But she is still damaged and unconscious, which is why she was absent from the meeting earlier. I'll fix her up for you and then you two can go back to her island."

"Thanks," said Hana. "I was wondering where I'd get all of the parts necessary to fix her up. For that matter, I was wondering where I'd get all of the manpower to do it. Thought I might have to hire some of the katabans here on World's End, which would be bad because most katabans are terrible shipwrights and charge way too much."

Just then, the sound of metal echoing against stone echoed throughout the room. This caused Malock to look to the right, where a familiar automaton—with a sword in its hand—entered. The automaton looked wet and its head was dinged, but otherwise seemed perfectly functional as it walked toward them with the usual efficiency that the Mechanical Goddess' automatons always displayed.

"Calir?" said Hana. "What are you doing here? I thought you got killed by the Sleeping Beast."

Calir shook its head and made a bunch of clicking and beeping noises. It all sounded like gibberish to Malock, but Hana listened with shock and great attentiveness.

"Oh," said Hana, putting her hand over her mouth. "Please forgive me, Mechanical Goddess. I didn't recognize you there at first. I thought you were still unconscious."

"Wait," said Quro, looking at Calir more closely. "I thought this automaton was different from the Mechanical Goddess."

"The Mechanical Goddess put her soul inside Calir's body," said Hana. "Says she didn't like being stuck on the beach while everything was going on, so she transferred herself into Calir so she would be less of a sitting duck."

"Of course," said Malock. "She's always been one to just sit around unprotected and hope everything turns out for the best, right?"

Calir made more clicking and beeping noises. Hana translated, saying, "She says she heard the sarcasm in your voice, but that it doesn't matter because she doesn't think she'll ever see you again. Says that she's just going to go home to Stalf and rebuild her children one by one until they're at the same numbers as before. She lost most of them when the *Clockwork Heart* was sunk earlier."

"Good luck with that," said Malock. "Oh, and ... thank you for helping us. Out of all of the southern gods, you've been both our best friend and worst enemy. I still don't understand or like you completely, but I do appreciate the help you gave us anyway."

The Mechanical Goddess simply nodded, as if that was all she needed to do. Then she gestured for Hana to follow her, turned around, and began walking out of the Throne Room, metal feet brushing aside the sand on the floor as she did so.

"Guess I'd better leave," said Hana. "Good bye, you guys. The Mechanical Goddess isn't very patient or tolerant of servants who delay, so I must be going. See you ... uh, some time, maybe."

With that, Hana dashed after the Mechanical Goddess and soon both of them had left the Throne Room. Malock was both happy and sad to see them go; happy because, despite all of their help, he didn't really like either of them very much; sad because, despite his dislike of them, he found the idea of never seeing them again slightly depressing.

"Seeing as Rint is going to stay here, I think I should teleport you three out of here now," said Skimif to Malock, Jenur, and Quro. "I know Malock has decided that he wants to go back to Carnag, but what about you two? The Dark Tigers live in Ruwa, so do you want to go there?"

"Hell no," said Jenur, shaking her head furiously. "The Dark Tigers want me dead, and since Dad here has been missing for a few weeks now, I bet they think he's abandoned them, which means they probably want him dead, too."

"Then where do you want to go?" said Skimif. "Of course, if you want to stay in World's End like Rint, I won't stop you, but—"

"The Great Berg," said Quro, without hesitation. "The Dark Tigers don't have a presence there, mostly because very few people live there. If you could take us there, that would be good."

"The Great Berg, eh?" said Skimif. "I've never been there, but I've heard it's a harsh place, very cold."

"We know," said Jenur. "But I agree with Dad. At least for now, it's where we'll go until we figure out what we want to do next."

"Carnag Hall is always open to you two," said Malock. "If you want, I could give you positions as Justice Enforcers or even as sailors in the Carnagian Navy. Making false identities for you should be easy enough."

"Nah," said Jenur. "That would make us too high profile, far too easy for the Dark Tigers to find us, even if we took fake identities. No, for now, the Great Berg is our best bet."

"If you say so," said Skimif. "Now that we've got that out of the way, I want us all to hold hands because I will be taking you three back to the Northern Isles together."

"Hold on," said Rint. "I need to say something to Jenur and Quro."

Jenur and Quro looked at him curiously.

"What is it?" said Jenur.

"I wanted to thank both of you," said Rint, sounding slightly emotional. "I wanted to thank you, Quro, because you killed the woman who ruined my brother's life. I would pay you in full for it right now, but because the Priestly Guard took away my money, I unfortunately cannot."

"No need for that," said Quro. "After all we've been through, money is the last thing on my mind."

"No, I will have to pay you," said Rint in a firm voice. "Once I get the exact amount we agreed on, I will find a way to send it to you. No arguments."

Quro shrugged but said nothing to the contrary.

"As for you, Jenur," said Rint, turning his attention to her. "I want to thank you because—despite how irritating you often are—if it wasn't for you, I would never have known the truth about my brother and his death. I wish I could repay you, too, but I know no amount of money would ever suffice for the knowledge that you gave me."

Jenur looked away, like she was embarrassed. "Oh, it's not a big deal. Really, you don't have to thank me. It was nothing."

"You can say that, but it's not true," said Rint. "But whether we agree or not, just accept my thanks. I hope we see each other again someday, whenever that might be."

This was all very heartwarming to Malock, but then a thought occurred to him that he could not let slip by.

"Skimif, what about the Brotherhood?" said Malock. "What will happen to them? You can't be the leader any more, now that you're a god yourself."

Skimif frowned. "Yes, I've been thinking about that. When we go to Carnag, I'll personally talk to the Brotherhood. I don't think it will be around anymore, but I will make sure that none of the Heathens get arrested or harmed for their involvement in the movement. I still don't have it all figured out just yet, but I do have that much thought out. The rest, as usual, I will figure out as I go along."

Malock nodded. "I could help. As Prince of Carnag, I could pardon the Heathens. Assuming, of course, I can convince my parents that they deserve to be pardoned."

"You may try," said Skimif. "But the Brotherhood is my responsibility, so don't feel like you have to do anything, all right?"

"Okay," said Malock. "But if you need any help, feel free to ask."

Skimif chuckled. "You do realize I'm the God of Martir now, right? That means, if anything, it ought to be *you* asking *me* for help."

"Even the God of Martir needs help every now and then, doesn't he?" said Malock. "Either way, I'm sure you'll do just fine and make the right decision, whatever it may be."

"I hope so," said Skimif. "Anyway, is that all everyone has to say?

Any last words?"

Everyone shook their heads.

With a smile on his face, Skimif said, "All right, then. To a new era!"

After Skimif said those words, everything around Malock shifted and altered. Even as they teleported out of the Throne Room, Malock knew that, whatever the future held in store for them, whatever might happen in this new era, they could handle it. He was sure of it.

Chapter Nineteen

In a dark place, where Nimiko refuses to shine his light and where even the blackest souls refuse to walk ...

RAMUFA SAT ON THE cold, stone floor of his room, wrapped in a bundle of old robes that he had used as a blanket ever since he was a child. A soft, comfortable bed, with a springy mattress and clean white sheets, sat opposite him, tempting him to lie on it and rest his aching back.

But Ramufa didn't move over to it, mostly because he knew his master well enough to know that the bed likely had some sort of trap in it. Master Hollech wasn't the kind of god who would ever just give his servants nice things, as Ramufa had learned again and again over the years since entering his servitude. As the God of Deception, Thieves, and Horses, little was what it seemed with Hollech, which was why Ramufa refuse to sleep on that bed, even if it did look nice.

This wasn't to say that Ramufa hated his master. Hollech was very much like a father to him, having raised Ramufa from childhood. It was just that Ramufa was not interested in getting thrown into the ceiling or discovering that the bed was actually a cauldron full of burning hot water tonight. He just wanted to sleep and the stone floor—as cold and bad for his behind as it was—was the only sure way of getting that much-needed sleep.

The only problem was that he kept drifting between reality and dreams. Every now and then he would think that Skimif or that cursed dragon was standing right before him, ready to tear him to shreds, only to pinch himself and discover that it was just his imagination. It was difficult for him to forget being picked up by a dragon and thrown into a building, mostly because it had never happened to him before. Granted, he had avoided the worst of it by slipping into the shadows before he collided with the building itself, but that had not stopped or even slowed down his velocity.

Good thing I only knocked over three trash cans and one cart, Ramufa thought. *Otherwise, I might have actually killed myself.*

Since then, he had spent the rest of the week in his room alone, trying to recover. While Ramufa normally hated sitting alone and still in his room, Master Hollech had told him to stay here because his help was not required of him anymore. Hours before, Hollech had left their home, telling Ramufa that he was traveling to World's End to aid his brothers and sisters in stopping Prince Malock and his band of idiotic friends from going beyond the Void. Ramufa had wanted to come along, but he knew better than to disobey Master Hollech's orders. He had been taught well.

Just then, the scent of horse hair entered his nostril. He almost sneezed, but he held it in because—although he desperately wanted to sneeze—he knew that Master Hollech hated anyone who sneezed in his presence. Ramufa looked up and saw Master Hollech standing before him, even though he had not heard Hollech open the door or enter the room at all.

Then again, Ramufa thought, *Master Hollech is the inventor of the Thief's Way.*

Master Hollech looked like he always did. A tall, muscular human body, wearing a dark coat that seemed to be one with the darkness. His large feet were covered with lightweight shoes made of fine silk that made no noise whenever the god moved.

But it was his head that Ramufa had to look at. Though the rest of Hollech's body was humanoid, his head resembled that of a horse's. But his eyes were far more intelligent than that of a normal horse and far more angry as well, making Ramufa wonder if he had done something wrong.

"Master Hollech," said Ramufa, scrambling to his feet, his coarse blanket falling off his body as he did so. "I am glad to see you have returned. Did you and your fellow gods succeed in stopping Malock and his friends?"

Hollech snorted in anger. "No."

"Oh," said Ramufa. "Then are we all going to die?"

"No," said Hollech again, this time shaking his head. "Malock and his friends succeeded in convincing the Powers to spare Martir. We will all live for the foreseeable future."

"How did they accomplish that, Master?" said Ramufa. "I thought the Powers were above and beyond anything us mortals."

"I have no idea," said Hollech. "All I know is that this news is not nearly as good as it sounds."

"It's not?" said Ramufa. "I mean, not to contradict you, Master, and I certainly hold no respect for Malock or Jenur or any of those others mortals, but isn't survival better than destruction?"

"It would be, Ramufa, if the Powers had not dramatically altered the gods' hierarchy as part of the deal," said Hollech. "Or rather, I should say, if the Powers had not created a hierarchy entirely."

"What do you mean?" said Ramufa. "I thought that the gods were all equals, with no one god wielding more power than the other."

"Originally, that was how it was," said Hollech. Then his eyes narrowed. "But the Powers decided that that system had failed. Rather than take one of us preexisting gods and making us ruler over the others, the Powers chose the mortal, Skimif of Tunya, to become the God of Martir. That means he is the boss of all of us, including me."

Ramufa gasped. Although the story was hard for him to believe—made even harder by the knowledge that Hollech didn't always tell the truth—Ramufa had long learned to tell when his master was telling the truth and when he wasn't. Considering how annoyed Master Hollech seemed, Ramufa had no choice but to believe that this story was true.

"What does that mean for us, Master Hollech?" said Ramufa, putting his hands together anxiously. "What does Skimif plan to do?"

"At this point, I am not sure," said Hollech, shaking his head. "Skimif mentioned wanting to make the northern and southern gods get together, but no doubt that power of his will go to his head eventually. Mortals rarely respond well to abrupt and unexpected increases in power. No doubt this will all end up backfiring horribly, perhaps even prompting the Powers to step in again."

Ramufa gulped. "What do you suggest we do, Master? Attempt to overthrow Skimif?"

Hollech whinnied like a horse, although it was meant to be a harsh laugh. "Even I'm not dumb enough to try that. At least, not directly. We will have to work discretely. Skimif is not yet used to his new powers, but once he is, it will be impossible to do anything about him."

"Then what does that mean?" said Ramufa. "Do you have any plans, Master?"

"I do," said Hollech. "Normally, I rarely care about what the Powers do, but this time, they've overstepped their boundaries. It is time we caused a little chaos, Ramufa."

Ramufa liked Hollech's tone. His master sounded eager and excited, traits that Ramufa had always liked in his master. Granted, they were usually followed by Hollech doing something horrible, but this time, Ramufa didn't feel afraid at all.

"But we won't—and can't—do it alone," said Hollech. "I have recruited the help of a few other gods who share similar sentiments to me. They should be here any minute now."

At that moment, the temperature in the room fell ever-so-lightly, enough that Ramufa would not have noticed had he been wearing shoes. But the cold went up his bare feet, causing him to jump onto his fallen blankets to keep his toes from freezing.

Then, from out of the floor near the door, a pillar of ice arose. It rose and rose until it almost touched the ceiling. It was crystal clear, with patches of whiteness scattered randomly on its surface, like paint splattered by a child.

The ice pillar shook. An arm broke through the right half of the pillar, followed by a left arm on the other side. Two legs—strong, powerful, and lithe—smashed through the bottom and then a head broke through the top, sending shards of ice flying everywhere. Hollech didn't bother to move out of the way of the shards, which bounced off his body harmlessly.

Dusting ice chips off his shoulders, the newcomer stepped out of the remaining chunks of ice and waved one of his large hands. The remaining chunks latched onto his lanky body, conforming to his shape and giving him extra bulk.

The newcomer looked like a perfectly sculpted statue, like the ice sculptures created by pagomancers from ice from the Great Berg. His chin was square and firm, while his chest was broad and thick. He looked like an arena fighter, though his expressionless eyes made him seem more like a corpse.

"There you are," said Hollech, without turning to look at the newcomer. "I was wondering where you were. Thought you might have taken a detour through the Konez Isles. I hear they're very warm this time of year."

The newcomer didn't smile at the joke. "I am here because you asked me to be here, brother, not because I wanted to be here."

"Nice of you to come anyway," said Hollech. "Anyway, Ramufa, this is Xocion, the God of Ice. I don't believe you've had the pleasure of meeting my icy brother yet."

Xocion nodded at Ramufa, which surprised the thief. The last few gods Ramufa had met had barely acknowledged his existence, even after Hollech introduced him to them. That Xocion actually nodded at him made Ramufa wonder what was up.

"He's not the only one who is going to be here," said Hollech. "One of my beautiful sisters is on her way here. Granted, it's not always easy to tell when she's going to get here, seeing as she's always been very unpredictable, but she assured me she would be here soon."

Xocion grunted. "She's always late. She's even worse than the God of Sloth when it comes to arriving on time."

Ramufa was about to ask who they were talking about when the door burst open and a black blur dashed into the room. The blur almost rammed into Ramufa, missing him only because he teleported to the bed. From his position on the bed—which apparently wasn't a trap, much to his relief—he watched the blur slam into the opposite wall and stop.

Much to his astonishment, the blur turned out to be a little girl. She couldn't have been older than six, with coal-black hair that stood on end like lightning bolts. Her clothing was a strange mishmash; a gray skirt, blue leggings, pink shoes, and a bright green top. And despite having rammed headfirst into the wall—leaving a massive hole that Ramufa would have to fix—she didn't seem at all damaged by it. She just stood up, giggling like she had had a lot of fun, and then whirled around to face the others.

"There she is," said Hollech, sounding bored. "How was the trip, sister?"

The little girl giggled. "It was fun. I went all over the southern seas and Northern Isles and didn't think I'd ever make it until I found your front door. It's broken now, by the way. I rammed through it."

"We didn't think you'd ever make it, either," Xocion muttered while Hollech just sighed.

Then the little girl noticed Ramufa. She pointed at him excitedly and said, "Is *he* lunch?"

"No, sister, he is my servant," said Hollech. "Remember the Treaty. You can't eat any mortals while in the Northern Isles."

The little girl pouted. "I hate the Treaty. It's stupid and boring and orderly. I hate order."

"By the way, Ramufa," said Hollech, glancing at his servant, "this is the Chaotic Goddess, Goddess of Chaos. She's a southern goddess, if you couldn't tell, but she's just as much committed to ruining things for Skimif as we are. Isn't that right, sister?"

"Yes," said the Chaotic Goddess, nodding enthusiastically. "Skimif made it sound like he's gonna make everything more orderly. And that would be *boring*."

She said 'boring' like it was the worst word she could come up with.

"Master Hollech," said Ramufa, edging away from the Chaotic Goddess, "are these the only two gods you could get on your side?"

"Oh, no," said Hollech. "There are many more, but these are the two most important, besides myself, of course. Together, we're going to ensure that Skimif doesn't get too uppity and that he knows how we wish to be treated. Right, siblings?"

"I simply don't want anyone telling me what to do," said Xocion. "I've live thousands of years without a boss and I will spend the next several thousand just the same, if I can get away with it."

"I just don't want things to get boring around here," said the Chaotic Goddess. "Think about how boring it would be if Skimif united the gods again and stuff. Ugh."

Ramufa didn't know what to think about Xocion or the Chaotic Goddess, but he supposed that if Master Hollech could trust them, then he could, too.

"Now that the introductions are out of the way," said Hollech, a smile crossing his equine lips, "why don't we get started on that plan?"

Concluded in:

The Coronation of Prince Malock

Book Four in the Prince Malock World

Now available wherever books are sold!

About the Author

Timothy L. Cerepaka writes fantasy stories as an indie author. He is the author of the Mages of Martir fantasy novels, the Tournament of the Gods fantasy novels, and The War-Torn Kingdom fantasy novels.

Find out more at his website: www.timothylcerepaka.com

Other books by Timothy L. Cerepaka

www.ingramcontent.com/pod-product-compliance
Lightning Source LLC
Chambersburg PA
CBHW032243010726
47494CB00002B/613